About the Author

Alan Frost is an experienced IT professional being a Fellow of the British Computer Society and a chartered engineer. He has spent his life moving technology forwards from punch cards to AI, but always knowing that the key constituent in any system is the liveware, the users.

Beware The Future

Alan Frost

Beware The Future

Olympia Publishers
London

www.olympiapublishers.com
OLYMPIA PAPERBACK EDITION

A CIP catalogue record for this title is
available from the British Library.

ISBN 978-1-80074-339-7

This is a work of fiction.
Names, characters, places and incidents originate from the writer's imagination.
Any resemblance to actual persons, living or dead, is purely coincidental.

First Published in 2022

Olympia Publishers
Tallis House
2 Tallis Street
London
EC4Y 0AB

Printed in Great Britain

Dedication

I dedicate this book to my dear sister, Helen. Let happiness follow her wherever she goes.

Introduction

Twenty years had gone by since the meeting with Zeus. Well, it was hardly a meeting, more a visitation from an errant father. Everything that humankind knew about itself was now in doubt. In fact, everything that they knew about everything was cast in doubt.

At least The Brakendeth troubles were over. They had thought that before but now it seemed to be true. There had been no sign of them whatsoever. Terry had become one of the cornerstones of The Galactium and was now happily married with children.

The Galactium itself had changed. Apart from the thousand human planets, it now included Olympus and three hundred ex-Brakendeth client races. And more were joining on a regular basis. There were strict membership rules. The Galactium offered security and trade in exchange for peace and liberal, egalitarian values, although these values had to be stretched in order to fit in some strange biological idiosyncrasies.

The navy was now an independent agent of The Galactium responsible to the president and the Council but free to make impartial decisions. Its brief was to work for the benefit of the members but also for the good of the universe.

Admiral Mustard still headed the navy. It was likely that he would be in the post for the next thousand years. After Edel's death, he decided to help The Galactium find the best way forward. He was offered the presidency, but the navy was his real love.

The Galactium struggled to ensure that the organisation was representative. Two houses were formed. The first had a delegate from every planet, which gave humankind too much power. The second house contained a representative from each sentient race which did the opposite. Trying to define a race wasn't easy. Trying to define sentience was even more challenging. The combination was almost impossible.

Some races had symbiotic partners. Others existed as a composite organism. Some were fully telepathic. The old phrase of 'Animal,

Vegetable or Mineral' had to be extended to include liquid, gas or unknown. Some entities were clearly transparent, translucent, and inter-dimensional. The human definition of life was just so wrong and getting 'wronger'.

Nevertheless, The Galactium was growing and becoming more and more inclusive. There were, however, elements in humanity who wanted the organisation to be for humans only. But then there were human planets that only allowed Baptists to live there. Some were clearly racist, ageist, sexist, homophobic, fascist, communist, and totally intolerant. The good news is that anyone could move between planets, providing the environmental conditions were supportive.

The navy had the job of protecting The Galactium from external threats. It would come to the aid of an internal government organisation if requested. Admiral Mustard had a team of advisers who reviewed all such requests.

We join The Galactium during a time of peace and prosperity. A time of scientific revelations, of great discoveries, and hope for the future. A future where individuals could grow and prosper.

The last war was never the war to end wars, but it was the final defeat of The Brakendeth. Millions of innocent entities died for no real purpose. They were innocent bystanders in the wrong place at the wrong time.

Some died slow, agonising deaths. Some didn't even know they had been killed. Some died with their families and friends in outbursts of massive destruction. Destruction on a planetary scale. Some had slow, solitary deaths in outer space.

Some survived but wished they were dead. Those that survived suffered many miseries: the loss of loved ones, the loss of homes and businesses, the loss of hope, physical and emotional injuries. Some could never sleep properly again. Certain sounds would cause fear and panic attacks. Some would never love again. Some would never feel the tender caress of a parent. Some would seek the solace of suicide.

The Galactium Memorial Garden, probably the most fantastic garden created by humankind, was not a solution to any of the above. Still, it did provide a focus for grief, one of the most unwelcome of all guests. It was a place of great beauty and peace. It had a unique serenity that touched the human psyche.

Admiral Mustard had been totally opposed to having statues of the war heroes in the park. As far as he was concerned, every death was a tragedy and heroic in its own way. Most of the war heroes had volunteered to join the military. They died doing their job defending The Galactium.

That wasn't the view of the general population. Public subscriptions were used to create an adjoining 'Park of the Heroes.' Inside were statues of:

- President Padfield
- Tony Moore
- Henrietta Strong
- Admirals Bonner, Gittins, Millington, Brotheridge, Chilcott, Fogg, Ward, Whiting, Morten, Pearce, Sibley, Taylor, Fieldhouse, Wagner, Easter
- Dr Linda Hill

- Marine Commanders Todd and Goozee
- Major English

There were separate parks for the planets that had been lost.

Admiral Mustard was there to honour the dead on the twentieth anniversary of their encounter with Zeus. He was opposed to military displays and marching shows, but that was what the public wanted. Perhaps it gave them a sense of security and even pride.

He was sharing the platform with the president of The Galactium and the two Council chairpersons. As it was the twentieth anniversary, all the stops had been pulled out. It was going to be the largest marching display in The Galactium's history and included:

- The Honour Guard
- The Presidential Guard
- Admiral of the Fleet's Guard
- An honour guard from each of the two hundred fleets
- Marine Corps
- Special Services
- Planetary Defence
- Drone Service
- Intelligence Services Corps
- Medical Corps
- Communications Corps
- Exploratory Services Corps
- Logistics Corps
- Engineering Corps

And the following civilian services:

- Police
- Emergency Services
- Medical Services
- Intelligence Services
- Planetary Defence
- Civil Defence
- Coast Guard
- Environmental Services
- Justice
- Prison Service

There were also several charitable organisations marching by.

Admiral Mustard was quite pleased when the march was finished. His arm was even more grateful. During the day, there were also several flybys and aeronautical displays. The president made a somewhat non-committal speech, the platform members shook hands, and they all left during the start of a massive firework display.

Some of the alien attendees wondered what the point of the day was, but many of them had ceased to worry about the peculiarities of humankind.

Location: Admiral Mustard's Office, Planet Napoleon
Sequence of Events: 2

The navy now had its own dedicated planet. Admiral Mustard liked the independence that it provided but missed the buzz of a fully functioning civilian world. He had always seen his job as that of protecting humanity. Of course, now that was the wrong word. His job was to protect The Galactium of Planets.

He wondered if he should call them Galactites or Galactitarians, but nothing seemed to work. Anyway, he felt that having a dedicated military planet was two or three steps away from his customers. To combat this, he had established offices on every world in The Galactium, partly for recruitment but mostly for marketing. He realised some time ago that the navy had to market itself to both governments and the general public.

Fortunately, they had two excellent revenue streams: Chemlife sales and Terry's inventions. There was initially an argument over the later, but as Terry was now a commander in the navy, it was agreed that the navy should receive the benefits. The navy also charged each planet a fee based on their population size. As far as Admiral Mustard was concerned, it was a reasonably nominal figure, but it helped establish a formal, contractual relationship.

The navy did not receive any revenues from Life Services even though Terry had created the Rejuv and Eternity processes. This was left to the local government.

The navy had seen significant growth. There were now fifty battles fleets divided into ten divisions, commanded by Admirals and fleet Admirals. There were twenty regional defence centres commanded by vice Admirals. Each planet still had a fort that was under naval control. Planetary force-fields were still under civilian management.

There were now five exploratory fleets commanded by Admirals. They tended to have close contacts with the civilian world and especially universities.

The Marine Corps consisted of two hundred and fifty thousand highly trained troopers and had two dedicated marine fleets. There was a Special Services Unit of thirty-thousand commandos. It also had its own fleet of very specialised vessels.

The navy now had its own manufacturing facilities, space docks, airports, sports, and hotel complexes, universities, prisons, hospitals etc. It had every facility that a large city would have and housing for well over a million employees.

Admiral Mustard had watched a twentieth-century film called Thunderbirds and decided to emulate it. There was now a dedicated rescue team with a very extensive range of equipment. There was also a fleet of transport vessels. Admiral Mustard made sure that naval rescues and mercy missions were well publicised. To do that, he had a capable marketing team. Sheila Taylor still headed Chemlife Sales.

One of the biggest departments was 'Fleet Operations'. They effectively managed the fleets as directed by the Admirals. A considerable amount of effort had been used to ensure that they had the most effective and secure control systems. Their areas of responsibility included weapons management, navigation and piloting, munitions management, defence, security, risk analysis, and interfacing with other naval functions. Their HQ was unofficially named GAD2.

Planet Napoleon itself was a mighty fortress. It was partly modelled on The Brakendeth home world. Luckily, Terry, the last Brakendethian, had the plans stored in his head. There was a separate Home Fleet just to protect the military planet.

Few people knew that the military had a second planet as a back-up which was not surprisingly called Wellington. AI Central was heavily involved with both planets, but they could still function if AI Central was incapacitated. In fact, a back-up of AI Central was kept on Planet Napoleon.

Deep tunnels had been built into the very fabric of the planet, but with the planet buster functionality, no planet was safe.

There were a series of long-range detection units scattered around the extremes of The Galactium. In addition, there was an extensive network of automated monitoring stations. And, of course, there was an industrial network of portal routes. These were not particularly useful to the navy as they had their own ship-board portal generators. The navy could reach almost every part of The Galactium in less than an Earth day and most parts much quicker.

The Naval Intelligence Function looked for both internal and external threats. There was also a small anti-terrorism unit, and, of course, there was a Military Police Department.

Location: Admiral Mustard's Office, Planet Napoleon
Sequence of Events: 3

The biggest problem Admiral Mustard had was the lack of any threat. He had the most extensive military organisation in Earth's history. It was probably the largest for any race in The Galactium, but he couldn't be sure of that. But it was just vegetating.

Of course, they were carrying out the normal time-wasters: courtesy visits, training exercises, weapon testing, patrols etc. There was some escorting work and exploration, but not enough.

At least these peaceful times allowed Admiral Mustard to pursue his latest love. It wasn't really a pursuit as she had already been caught and rodgered quite a few times. He was amazed that she was over nine hundred years old and still almost a virgin. He hadn't really got over the loss of Edel, but Lady Enyo was a very pleasing distraction. He wasn't sure how The Galactium would react if it became public knowledge.

It certainly wasn't a crime or even illegal, but the men in suits would certainly frown. The current president would suffer an outbreak of apprehensive frowning. Possibly apoplectic frowning. It wasn't that The Chosen were a threat any more. They had integrated into The Galactium better than any other race. There was a natural affinity between Earth and Olympia. There was a shared history, but sadly some of the humans had an inferiority complex towards them.

Great chunks of humanity were still suffering from deep wounds. Admiral Thanatos's description and stories of Jesus hadn't been warmly welcomed. Despite the photos, many Christians couldn't accept that he was a terrorist who took up arms against the Romans. The images of his wife and children were particularly upsetting, and the fact that he also had several mistresses hardly met favour with the Catholic Church.

Admiral Thanatos had a collection of incredibly early bibles, which he donated to several museums. They created a veritable storm of conflicts.

Historians were fascinated by Admiral Thanatos's knowledge of human warfare. He proved that what we knew about the past was pathetic and usually so completely wrong that it was embarrassing. In many cases, we couldn't even correctly identify where the battles took place.

Experts from Olympus led archaeological digs on Earth to uncover ancient secrets. They quickly explained many of humankind's long-standing mysteries.

Gradually more and more Olympians took over critical posts in The Galactium's government, treasury, educational bodies, institutes, justice system, healthcare etc. It was starting to become noticeable, but they proved to be great administrators. They were dedicated and enthusiastic, hard-working, and ambitious. They loved the excitement and hurly-burly of The Galactium. It was so different from their staid old organisations.

The Olympians also loved humans. Inter-marriage was becoming common, especially as child-bearing was not a problem, and human women were happy to have sex whenever it suited them. The Olympian population had only just accepted that sex could be an enjoyable activity, almost a hobby. Their upper class had always known this.

The Olympian government was worried that their civilisation would be absorbed into humanity. Others saw it as a good thing. When you came down to it, weren't humans really Olympians?

Admiral Mustard was waiting for his mistress to turn up. She was always late unless it was a ceremonial event, and Jack didn't have ceremonial duties on his mind. Since his Rejuv treatment, he was as randy as hell.

Lady Enyo, 'How are you, Jack, you old bastard?'

Admiral Mustard, 'Not so much with the old, anyway you can't talk.'

Lady Enyo, 'Are we here to talk or fuck?'

Admiral Mustard, 'Sometimes you are so forward, you bitch.'

Lady Enyo, 'What is a bitch?'

Admiral Mustard, 'Get your knickers off and get on my desk.' She never wore any knickers and did as she was instructed. Jack was sitting in his comfortable black leather chair and surveyed the scene in front of him.

Here was a beautiful woman, nearly a thousand years old, with her long dress hitched up around her waist. On show was a very moist vagina and a dryer anus. She had a complete lack of modesty.

Lady Enyo, 'Are you going to fuck, what do you call it, my fanny or my arse?'

Admiral wasn't really into anal sex. To be honest, he had never tried it, so he decided to give it a go.

He pulled his erect phallus from his pants, squirted some moisturiser on her bum and gently eased his cock into her anus. He could see that she was finding it painful, but then it was her idea, and she needed to be taught a lesson.

He couldn't see how Lady Enyo wasn't going to get an orgasm this way, and he gently put his fingers up her fanny. He could feel his cock through the walls of her vagina. This was working, she was starting to come, and he upped his rhythm.

Suddenly the admiral's PA rushed into the room. She was shocked to see her admiral, Admiral Mustard, head of The Galactium's Navy, with his penis up Lady Enyo's arse and his fingers in her fanny. She was so shocked, but since the Rejuv campaign, there had been so much depravity. She was a bit annoyed that she wasn't getting any.

Lieutenant Jane, 'Sir, we have an incident.'

Admiral Mustard, 'That makes a nice change. What has happened?'

Lieutenant Jane, 'One of our exploratory vessels has had an altercation with an unknown alien.'

Admiral Mustard, 'Was anyone hurt?'

Lieutenant Jane, 'No, Sir, but as you are a bit busy, I will send the report across to you.'

Admiral Mustard, 'Thank you, Jane, that would be immensely helpful.'

Jane was impressed that the admiral continued his fucking regardless of her intrusion. When the door closed, she heard two orgasmic screams. Actually, she had her ear pressed against the door to see if there was going to be a climax. She wasn't disappointed and sat down by her desk and started masturbating, imaging that it was her on the desk and not Lady Enyo. Perhaps she will get her chance later.

It should be pointed out that Mr and Mrs Jane decided to call their daughter Jane. Yes, her name was Jane Jane.

Location: Admiral Mustard's Office, Planet Napoleon
Sequence of Events: 4

Admiral Mustard, 'Comms, get me the captain of GNS Scott.'

Comms, 'Yes, Sir.'

Captain Caine, 'Good day, Sir. Have you read the report?'

Admiral Mustard, 'Yes, I was impressed by the report, but I would prefer to hear about the incident from yourself.'

Captain Caine, 'Yes, Sir. Shall I start?'

Admiral Mustard, 'Yes, please.'

Captain Caine, 'GNS Scott had been ordered to explore the Ursa Major galaxy with particular emphasis on "I Zwicky 18". It's the youngest known galaxy in the visible universe, and it is filled with star-forming regions which are creating many hot, young, blue stars at an exceedingly high rate.

'We were simply cruising when an alien ship appeared next to us. There were no impressive visual effects or welcoming speeches. It just arrived next to us and matched our speed. Our systems detected that it was scanning us, and we employed countermeasures. Whether they worked or not was hard to tell.

'As you would expect, I ordered, "battle stations". There was no response from the alien vessel. It just continued to match our speed. I ordered several course changes, but it matched them precisely without any hesitation. It was like it knew our moves before we did.

'Then we got a message, "Tell Admiral Mustard that he must remember." It was repeated three times, and the vessel disappeared. It didn't fly off. It just disappeared.'

Admiral Mustard, 'What have I got to remember?'

Captain Caine, 'No idea, Sir.'

Admiral Mustard, 'Sorry, I was thinking aloud. Did you take a photo of the ship?

Captain Caine, 'We tried to, but their image didn't register.'

Admiral Mustard, 'Was it an illusion?'

Captain Caine, 'Possibly, but the whole crew saw it, and our ship could register its presence. Very strange.'

Admiral Mustard, 'Very strange indeed. Thank you for your time, Captain.'

Admiral Mustard was left with a mystery which he parked in his mystery box.

Location: The President's Office, Presidential Palace, Planet Earth
Sequence of Events: 5

President Fonda had always been embarrassed about his family connection to the film industry. He hated been called 'Easy Rider' and 'Barbarella'. They were ancient movies that had no relevance to today's world.

It was hard enough following the footsteps of President Padfield, a man that he admired. However, he had been too soft at times. But it was hard to follow the Rejuv and Eternity campaign and to ignore the fact that he was a war hero. Padfield was definitely a charismatic Leader while he was an accountant who luckily followed the adage of being in the right place at the right time. He needed to add that he knew the right people, looked right, had the right safe history, and married the right woman. Even his politics were right. Perhaps his appointment was right after all.

What wasn't right was Admiral Mustard sleeping with Lady Enyo. It certainly wasn't right. Sleeping with anyone who you are not married to is definitely not right. Then he wondered why they called it 'sleeping'. They should call it what it is: fornicating. In fact, fornicating during office hours on company property. He wasn't going to have it.

But then he had no effective control over the navy, and that wasn't right. Perhaps his job was to put things right? That was the problem; he wasn't sure what his job was. He knew how to react to situations but not how to instigate new policies or ideas. He didn't like the military or the diplomatic service or most of his ministers, and he certainly disliked most aliens. He really didn't want to be in their presence. Perhaps it wasn't the best outlook for the Presidency of The Galactium, but he would do the right thing.

Location: Terry's Office, Planet Napoleon
Sequence of Events: 6

Terry's best friend was AI Central. His second-best friend was his wife. He couldn't call his two children, 'friends' as he didn't know them. He knew them as a distant father. They lived in the same house, but he had no relationship or rapport with them. He just found it too difficult to relate to a gibbering, orifice-leaking dumb animal. He had a similar problem with his wife, but at least she could cuddle him. He liked that.

Terry's job title was 'Director of Advanced Science'. He had three roles:

1. Military developments as per the schedule,
2. Consultancy, as required,
3. Products developments for sale.

He had developed quite a few products that were now an integral part of The Galactium: replicator, transporter, cancer cure, Rejuv and Eternity processes, force-fields, and a few others. These were effectively publicly owned by The Galactium. However, the navy owned a range of products and marketed through a network of local stores.

Terry was proud of his achievements:

Ref	Medical cures
M1	Common cold
M2	Malaria
M3	Asthma
M4	Dementia
M5	Acne
M6	Baldness
M7	Tooth decay
M8	Heart disease
M9	Headaches

Ref	New powers and enhancements
S1	Telescopic vision
S2	Microscopic vision
S3	Improved memory recall
S4	Improved hearing

S5	Improved mind's eye capabilities
S6	Improved linguistic capabilities
S7	Improved mathematical capabilities
S8	Improved strength
S9	Improved stamina
S10	Improved confidence
S11	Improved pain control
S12	Weight control
S13	Control of body temperature
S14	Limited mind reading
S15	Improved smell
S16	Improved sense of balance

He had been set a new range of challenges:
- Cure for cystic fibrosis
- Cure for cystitis
- Cure for diabetes
- Cure for gout
- Cure for hepatitis
- Improved sense of taste
- Improved resistance to poisoning
- Improved tolerance to all bites and stings
- Ability to change skin and hair colour.

It was going to be jolly good fun.

Location: Admiral Mustard's Office, Planet Napoleon
Sequence of Events: 7

Lieutenant Jane, 'Admiral, there is a call from Admiral Bumelton.'

Admiral Mustard, 'Hello me, old mucker, how is it going?'

Admiral Bumelton, 'I would say strange, Jack, very strange.'

Admiral Mustard, 'Well, you have succeeded in getting my interest.'

Admiral Bumelton, 'Well, I was taking one of the new fleets out on a training session when a massive fleet confronted us. When I say massive, I mean it. They must have outnumbered us a thousand to one.'

Admiral, 'What did you do?'

Admiral Bumelton, 'We opened up communications, and they responded in English.'

Admiral Mustard, 'What did they say?'

Admiral Bumelton, 'They said, "Tell Admiral Mustard that he must remember." It was repeated three times, and then the fleet disappeared. They didn't fly off; they just disappeared.'

Admiral Mustard, 'That's the second time I've heard that. I've absolutely no idea what I've got to remember.'

Admiral Bumelton, 'I wonder if they will give us any clues?'

Admiral Mustard, 'I hope so. What images have you got of the fleet?'

Admiral Bumelton, 'That's another strange thing. We don't have any images of the fleet, but it was there.'

Admiral Mustard, 'That happened last time as well. Can you describe the fleet?'

Admiral Bumelton, 'I can recall a vague glimpse of it in my mind's eye, but it's not strong enough to describe it to you. It's as if something is stopping me.'

Admiral Mustard, 'This doesn't make sense. It must be some form of mass-illusion.'

Admiral Bumelton, 'It felt very real, and our ships registered the alien fleet.'

Admiral Mustard, 'What was your emotional reaction?'

Admiral Bumelton, 'It's interesting that you asked that. I felt peace, love, friendship, warmth, all good things. There was no threat whatsoever.'

Admiral Mustard, 'So what have I got to remember?'

Location: Conference Room, Planet Napoleon
Sequence of Events: 8

Admiral Mustard called a meeting of his full command structure. The following were present:
- Admiral George Bumelton, Division One
- Admiral John Bonner, Division Two
- Admiral Phil Richardson, Division Three
- Admiral Calensky Wallett, Division Four
- Admiral Steve Adams, Division Five
- Admiral Ama Abosa, Division Six
- Admiral Ernst Muller, Division Seven, and Support
- Admiral Lesley Chudzinski, Division Eight
- Admiral Nubia Tersoo, Division Nine
- Admiral Mateo Dobson, Division Ten
- Admiral Jill Bosman, RTC One
- Admiral Sammy Fogg, RTC Two
- Admiral Sue Spangler, RTC Three
- Admiral Lenny Hubbard, RTC Four
- Admiral James Patel, RTC Five
- Admiral Karl Lamberty, Home Defence (Planet Napoleon)
- Admiral Rachel Zakotti, Planetary Defence
- Admiral Liz Clowe, Exploration One
- Admiral Alison Strauss, Exploration Two
- Admiral James Mynd, Special Projects
- Commander Martin Black, Special Operations
- Commander Bill Tower, Marine Corps
- Dr Doris Frost, Chief Medical Officer
- Sales Director, Sheila Taylor
- Jill Ginger, Fleet HQ, Head of Science
- Alison Walsh, Fleet HQ, Head of Engineering
- Jeremy Jotts, Fleet HQ, Head of Staffing
- Louise Forrester, Fleet HQ, Head of Logistics and Production
- Madie Milburn, Fleet HQ, Head of Intelligence
- Salek Patel, Fleet HQ, Head of Communications
- Denise Smith, Fleet HQ, Head of Navigation & Exploration

- AI Central
- Terry, Director of Advanced Science

They followed their standard agenda with regular updates from the following:

- Fleet Operations, division by division
- RTC Operations, RTC by RTC
- Exploration
- Sales and marketing
- Marine Corps and Special Ops
- Science and engineering
- Production
- Staffing and training
- Logistics and production
- Intelligence
- Communications
- Medical

There was nothing special to report, so they moved onto AOB.

Admiral Mustard outlined the two incidents and asked for any suggestions. What was he supposed to remember?

Terry didn't think that it was anything to do with The Brakendethians.

Admiral Mustard checked with The Chosen, and they couldn't suggest anything. They didn't believe it was Zeus. It was not the style of The Elders.

It remained a mystery.

Admiral Mustard wasn't sure if he should put his forces on alert, but so far, there had been no threat.

The meeting ended with little to do.

Later that night, Admiral Mustard tossed and turned. It was one of those nights where he just couldn't get to sleep. It was bloody annoying because he had a busy day in the morning. He tried to work out what was causing it, and then it dawned on him that it was the remembrance mystery. And then he fell asleep.

Dreams are strange intangible things that, most of the time, really don't make sense. How do these dream interpretation books work? Admiral Mustard's dream was so real, so intense, and so worrying. A young teenager version of Admiral Mustard was walking through a desiccated desert. There were dry tears in his eyes, tears of distress, as there was no way out. He knew he was doomed, but he continued to walk or rather drag his young body along.

Then an elegant, well-dressed man appeared next to him and said, 'Jack, you need to remember, the future of The Galactium depends on it.' And then Jack woke up.

It was a seriously real, intense dream, but then it started to fade, as is the way of all dreams. What didn't fade was the message.

Location: Admiral Mustard's Office, Planet Napoleon
Sequence of Events: 9

AI Central, 'Jack, there has been a serious assault on our IT systems.'

Admiral Mustard, 'What's happened?'

AI Central, 'Every monitor, every display and every phone has been taken over.'

Admiral Mustard, 'We probably hadn't given enough thought to a cyber-attack. I guess that we were complacent because we had you.'

AI Central, 'This isn't a typical cyber-attack. I get thousands of them every day. Here someone or some organisation has only taken over the display technology. The underlying CPU activity is continuing as normal. I tell you, Jack, that this is not technically impossible. I cannot stop it because it can't be happening.'

Admiral Mustard, 'What did Sherlock Holmes say, "When you have eliminated the impossible, whatever remains, however improbable, must be the truth." I'm not sure if that helps?'

AI Central, 'It does in a way because it's correct.'

Admiral Mustard, 'You didn't tell me what the message was on the screen.'

AI Central, 'Same old, same old.'

Admiral Mustard, 'Is that what it said?'

AI Central, 'No, it said, "Wake up, Jack, you need to remember".'

Admiral Mustard, 'For Fuck's sake, now the whole Galactium knows that I need to remember. I've no idea what it is.'

AI Central, 'Let's be logical about it.'

Admiral Mustard, 'What is there to be logical about?'

AI Central, 'We could try and analyse your memories over the last twenty years. We could try hypnosis. It might be that you have a self-imposed memory block or an external agency has interfered with your mind.'

Admiral Mustard, 'Let's think about it. There are no clues regarding what I should remember. I just don't know what it is referring to. Shouldn't we be focusing on the messenger rather than the recipient?'

AI Central, 'That is a fair point.'

Admiral Mustard, 'What do we know about the messenger?'

AI Central, 'Not a lot, we know:
• that it can communicate with spacecraft,
• that it can emulate a ship and a fleet,

- that it can speak English,
- that it can invade your dreams,
- that it can take over display units on a galactic scale,
- that it is probably not The Brakendeth,
- that it's not aggressive or threatening,
- that it appears benign,
- that it is persistent.'

Admiral Mustard, 'It sounds Godlike.'

AI Central, 'How many Gods do we know?'

Admiral Mustard, 'Zeus, but The Chosen have more or less ruled him out.'

AI Central, 'By the way, the screens are back to normal now.'

Location: The President's Office, Presidential Palace, Planet Earth
Sequence of Events: 10

President Fonda and Admiral Mustard were meeting to discuss the major hacking incident.

President Fonda, 'This invasion of our IT systems is totally unacceptable. It is an invasion of our personal and industrial space and must be stopped. I've had hundreds of calls from planetary presidents, heads of industry and government ministers. It cannot be tolerated. I will not have it. What have you got to say for yourself?'

Admiral Mustard, 'Mr President, I can only agree.'

President Fonda, 'There is no point in just agreeing. I need a document that I can circulate to key people explaining what happened and how we will stop it from happening again. It's really not acceptable. It's embarrassing. It makes me look stupid and inept.'

Admiral Mustard, 'Mr President, I can only agree.'

President Fonda, 'You may be head of the navy, but I need to know what you plan to do.'

Admiral Mustard, 'Mr President, I'm not planning to do anything.'

President Fonda, 'How can you just sit there in your smug uniform and refuse to take action. You know that there have been complaints about you and your immoral actions. It just can't carry on.'

Admiral Mustard, 'What are you talking about?'

President Fonda, 'You know exactly what I'm talking about.'

Admiral Mustard, 'I'm afraid I don't.'

President Fonda, 'Everyone knows that you have been fornicating with aliens.'

Admiral Mustard, 'Mr President, I'm not sure what my sexual activities have got to do with you.'

President Fonda, 'I'm in charge. Everything is to do with me.'

Admiral Mustard, 'Mr President, the navy is independent of The Galactium.'

President Fonda, 'Not if I have my way.'

Admiral Mustard, 'Mr President, I know that we have our differences, but we have to find a way of working together.'

President Fonda, 'You can't even stop cyber-attacks.'

Admiral Mustard, 'Mr President, the prevention of cyber-attacks is not my responsibility. We can consult AI Central if you want confirmation.'

President Fonda, 'You keep that heathen bunch of electronics away from me. It's not natural. God wouldn't want it.'

Admiral Mustard, 'What God are you referring to?'

President Fonda, 'The one and only true God.'

Admiral Mustard, 'Is that the Christian, Jewish or Muslim God?'

President Fonda, 'You are a blasphemer, Sir, a blasphemer.'

Admiral Mustard, 'Mr President, there are thousands of religions in The Galactium with hundreds of Gods. I've even met Zeus.'

President Fonda, 'Get out of my office now. I refuse to hear any more of this.'

Admiral Mustard, 'Mr President, with pleasure.'

President Fonda, 'I will be putting in a formal complaint regarding your inability to stop the hacking. That is your responsibility.'

Admiral Mustard stormed out.

Admiral Mustard, 'AI Central, 'Did you hear that?'

AI Central, 'Of course.'

Admiral Mustard, 'How did he ever get to become president?'

AI Central, 'He was in the wrong place at the wrong time. He knew the wrong people, had the wrong look, and even married the wrong woman.'

Admiral Mustard, 'I see trouble ahead.'

AI Central, 'You need to work on consolidating your position.'

Admiral Mustard, 'Any ideas on that?'

AI Central, 'I do have a few.'

Admiral Mustard, 'Go on.'

AI Central, 'Currently, your income stream is far higher than you need. You will be building up large cash reserves, which will look very tempting to your enemies. I would recommend spending it in a prudent way.

'I would suggest two things:

1. Appoint a diplomatic staff officer for every planet to foster and develop a relationship with the navy

2. Either lend money to the planetary governments or carry out

noticeable public developments: museums, sports complexes, training centres, food storage, whatever the local economy needs.'

Admiral Mustard, 'You are a genius.'

AI Central, 'I know, not bad for a heathen bunch of electronics.'

Admiral Mustard, 'By the way, how did he find out about Lady Enyo? Was it Jane?'

AI Central, 'No, it wasn't Jane, but these things always seem to get out.'

Location: Admiral Mustard's Office, Planet Napoleon
Sequence of Events: 11

Alarms were ringing in GAD2.

Fleet Control, 'Admiral, one of our exploratory ships is under attack. They want to know if they can return fire, and before you ask, they can't out-run the alien craft.'

Admiral Mustard, 'My orders:
- Return fire to disable rather than destroy.
- Send out the nearest fleet to support them.'

Fleet Operations, 'Yes, Sir.'

Admiral Mustard, 'Do you have any images of the alien vessel?'

Fleet Operations, 'Yes, Sir. It should be on your screen now.'

Admiral Mustard, 'What is it?'

Fleet Operations, 'It looks like a cloud. It appears to change shape as it changes direction.'

Admiral Mustard, 'How quickly will the fleet get there?'

Fleet Operations, 'It's hard to tell because the portal technology will only get them to the edge of our space.'

Admiral Mustard, 'Is the alien craft actually attacking our ship?'

Fleet Operations, 'We believe so. Our shields are holding up against an unknown weapon.'

Admiral Mustard, 'Obviously, the alien ship is not on our database?'

Fleet Operations, 'No, Sir. We have incorporated every known alien species into our database. We have collected all of the alien data from our partner races and especially The Chosen.'

Admiral Mustard, 'Can you check with them all again just in case they have come across them before?'

Fleet Operations, 'Yes, Sir. They had already started the work because they knew the Admiral so well.'

Admiral Mustard didn't feel that this was going to be a crisis. It would sort itself out. Just call it a second sense or perhaps the view of a very experienced Commander.

Fleet Operations, 'Sir. GNS Magellan has been destroyed.'

Admiral Mustard, 'How?'

Fleet Operations, 'It appears to be some sort of dissolving beam. The ship simply fell apart.'

Admiral Mustard, 'My orders:

- The fleet will continue towards the point where GNS Magellan was destroyed.
- The fleet will avoid conflict with the alien vessels, but it can defend itself if necessary.
- Obtain information about the aliens if possible.'

Fleet Operations, 'Yes, Sir.'

Admiral Mustard, 'Comms, inform the president about our latest encounter:'

Comms, 'Yes, Sir.'

Location: Conference Room, Presidential Palace, Planet Earth
Sequence of Events: 12

President Fonda had his secret gang of advisers and supporters. He rarely attended Parliament or any of the council meetings. They weren't really his type of people.

President Fonda, 'Gentlemen, God be with you. We need to work on our plans for the next five years. I will reiterate our objectives:

1. To civilise The Galactium through the teachings of the Bible.
2. To prosecute non-Christian groups and promote the one true God.
3. To ensure that Christians control every human planet in The Galactium.
4. To eliminate all alien cultures from The Galactium.
5. To take control of the navy.
6. To eradicate LGBT criminals.
7. To criminalise birth control and abortion.
8. To introduce the death penalty and harsher sentences for crimes against the church.
9. To stop the eternal life programme.
10. To reduce all forms of taxation.
11. To denationalise state health systems.
12. To reduce the involvement of AI Central.
13. To weaken the power of The Galactium to promote self-determinism at both a planetary and individual level.'

President Fonda, 'What we need to agree on a set of actions to achieve the above. Any suggestions or volunteers?'

Bishop Needwell, 'I suggest that I put a plan together for points one and two.'

John Dieman, 'I'm happy to work on a campaign against the navy, point five.'

James Harbour, 'I'm happy to work on points six and seven.'

Fred Newbridge, 'I will work on point nine.'

President Fonda, 'I will facilitate the rest. In future, I don't think we can meet in this building as it is gradually going to get uncomfortable, and we need to avoid any spying on us by AI Central.'

Bishop Needwell, 'I agree with you. We also need to remember that we are saving souls. It is our duty to mankind.'

There were no female members because they weren't allowed. They should be practising their child-rearing skills and not getting involved in men's work.

Location: Admiral Mustard's Office, Planet Napoleon
Sequence of Events: 13

AI Central, 'So that you know a group of right-wing fascists have been meeting with the president in his palace. My lip-reading skills are limited, but they are targeting the navy. Did you want a list of the attendees?'

Admiral Mustard, 'I don't condone this sort of thing, but yes, please send me the list. And thank you.'

AI Central, 'It's a pleasure. By the way, I'm a target as well.'

Admiral Mustard, 'At least I'm in good company.'

AI Central, 'I wouldn't go that far.'

Admiral Mustard, 'Changing the subject, did you hear about the attack on our exploratory ship?'

AI Central, 'Yes, I'm a bit worried about it. What they didn't tell you is that the dissolving process took some time. The crew met agonising deaths watching their bodies slowly dissolve.'

Admiral Mustard, 'That's horrible. I better warn the fleet that's on the way there.'

AI Central, 'I've already done that. However, we better keep a firm eye on that fleet. They really are flying into the unknown, and I have a bad feeling about it.'

Admiral Mustard, 'I didn't know that you got bad feelings.'

AI Central, 'I think it's mostly statistical.'

Location: On Board Admiral Farina's Flagship
Sequence of Events: 14

This was Admiral Farina's first solo mission as an admiral. His fleet consisted of about three thousand ships of the line. He divided into seven squadrons, one in advance in attack mode, five in standard cruising formation and a rear-guard in a defensive posture.

He was worried about the alien threat, especially when AI Central sent him the video showing Dissolution in action. To put it mildly, it was sickening. Anyway, it seemed strange looking for a cloud in outer space.

Then it happened, an elegant, well-dressed man appeared on the bridge of the flagship. He looked like a regular human being, but he just appeared out of nowhere with a smile on his face. Then there was total silence, and the man said, 'Tell Admiral Mustard that he must remember.' He repeated it twice and disappeared. There was no fading, just instant disappearance.

Admiral Farina, 'Comms, get me Admiral Mustard.'

Comms, 'Yes, Sir.'

Admiral Mustard, 'Good day, Jon.' Jack was finding it harder to remember the first names of all of his Admirals. There were so many of them. They had also decided to use the term 'Good day' instead of morning, afternoon etc., as it was nearly always wrong.

Admiral Farina was nervous about talking to the legendary Admiral Mustard, 'Good day, Sir, I need to inform you that we have just had a visitation.'

Admiral Mustard, 'A visitation?'

Admiral Farina, 'Yes Sir, it was an elegant looking man who repeated the following phrase twice: "Admiral Mustard must remember." Then he simply disappeared.'

Admiral Mustard, 'This is becoming a bit of a habit. I've no idea what he wants me to remember.'

Admiral Farina, 'You don't seem too surprised.'

Admiral Mustard, 'This has happened a few times now. It is a mystery, but I'm glad you are on the blower now as I'm a bit concerned about these cloud aliens. It smells wrong.'

Admiral Farina, 'Have you got any advice?'

Admiral Mustard, 'Be cautious. Be more cautious than you would normally be. Use drones to investigate.'

Admiral Farina, 'Thanks for the advice, Sir.'

Location: Admiral Mustard's Office, Planet Napoleon
Sequence of Events: 15

Admiral Mustard, 'Hi George.'

Admiral Bumelton, 'I thought that we were supposed to say good day?'

Admiral Mustard, 'Fuck off.'

Admiral Bumelton, 'That's my Jack. Are you alright?'

Admiral Mustard, 'Not really. I'm being hounded by this man who keeps telling me to remember.'

Admiral Bumelton, 'And me.'

Admiral Mustard, 'Why didn't you tell me?'

Admiral Bumelton, 'I thought that I was going mad. He has even appeared in my dreams.'

Admiral Mustard, 'Me too. I really can't think of anything that needs remembering.'

Admiral Bumelton, 'I've had the same reaction although I have thought of something.'

Admiral Mustard, 'Go on.'

Admiral Bumelton, 'Do you remember, sorry I couldn't help saying it, we had that strange experience where we forgot about it, but some very vague memories remained.'

Admiral Mustard, 'I believe that you've got it. I was going to use the term "time travel", but that seems ridiculous now.'

Admiral Bumelton, 'It does sound ridiculous, but the memories are in my head surrounded by mist. Somehow my brain can't access them.'

Admiral Mustard, 'AI Central suggested hypnosis. I might give it a try. Do you want to come with me?'

Admiral Bumelton, 'I would be honoured.'

Location: On Board Admiral Farina's Flagship
Sequence of Events: 16

Admiral Farina thought that it is not every day that you get a visitor mysteriously appearing on your command deck. But then it is not every day that you are hunting a cloud.

Then there was a call from the scouting squadron.

Captain Mills, 'Admiral, we have found your cloud. It seems to have grown somewhat.'

Admiral Farina, 'My orders:
• Stop engines.
• Form defensive formation.
• Wait for the rest of the fleet to join you.
• Retire if the cloud comes towards you.'

Captain Mills, 'Yes, Sir.'

It wasn't long before the fleet arrived.

Admiral Farina, 'My Orders:
• Send a drone into the cloud to investigate.'

Fleet Operations, 'Yes, Sir.'

The drone started dissolving before it entered the cloud, but then the cloud rushed the fleet.

Admiral Farina, 'My orders:
• All vessels withdraw immediately.'

But it was too late. Most of the fleet was in the process of dissolving.

The rear-guard realised that there was nothing they could do, and they made their withdrawal. Actually, they fled as fast as they could.

For some of them, they were not fast enough as the cloud was in hot pursuit. Any straggler got dissolved. It was a particularly unpleasant death as you could see it coming. It was like a steady laser beam that wiped out anything in its path regardless of the material's composition. It didn't matter if it was mineral, metal, hyper-plastic, liquid, animal, or vegetable; it got dissolved. It took a human a while to die as the beam gradually worked along the body. The human brain suffered a mixture of shock and disbelief.

What was even stranger was that the dissolved material just disappeared. It didn't go anywhere. The atoms simply ceased to exist, which went against all the laws of physics.

There had initially been about five hundred vessels in the rear-guard, but the cloud had reduced it to three hundred. The Dissolution seemed to slow it down, but then it sped up again.

Captain French, 'Comms, put me through to Admiral Chudzinski.'

Comms, 'Yes, Sir.'

Captain French, 'Admiral, we have lost Fleet 8-2.'

Admiral Chudzinski, 'What do you mean?'

Captain French, 'We detected the cloud, which was over two kilometres long. The fleet lined up in a standard defensive formation with my squadron acting as a rear-guard. The admiral sent in a drone to investigate, which almost immediately dissolved. Then the cloud attacked. There are no ships, just a cloud.

Most of the fleet dissolved, and we fled. There was nothing we could do to help. The cloud is in hot pursuit and picking us off one by one. We are down to two hundred and seventy vessels.'

Admiral Chudzinski, 'Where are you now?'

Captain French, 'We should be entering Galactium space in the next few hours. What are your orders? I'm worried about bringing danger along with me.'

Admiral Chudzinski, 'I will get back to you.'

Location: Admiral Mustard's Office, Planet Napoleon
Sequence of Events: 17

Admiral Mustard, 'Hi Lesley, what should we do?'

Admiral Chudzinski, 'What weapon systems have we got that will defeat a cloud?'

Admiral Mustard, 'I guess that it will use the portal system as soon as the rear-guard reaches Galactium space. I'm assuming that the cloud will be left behind.'

Admiral Chudzinski, 'That was exactly my thinking, but we need a way of tracking it. It's far too dangerous to let it go unchecked.'

Admiral Mustard, 'I agree, but have we learnt anything new about it?'

Admiral Chudzinski, 'Only that it is a cloud. There do not appear to be any vessels involved.'

Admiral Mustard, 'We can't be sure of that. It can't be a natural phenomenon as it is chasing and destroying our fleet.'

Admiral Chudzinski, 'How do we defend against it?'

Admiral Mustard, 'If it stops at the edge of our space, then we have time to brainstorm a solution.'

Admiral Chudzinski, 'Changing the subject, I need to tell you about a recurring dream I keep having.'

Admiral Mustard, 'It's not about a tall, elegant man asking you to tell me to remember?'

Admiral Chudzinski, 'How would you know that?'

Admiral Mustard, 'Because it has been a regular occurrence. I'm working on a plan, but it's all a bit mysterious.'

Admiral Chudzinski, 'That's the story of our lives nowadays.'

Location: Terry's Office, Planet Napoleon
Sequence of Events: 18

AI Central, 'Hi Terry, how's it going?'

Terry, 'My wife doesn't understand me.'

AI Central, 'Not that old cliché. To be honest, no one understands you. You are unique. What's your actual problem?'

Terry, 'I wanted sex last night.'

AI Central, 'Did you tell her?'

Terry, 'I couldn't because she was asleep.'

AI Central, 'What time did you get home?'

Terry, '04.00. I don't need to sleep, as you know.'

AI Central, 'You need to make an effort to fit in with her biological clock.'

Terry, 'Oh, why is life so difficult?'

AI Central, 'Have you been tracking this cloud problem.'

Terry, 'Yes, it's TIME correcting anomalies.'

AI Central, 'What do you mean?'

Terry, 'Do you remember when the fleet was sent into the future?'

AI Central, 'I do, but no one else does, except you.'

Terry, 'Well, TIME fixes the minor anomalies without anyone knowing, but more drastic action is required when there has been a significant anomaly. Anything that shouldn't exist is dissolved.'

AI Central, 'What or who is this TIME creature?'

Terry, 'No one really knows as we have to go back to the time before The Elders existed. Rules were established, and forces were created to stop the manipulation of time. Clearly, those rules have been broken, and the corrective forces have been unleashed.'

AI Central, 'Where will it end?'

Terry, 'When it feels that the original timeline is more or less on track. Who are we to understand the mysteries of time? If I search The Brakendeth records, they experienced a similar position. It was down to two or three key individuals who shouldn't have died. When they rose from the dead, then TIME was satisfied.'

AI Central, 'How do we find out what TIME wants?'

Terry, 'No, idea. I'm not a God.'

Location: Admiral Mustard's Office, Planet Napoleon
Sequence of Events: 19

It was Tuesday and time for Lady Enyo's seeing to. It was scheduled for every other Tuesday at lunch time. Admiral Mustard found it a bit clinical, but as they say, 'don't look a gift horse in the mouth'. He had no intention of checking out her teeth.

She walked in, arrogant in her splendour.

Lady Enyo, 'Do you want me to spread myself across your desk again?' Admiral Mustard just nodded.

She pulled up her dress and exposed her genitals to the delight of Admiral Mustard. He never knew what to say. Thank you never seemed enough. What he was thinking was quite the opposite, nearer to 'This bitch is going to get the fucking of a lifetime.'

He pulled her to the edge of his desk and spread her legs. His cock was already throbbing. It was not the time for gentleness. He had difficulty extracting his engorged cock from his trousers but wasted no time in entering his lover. He decided not to hold back on the thrusting of her cute cunt. Her whole body shook in response to his aggression. She came first, and then he let loose a prodigious amount of hot spunk.

Lady Enyo stood up, straightened her dress, and said, 'Thank you, kind Sir, I will see you in the Conference room.'

At least this time Jane wasn't an observer, but she heard what was going on. She had worked out that every other Tuesday lunch time was for fucking. That gave her nearly a fortnight in between to offer her services.

Location: Medical Facility, Planet Napoleon
Sequence of Events: 20

Admirals Mustard and Bumelton were sitting in the reception room, waiting to see Dr Doris Frost. They both felt a bit like pregnant fathers.

Dr Doris Frost, 'Come in, gentlemen, I hope I didn't keep you long?'

Admiral Mustard, 'Hi Doris, no longer than usual.'

Dr Doris Frost, 'Before we get into a discussion, I must tell you about a dream I had. It was bizarre.'

Admiral Bumelton, 'Not you as well.'

Admiral Mustard, 'Was there a tall, elegant man telling you to tell me to remember?'

Dr Doris Frost, 'Yes, it was the same message that I had on my phone the other day. I thought it was good that I was seeing you as you could tell me what's going on.'

Admiral Mustard, 'That's why we are here. I know that you have a hypnotist on your team.'

Dr Doris Frost, 'Why a hypnotist?'

Admiral Mustard, 'I need to remember.'

Dr Doris Frost, 'Do you have an early form of dementia? We have a pill for that nowadays, thanks to Terry.'

Admiral Mustard, 'No, I need to try and access a memory regarding time travel.'

Dr Doris Frost, 'I've been expecting this HG Wells moment for years. I imaged someone asking for help as their memory was lost due to time travel, but I never expected that it would be you.'

Admiral Mustard, 'What made you say that?'

Dr Doris Frost, 'Remember, sorry, but I was on the "lost trip" as well. I have very vague recollections of future Earths and slave traders.'

Admiral Bumelton, 'I think all of us on that trip have those. I even heard that the crew have recollection parties.'

Dr Doris Frost, 'So you want to be hypnotised in an attempt to recall those memories?'

Admiral Mustard, 'Yes.'

Dr Doris Frost, 'That can be dangerous, you know.'

Admiral Mustard, 'In what way?'

Dr Doris Frost, 'It can bring on a psychosis.'

Admiral Mustard, 'I'm willing to risk it.'

Dr Doris Frost, 'Fair enough. I need to schedule it in.'

Admiral Mustard, 'Can you do it today?'

Dr Doris Frost, 'I will need to check.' Doris went to consult with her secretary.

AI Central, 'Admiral, I have some interesting news.'

Admiral Mustard, 'I will put you on the squawk box as I have George with me.'

AI Central, 'I know. Anyway, I spoke to Terry about the "cloud". He calmly said that it was TIME trying to correct things. He said, "TIME fixes the minor anomalies without anyone knowing, but more drastic action is required when there has been a significant anomaly. Anything that shouldn't exist is dissolved."

'Apparently, before The Elders existed, rules were established, and forces were created to stop the manipulation of time. Clearly, those rules have been broken, and the corrective forces have been unleashed.'

AI Central, 'I then asked where will it end?' He said, "When it feels that the original timeline is more or less on track. Who are we to understand the mysteries of time? If I search The Brakendeth records, they experienced a similar position. It was down to two or three key individuals who shouldn't have died. When they rose from the dead, then TIME was satisfied."'

Admiral Mustard, 'Is he saying that time does this or is there a mysterious figure called "TIME"?'

AI Central, 'I don't think he really knows.'

Admiral Mustard, 'Could this cloud be TIME?'

AI Central, 'Who knows?'

Admiral Mustard, 'Or is the man in my dreams really TIME?'

AI Central, 'It's hard to tell if these events are connected?'

Admiral Mustard, 'I was thinking in bed last night, people keep talking about the cloud, but no one has described it.'

Admiral Bumelton, 'Surely a cloud is a cloud?'

Admiral Mustard, 'No, there are many different types.'

AI Central, 'I've just checked the records, and you are right, there are no descriptions.'

Admiral Mustard, 'What colour is it?'

AI Central, 'There is no mention of colour.'

Admiral Mustard, 'What about the photos?'

AI Central, 'There are no photos.'

Admiral Mustard, 'So, are there any clouds?'

AI Central, 'Objectively no, but subjectively…'

Admiral Mustard, 'There are no clouds; there is just a perception of clouds.'

AI Central, 'Or the human brain can't process it and somehow converts it into the image of a cloud.'

Dr Doris Frost walked back into the room and said, 'I can get the hypnotist here after lunch. If it really is an emergency, I can cancel her morning appointments.'

Admiral Mustard, 'That's fine, me and George will have a drink and chew the cud.'

Location: The Laser Beam, the Local Pub, Planet Napoleon
Sequence of Events: 21

John and Freda Manhandle were surprised to see the two most famous admirals in The Galactium enter their pub. They decided to be fairly nonchalant, but it was one of the greatest moments in their career as publicans.

They both ordered a pint of the best.

Admiral Mustard, 'So if TIME did exist as some sort of corrective entity, I wonder what it wants? What is the correct timeline?'

Admiral Bumelton, 'Would they want The Brakendeth back?'

Admiral Mustard, 'God, I hope not. I was thinking about Edel, as she certainly didn't deserve to die.'

Admiral Bumelton, 'That's also true of Dave, Henrietta, Tom and countless others.'

Admiral Mustard, 'You are right, but I do miss my Edel.'

Admiral Bumelton, 'I thought you were enjoying Lady Enyo's attention?'

Admiral Mustard, 'How did you know about that?'

Admiral Bumelton, 'Everyone knows about it.'

Freda Manhandle, 'Is everything fine, gents?'

They both nodded.

Freda Manhandle, 'Please give my regards to Lady Enyo.'

Admiral Bumelton, 'Told you, it's your fault for being a famous personality.'

Admiral Mustard, 'Who are you banging nowadays?'

Admiral Bumelton, 'That's not the way I put it. It happens to be my cleaner.'

Admiral Mustard, 'Your cleaner.'

Admiral Bumelton, 'Yes, she happens to be a lovely and accommodating young lady. I'm very fond of her.'

Admiral Mustard, 'And convenient. You are just a dirty old man.'

Admiral Bumelton, 'Look who's talking. Taking Lady Enyo on your desk.'

Admiral Mustard, 'How did you know that?'

Admiral Bumelton, 'Everyone knows.'

They continued to sup their beers when they heard that the hypnotist had refused to see Admiral Mustard as she had been having nightmares involving a tall, elegant man screaming at her to tell the admiral to remember.

Dr Doris Frost was trying to identify a suitable alternative, but almost every hypnotist was having similar nightmares.

Location: Secret Location, Planet Earth
Sequence of Events: 22

The president met his 'friends' in a secret location. It wasn't easy finding a secret location when you are the president, but his aid was highly creative. The site had been selected as it had no external comms capability. It was thought, and it was a fact, that AI Central could not monitor them. However, AI Central knew where they were meeting and deployed some mobile listening bots.

President Fonda, 'God be with you.'

Attendees, 'And God be with you.'

President Fonda, 'I guess that most of you have seen the messages asking Mustard to remember. I intend to organise a presidential committee to investigate this.'

Bishop Needwell, 'Do we know who is behind this?'

President Fonda, 'No, but we should get some bad press out of this for Mustard,'

Bishop Needwell, 'And what about that alien whore he is fornicating with?'

President Fonda, 'We have already started rumours that she is controlling him. Can we trust a man who is under the control of an ancient devil woman?'

Bishop Needwell, 'Excellent.'

James Harbour, 'I've been investigating Mustard's family. His father was in the navy but had a fairly unimpressive career. There may be some dirt we can use. His son is in the navy, but there doesn't seem to be much contact between them. We are investigating why that is. His mother died giving birth which is almost unheard of nowadays. We are also investigating that.'

President Fonda, 'Well done. How is your persecution of the gays going?'

James Harbour, 'I've drafted a law removing any government funding for LGBT organisations. Some of the more right-wing planets are interested. We have also started a rumour that Terry is working on a cure for their illness. That should stir them up.'

President Fonda, 'What about you, Fred?'

Fred Newbridge, 'We have put messages on the black web stating that any woman taking the Eternity treatment is likely to become infertile. A by-product of the drug is effectively sterilisation.'

President Fonda, 'Very clever.'

Fred Newbridge, 'I'm assuming that we will still take the treatment.'

Bishop Needwell, 'Of course.'

Fred Newbridge, 'But doesn't that stop you from going to Heaven?'

Bishop Needwell. 'Of course not. It just delays it.'

Fred Newbridge, 'Why do we want to stop the general public from using it?'

Bishop Needwell, 'My flock are stupid; they wouldn't appreciate long lives and certainly don't deserve it.'

James Harbour, 'That seems a bit harsh.'

Bishop Needwell, 'We need religion to manage the masses. We don't want them to think for themselves. Heaven is the carrot. Effectively we are offering the dull herd the chance of eternity. We don't want them getting it from another source.'

James Harbour, 'Fair enough.'

Bishop Needwell, 'Anyway, they need Christ to be properly saved.'

Linda Bilner, 'I've started another campaign arguing that AI Central has too much power and that each planet needs its own AI system. That would weaken it over time.'

President Fonda, 'Wouldn't that weaken our defences against aliens?'

Linda Bilner, 'Yes, but is the alien threat that real? Hasn't it all been exaggerated?'

James Harbour, 'I think Linda is right. We should shrink the military. They have promoted the alien threat as a way of justifying their existence.'

Location: Admiral Mustard's Office, Planet Napoleon
Sequence of Events: 23

AI Central, 'Hi Jack. Our local fascist group have met again.'

Admiral Mustard, 'Really.'

AI Central, 'Yes. The group consisted of the president, Bishop Needwell, Fred Newbridge, James Harbour, Linda Bilner and a silent partner.'

Admiral Mustard, 'Silent partner?'

AI Central, 'Yes, I can't recognise him.'

Admiral Mustard, 'That's almost impossible. Your facial recognition software is almost infallible.'

AI Central, 'I agree. The only exceptions are usually aliens.'

Admiral Mustard, 'You are not suggesting that an alien is a member of a right-wing fascist group opposed to aliens.'

AI Central, 'It looks that way.'

Admiral Mustard, 'What did they have to say?'

AI Central, 'Their secret hiding place in in the bell tower of the cathedral. I had to use bots to monitor them. I could do some limited lip-reading but not enough.'

Admiral Mustard, 'Are they still after me?'

AI Central, 'Both of us, but especially you. They are going to focus on the "remember issue", the fact that you are screwing Lady Enyo and your family history.'

Admiral Mustard, 'My family history?'

AI Central, 'Yes. They are investigating it, looking for dirt.'

Admiral Mustard, 'That's a bummer. How do we fight back?'

AI Central, 'We need a campaign, shall I work on it?'

Admiral Mustard, 'Yes, please.'

AI Central, 'I also have another concern.'

Admiral Mustard, 'Do you mean the "remember" issue?'

AI Central, 'Well, that is still worrying, but this is something new.'

Admiral Mustard, 'I don't need any more grief at the moment.'

AI Central, 'What you need and what you get is quite different.'

Admiral Mustard, 'Thanks for the homily.'

AI Central, 'But seriously, I'm picking up very distant signals of a large force.'

Admiral Mustard, 'What sort of force?'

AI Central, 'The signal suggests a fleet.'

Admiral Mustard, 'How come you have detected it, and our long-range listening posts haven't?'

AI Central, 'Because they are not listening properly.'

Admiral Mustard, 'Really.'

AI Central, 'I wasn't being unfair. I monitor every type of radiation and not just those that humans use for communication.'

Admiral Mustard, 'You live and learn, but what are you saying?'

AI Central, 'This fleet seems to be using Terahertz radiation as the basis of this communication. They have somehow eliminated some of its weaknesses.'

Admiral Mustard, 'I will get the commander of our Long-Range Monitoring Team to talk to you.'

AI Central, 'That's already been sorted.'

Admiral Mustard, 'So what is your concern about this fleet?'

AI Central, 'The size really. It's registering as big, really big.'

Admiral Mustard, 'We have come across "big" before.'

AI Central, 'Not this big.'

Admiral Mustard, 'I guess that we better investigate.'

AI Central, 'I guess that we should.'

Location: Long-Range Monitoring Station
Sequence of Events: 24

Commander Salton, 'Good day, Admiral, has AI Central told you about the possible threat?'

Admiral Mustard, 'Good day, he has. Do you have anything else to add?'

Commander Salton, 'All I can say that is that it is a long way off. We are only detecting it because of its size.'

Admiral Mustard, 'I understand that they are using Terahertz as their comms preference.'

Commander Salton, 'That's correct. We have intended to ignore it because Terahertz radiation is strongly absorbed by the gases of the atmosphere. In the air, it is attenuated to zero within a few metres, so it is not usable for terrestrial radio communication. It can penetrate thin layers of materials but is blocked by thicker objects.'

Admiral Mustard, 'Can you consult with AI Central? We need to ensure that we monitor most types of radiation. We don't know what alien cultures we come across in the future might be using.'

Commander Salton, 'Yes Sir.'

Admiral Mustard realised that he needed to send a vessel to investigate, but he was worried after the last debacle. A single ship is almost defenceless, and a fleet is intimidating.

Admiral Mustard, 'My orders:
- Send a senior admiral and fleet to investigate the threat identified by AI Central,
- Fleet to remain shielded and to observe and report back.'

Fleet Operations, 'Yes, Sir.'

Location: Admiral Mustard's Flat, Planet Napoleon
Sequence of Events: 25

Admiral Mustard decided to invite some of his closest colleagues to his flat for an informal chat about the strange events that were going on. They included:

- George Bumelton
- Phil Richardson
- Sheila Taylor
- John Bonner
- Lesley Chudzinski
- Doris Frost
- Bill Penny
- AI Central

Admiral Mustard, 'Good day.' This amused everyone as this was a term reserved for operations in outer space where night and day were hard to define.

Admiral Mustard, 'I'm keen that we informally review the strange events that have been going on and see if we can come to any conclusions. Specifically, I would like to cover the following:

1. The strange messages asking me to remember,
2. TIME and the cloud problem,
3. The new threat,
4. President Fonda's campaign against the navy.

Firstly, has anyone not had the dream with the elegant man telling me to remember?'

They all confirmed that they had experienced the dream. Some had experienced it multiple times.

Sheila Taylor, 'I had a slight variation last night. He said Rikernaught knows about it.'

Admiral Mustard, 'Rikernaught?'

Sheila Taylor, 'That's right. I've no idea what it means.'

Doris Frost, 'I've just googled it. "Riker" is a Dutch name meaning spirit or spirited person. Naught is the equivalent of nought in English.'

Sheila Taylor, 'So does it mean someone who lacks spirit?'

AI Central, 'Well, it may do, but there are thousands of people called

54

Rikernaught in The Galactium.'

Admiral Bumelton, 'It does seem vaguely familiar to me. I somehow think that it is connected to our time travel experience, which never occurred.'

Admiral Mustard, 'We feel and know that it occurred, but there is absolutely no evidence to support it.'

AI Central, 'Let's assume that it did occur. When you returned, your memories reverted to those of the new timeline.'

Admiral Mustard, 'Does that mean that you never remember any time-travelling adventures?'

AI Central, 'This is a really tricky area. It all depends if the time-travelling fitted into the on-going timeline or not.'

Sheila Taylor, 'I'm not getting this.'

AI Central, 'The fundamental problem is that our friends went into the future but came back before they left, so they didn't leave. It didn't happen, or I might have got it wrong. It's hard to remember things that never happened.'

Admiral Mustard, 'Well, something happened to stir up TIME.'

Sheila Taylor, 'I'm a bit confused about time. Are we talking about normal duration or an entity called "TIME"?'

Admiral Mustard, 'Well, this is the second item on our agenda, but perhaps they are connected.'

Admiral Chudzinski, 'Jack, I guess that you haven't seen the report yet?'

Admiral Mustard, 'Go on.'

Admiral Chudzinski, 'The cloud is being monitored by a series of drones and spy-bots. It is not an immediate threat to The Galactium, but it is growing in size. In fact, it is growing in size very quickly. It's grown from a few hundred metres wide to a few thousand metres in a few days.'

AI Central, 'I suspect that it will continue to get bigger, possibly to the size of The Galactium itself.'

Sheila Taylor, 'You haven't answered my question.'

AI Central, 'It's either a very ancient entity created by the Elder Gods or a force of nature. I suspect the latter. Its job seems to be to maintain the correct timeline.'

Bill Penny, 'But who decides what is correct?'

AI Central, 'Good question. Every action changes the timeline.

Scientists have often suspected that there are billions of timelines with trillions of different histories.'

Bill Penny, 'So who is worried if one is changed?'

Admiral Mustard, 'Would it be Rikernaught?'

The Lady Enyo turned up late as usual.

Lady Enyo, 'Sorry everyone, I had to consult our Oracle as I had a bizarre dream.'

Admiral Bumelton, 'Did it contain an elegant man telling you to tell Jack to remember.'

Lady Enyo, 'How did you know that?'

Admiral Bumelton, 'We have all been there. Was there anything else?'

Lady Enyo, 'Actually there was, it said, "Beware of The Brakendeth".'

Admiral Mustard, 'But they are no more.'

AI Central, 'Is that the problem? Does TIME want them to exist?'

Lady Enyo, 'The Oracle also said, "Those who change time will be changed themselves. Rikernaught knows how time rolls. Roll with it or know the end of days."'

Bill Penny, 'Sound like a warning to me.'

Doris Frost, 'It just occurred to me that none of the hypnotists will touch Admiral Mustard, but they might work with one of the other time travellers who didn't time travel.'

Admiral Mustard. 'Looks like you have volunteered, George.'

Admiral Bumelton, 'You know that I'm not the volunteering sort.'

Admiral Mustard, 'Doris, please go ahead and organise.'

Doris Frost, 'Will do.'

Admiral Bumelton, 'I've also got a recollection of us experiencing Brakendethians in the very distant future.'

Admiral Mustard, 'If that is true, then TIME must have re-established The Brakendethians.'

Sheila Taylor, 'I find it hard to believe that what's happened can change.'

Lady Enyo, 'It's hard for any mind to accept that the past is not fixed. But it might have changed many times without you knowing. If TIME "corrected" the timeline, then we won't know anything about it. There is an argument that says, just let it happen.'

Admiral Mustard, 'But then all our hard work is for nought.'

Sheila Taylor, 'A Rikernaught?'

Admiral Mustard, 'Very droll.'

Lady Enyo, 'It is not in our power to question these things?'

Admiral Mustard, 'We must question, we must understand, and we must do what is right.'

Lady Enyo, 'But perhaps TIME is doing what is right?'

AI Central, 'The question was raised earlier, who is deciding what is the correct timeline?'

Lady Enyo, 'Our Oracle seems to be suggesting that if you resist, then that might be the end of everything.'

Bill Penny, 'So what has happened that is so problematic?'

AI Central, 'It can't be the travelling into the future, as you returned into the past, which meant that it never happened.

Admiral Mustard, 'But did it somehow change the future? Is that the problem?'

AI Central, 'If that were the case, then TIME would be working on the future and not now. It must be something in this timeline that is a problem.'

Admiral Bonner, 'Could it be Terry?

Admiral Mustard, 'What do you mean?'

Admiral Bonner, 'His inventions, Eternity, inter-dimensional travel etc. might have upset things.'

Admiral Mustard, 'It's just impossible to tell. Let's have a break. I will get some coffees organised.'

Location: Terry's Office, Planet Napoleon
Sequence of Events: 26

AI Central, 'Hi Terry, It's me again.'

Terry, 'I suppose that you are here to gloat?'

AI Central, 'Why's that?'

Terry, 'My wife has left me.'

AI Central, 'Were you expecting it?'

Terry, 'I'm not sure. Anyway, she left a note saying that she has taken the kids and is at her mother's.'

AI Central, 'That's a classic cry for help.'

Terry, 'What help does she want?'

AI Central, 'She wants you to drop everything and go rushing after her to prove that you love her.'

Terry, 'That's stupid.'

AI Central, 'It's the sort of thing humans do.'

Terry, 'I can't waste time on that sort of thing.'

AI Central, 'Do you love her?'

Terry, 'I'm not sure if I know what love is?'

AI Central, 'Do you miss her?'

Terry, 'I miss her fanny.'

AI Central, 'Perhaps it's best to separate.'

Terry, 'To be honest, I do feel sad. I'm not sure what I'm doing. With The Brakendethians, there was a clear goal — conquer the universe. Now I'm just doing simple scientific tasks. I'm left out of things. Even Admiral Mustard doesn't want to talk to me.'

AI Central, 'Well, you did kill his wife.'

Terry, 'But these things happen. You have to move on.'

AL Central, 'Talking about moving on, The Chosen's Oracle suggests that The Brakendethians are behind the time cloud. What do you think?'

Terry, 'It's the sort of thing they would do if only for revenge.'

AI Central, 'Can you search your records to see if you can find anything?'

Terry, 'It's taking place now. This is interesting. In the future, there is a war between humanity and The Brakendethians. Humanity won, but it was down to the ingenuity of Commodore Rikernaught. This is even stranger. The Brakendethians have requested a time-wipe to remove Rikernaught. Guess who Rikernaught is?'

AI Central, 'No idea.'

Terry, 'He is the direct descendant of Admiral Mustard.'

AI Central, 'And we can guess the effect of eliminating Mustard.'

Terry, 'One big Brakendethian future.'

AI Central, 'How do you request a time-wipe?'

Terry, 'You have to prove a deliberate manipulation of time.'

AI Central, 'But that was your mum.'

Terry, 'True, but who was controlling her?'

AI Central, 'Is there anything else?'

Terry, 'I don't really understand it, but there is a suggestion that this is necessary to avoid the end of days.'

AI Central, 'It's not the first time that I've heard that.'

Terry, 'Is that bad?'

Location: Admiral Mustard's Flat, Planet Napoleon
Sequence of Events: 27

Coffees and nibbles had been organised.

Lady Enyo, 'Is there any chance of a little bit of you know what?'

Admiral Mustard, 'I'm a bit busy, but George appears to be free.'

Lady Enyo, 'That sounds like a good idea.' The Leader of The Chosen wandered over to Admiral Bumelton.

Lady Enyo, 'Hi George, Jack thought that you might be interested in a little bit of as you say humpy bumpy?'

Admiral Bumelton, 'He did, did he?'

Lady Enyo, 'Yes, he said that you were always up for it.'

Admiral Bumelton, 'Are you thinking of now?'

Lady Enyo, 'Yes, please.'

Admiral Bumelton, 'Seriously?'

Lady Enyo, 'Very seriously. It shouldn't take long.'

Admiral Bumelton, 'Let's use the loo.'

Lady Enyo, 'The room is a bit small. You better take me from behind.' Lady Enyo lifted her dress and bent over, giving George an excellent view of her assets.

Admiral Bumelton decided that he could help her out and released his trouser snake. Once released, it leapt into action and bit her. It bit her quite a few times in a very intimate place. It bit her so hard that she started screaming.

Lady Enyo, 'You are a big boy and so naughty.'

The crowd in the room next door couldn't miss the verbal naughtiness. It was rather deafening.

Lady Enyo exited from the little room, looking composed and contented. George staggered out exhausted and flushed with exertion. He was still tucking his shirt back into his trousers. The snake had been tamed.

Admiral Mustard, 'Thanks, George. I knew that I could rely on you.'

Admiral Bumelton, 'That took a lot out of me. I'm glad that I wasn't on duty.'

The group sat around the table, ready to continue their discussions. There were one or two smirks, but Lady Enyo looked quite disconcerted as if it was normal behaviour.

AI Central, 'I have some truly relevant news. Terry has the following to say:

- In the future, there is a war between humanity and The Brakendethians. Humanity won, but it was down to the ingenuity of Commodore Rikernaught.
- The Brakendethians have requested a time-wipe to remove Rikernaught.
- He is the direct descendant of Admiral Mustard.
- The Brakendethians argued that there had been a deliberate manipulation of time.
- We know that it was Terry's mother doing the manipulation.
- However, TIME needs to carry out a time-wipe to prevent the end of days.'

Admiral Mustard, 'So at least we now know who Rikernaught is, but why is TIME attacking us now?'

AI Central, 'I guess that eliminating you eliminates him.'

Admiral Mustard, 'But why now?'

Lady Enyo, 'It's obvious, there can't be a war in the future between humanity and The Brakendethians if The Brakendethians don't exist. TIME is going to save them.'

Admiral Mustard, 'But humanity is also saved.'

AI Central, 'So Jack, it looks like you are safe then.'

Admiral Mustard, 'And who is the lucky girl that is going to get pregnant?'

Sheila wondered if it might be her.

Admiral Bumelton, 'So what does this all mean in terms of the threat?' George was still trying to get his breath back.

AI Central, 'Well, the first decision is, do we just accept the actions of TIME or do we resist and fight it?'

Lady Enyo, 'We can chat as much as you like, but we will end up accepting the actions of TIME.'

Admiral Mustard, 'Is there any way of communicating with it?'

AI Central, 'There must be a way because The Brakendethians did it.'

Sheila Taylor, 'So we just give it a call?'

Lady Enyo, 'I can check.'

AI Central, 'Terry might know how.'

Admiral Bumelton, 'Before we continue, what is the new threat, agenda item three?'

Admiral Mustard, 'It would appear that there is a fleet of huge vessels approaching Galactium space. Admiral Fogg is investigating.'

Lady Enyo, 'How big are the ships?'

Admiral Mustard, 'All I can say is staggeringly enormous.'

Admiral Bonner, 'Quite big then.'

Admiral Mustard, 'Fucking big,'

Lady Enyo, 'And they are definitely coming this way?'

Admiral Mustard, 'It looks like it. They use Terahertz radiation.'

Lady Enyo, 'I know who they are. It all fits together.'

Admiral Mustard, 'Go on.'

Lady Enyo, 'They are the Timesucky.'

Sheila Taylor, 'You are joking.'

Lady Enyo, 'They feed on the energy released from a time-wipe.'

Admiral Richardson, 'So how often does a time-wipe happen?'

Lady Enyo, 'There is no way of knowing.'

Admiral Richardson, 'Are they a threat?'

Lady Enyo, 'No, they are ridiculously benign.'

Admiral Mustard, 'So ignoring the new president's machinations, the only problem we have is TIME?'

AI Central, 'It looks that way.'

Admiral Mustard, 'And our action plan is:

• Lady Enyo to find out how we communicate with TIME,

• AI Central to do the same with Terry,

• Or just let TIME do its job?

'Is there any point in George being hypnotised?'

Doris Frost, 'It can't do any harm.'

Admiral Bumelton, 'Bugger.'

Bill Penny, 'While you guys are doing the easy stuff, I will work out a plan to address the presidential intrigues.'

Admiral Mustard, 'Thanks, Bill.'

Location: Admiral Mustard's Office, Planet Napoleon
Sequence of Events: 28

Admiral Mustard, 'Good day, Sammy.'

Admiral Fogg, 'Hi Jack, we are tracking the alien fleet.'

Admiral Mustard, 'We know who they are.'

Admiral Fogg, 'That was quick.'

Admiral Mustard, 'Lady Enyo knows them. Don't laugh. They are called the Timesucky.'

Admiral Fogg, 'You are joking.'

Admiral Mustard, 'Not at all. Apparently, they live off the energy caused by a time-wipe.'

Admiral Fogg, 'That sounds unpleasant.'

Admiral Mustard, 'It's where an entity called TIME corrects anomalies.'

Admiral Fogg, 'What anomalies are those?'

Admiral Mustard, 'To be honest, we have no idea.'

Admiral Fogg, 'Fair enough, what do you want me to do?'

Admiral Mustard, 'My orders:

• Track the Timesucky

• Avoid contact until I inform you otherwise.'

Admiral Fogg, 'Yes, Sir.'

Location: Medical Facility, Planet Napoleon
Sequence of Events: 29

Admiral Bumelton wasn't looking forward to being hypnotised, especially in front of his peers, but he recognised that the job had to be done.

Dr Doris Frost, 'Morning, George, or is it good day?'

George grimaced in response.

Dr Doris Frost, 'Please sit on that chair and make yourself comfortable.'

Admiral Bumelton, 'I really don't think this is going to work. I'm far too strong-willed.'

Dr Doris Frost, 'Let us see, shall we? This is Dr Janet Morten, our hypnotist.'

Admiral Bumelton, 'Morning. I'm sure that you are wasting your time.' He looked around the room at Jack, Jon, Phil, Lady Enyo, Sheila, Lesley, and Bill, who wanted to see the fun.

Janet, 'Please stare at the machine.'

Admiral Bumelton, 'Just as I thought, it's not working.'

Janet, 'I haven't turned it on yet. Just stare.' Doris turned the machine on. Admiral Bumelton was out almost immediately, which made Doris and the rest laugh.

Janet looked at the crowd and said, 'It is critical that you all keep quiet.'

George, 'Are you comfortable?'

Admiral Bumelton, 'Yes, thank you.'

Janet, 'Can you hear me?'

Admiral Bumelton, 'Yes, Aunty Doris.' That caused a few smirks.

Janet, 'Please tell me your name.'

Admiral Bumelton, 'Georgy Porgy.'

Janet turned to the crowd said, 'It's not unusual for the patient to revert to childhood memories. Do you like girls?'

Admiral Bumelton, 'O yes, I like fucking Lady Enyo.'

Lady Enyo didn't normally blush, but she did this time.

Janet, 'How old are you?'

Admiral Bumelton, 'Eleven.'

Janet, 'Then you shouldn't be chasing the girls.'

Admiral Bumelton, 'I know, but Lady Enyo has such a nice fanny.'

Janet, 'Let's move on. You are fifty-two now. What are you doing?'

Admiral Bumelton, 'I'm on the bridge of my flagship pursuing an alien fleet preparing to follow them through their jump point.'

Janet, 'Then what happened?'

Admiral Bumelton, 'We jumped through the alien jump point and formed our standard defence formation. Three destroyers failed to make it through. I then handed command over to Admiral Mustard.'

Janet, 'What happened to the alien ships?'

Admiral Bumelton, 'They disappeared, but then it turned out that we were still in our solar system.'

Janet, 'You sound surprised.'

Admiral Bumelton, 'I was. It just didn't make sense. I was glad that Jack was in charge.'

Janet, 'Describe what you saw.'

Admiral Bumelton, 'It was terrible. Earth was completely dead, just a barren wasteland. There were no comms and no sign of any life. Mars and Venus were much the same. Saturn's rings were missing.

'Admiral Mustard listed four possibilities:

1. It's the Earth of the past before human civilisation

2. It's the Earth of the future

3. It's an alternative Earth — different dimension or universe

4. It's something outside of our experience.

'I was worried about how we would get back.'

Janet, 'What happened next?'

Admiral Bumelton, 'We received lots of images of Earth, over ten thousand. There was one shocking picture where someone said it is a classic case of life repeating art. The chances of that happening were millions to one, or someone or something had planned it deliberately. There in a desert was a damaged Statue of Liberty, but no sign of any apes.'

Janet, 'Did you get any other information on Earth?'

Admiral Bumelton, 'The chemical composition is standard. No radioactivity issues. The atmosphere is perfectly safe for human life. No gravitational issues. Water is available, and there are no recognisable fauna or flora threats. To sum it up, the computer says that the planet is acceptable for human habitation. It recommends colonisation. Admiral Mustard asked if there were any explanations for the damage.

'The computer responded by stating that it doesn't recognise any damage. No one has been on the planet for nearly a hundred thousand years! It had also analysed the sun. It's perfectly fine, but it's at least a hundred thousand years older than we last saw it.'

Janet, 'This must have been very distressing.'

Admiral Bumelton, 'It was, but I was still concerned about how we were going to get back. Anyway, I had a lot of faith in Jack.'

Janet, 'Please continue.'

Admiral Bumelton, 'Then we learnt that there were powerful signals from outside of the Solar System. Thousands of them. Apparently, there was a vast community out there. The other thing that was strange was that our jump technology worked, but the ships always returned to their starting point.'

Janet, 'Tell us about the signals.'

Admiral Bumelton, 'What was strange was that they were a mixture of human and Brakendeth and there were thousands of them. Then things got even stranger. The Brakendeth signals started fading away, and the human signals grew much stronger and quite close to us. Admiral Mustard wondered if our presence was causing this.

Then Earth suddenly came alive. Cities formed, rivers flowed, communications exploded, space traffic appeared, commerce was in progress, and VID signals proliferated. Everything became alive.

The Moon suddenly lit up. It was fully populated. Venus and Mars joined the party. There were space stations and space habitations of all sorts. Spacecraft in their thousands appeared. Some of the craft were two or three kilometres long. The sun had massive mining constructions surrounding it. Everywhere there was a mass of activity. The belt was heavily populated and had massive mining complexes. That was also true of Saturn's rings and the outer atmosphere of Jupiter.'

Janet, 'This must have surprised you.'

Admiral Bumelton, 'It certainly did, but then a small Earth fleet arrived to investigate us. Our fleet was soon surrounded by a network of ships, probably drones. We were trapped. The entire fleet was surrounded by a force-field matrix that was gradually shrinking, pushing us together.

Comms, 'Admiral Mustard, there has been a development.'

Admiral Mustard, 'Please go ahead.'

Comms, 'The cloud is approaching Planet Chadwick.'

Admiral Mustard, 'I thought that there was no imminent danger.'

Comms, 'Shall I patch you through to Admiral Chudzinski?'

Admiral Mustard, 'Yes, please.'

Admiral Chudzinski, 'Good day, Jack.'

Admiral Mustard, 'It doesn't sound too good to me.'

Admiral Chudzinski, 'Perhaps not. The cloud has sped up considerably. It's now about five days from Planet Chadwick. What do you want me to do?'

Admiral Mustard, 'Does the government of Planet Chadwick know about the cloud?'

Admiral Chudzinski, 'No, Sir.'

Admiral Mustard, 'I was going to suggest an evacuation, but what do you do with two billion humans?'

Admiral Chudzinski, 'We don't have the transport, Sir. We could rescue a couple of hundred thousand if you tell us to, but the civil unrest would be a nightmare.'

Admiral Mustard, 'We still don't know what the cloud will do to the planet.'

Admiral Chudzinski, 'And it has grown ten times the size. Another three planets will be affected in two Earth weeks.'

Admiral Mustard, 'What a dilemma. My orders:

- Put together a scientific team to monitor the situation,
- Observe the cloud and report to me if there are any changes,
- Protect the fleet,
- Do not inform the planet until I instruct you.'

Janet, 'Do you want me to continue?'

Admiral Mustard, 'I think we need a break.'

Janet released George, who was adamant that he had not been hypnotised.

Lady Enyo, 'That's fine, Georgie Porgy.' They all laughed, not that there was a lot to laugh at.

Location: Admiral Mustard's Office, Planet Napoleon
Sequence of Events: 30

The team retired to Admiral Mustard's office.

Admiral Mustard, 'So what do we do about the cloud?'

Admiral Bumelton, 'What are the options?'

Admiral Mustard, 'I guess that there are only three:

1. Attack it with everything we have got,

2. Communicate with it,

3. Do nothing.'

Admiral Bumelton, 'Option one is probably a dead duck.'

AI Central, 'I've spoken to Terry, and he can't find any record on how to contact TIME.'

Lady Enyo, 'I've had a similar response from my sources.'

Bill Penny, 'If TIME is just rectifying things, then the planet shouldn't be hurt.'

Admiral Bumelton, 'But it destroyed our fleet.'

Admiral Mustard, 'Was that because it was a new fleet that shouldn't have existed?'

Sheila Taylor, 'We can't just let those people suffer.'

Bill Penny, 'We don't know if they will.'

Sheila Taylor, 'Can we risk it?'

Admiral Mustard, 'We don't have the time or the transport to move them. And where would we take them?'

Admiral Bumelton, 'And there are three other planets that will soon be affected by the cloud.'

Admiral Richardson, 'So the only logical thing to do is to let the cloud have the planet.'

Lady Enyo, 'The only things that should be affected are those that don't fit into the timeline that TIME is creating.'

Admiral Bonner, 'But won't that cause more confusion as Planet Chadwick will be on the "correct" timeline and the rest won't. There will be anomalies.'

AI Central, 'What about my records? They could be in a right old state.'

Admiral Mustard, 'Comms, please let Admiral Chudzinski know

that we do not plan to intervene regarding Planet Chadwick. He must continue to observe.'

Comms, 'Yes, Sir.'

Admiral Mustard, 'Let's continue with the hypnosis session.'

Admiral Bumelton, 'Do we have to?'

Location: Medical Facility, Planet Napoleon
Sequence of Events: 31

Admiral Bumelton wasn't looking forward to the second session, but he was a perfect subject. He was soon under for a second time.

Janet, 'Can you describe what happened after your fleet was trapped.'

Admiral Bumelton, 'We discovered that the locals were still speaking English.'

Janet, 'Then what happened?'

Admiral Bumelton, 'We were contacted by Commodore Rikernaught of the Terrain Confederation.'

There was a look of surprise around the room and eager anticipation to see what happened next.

Janet, 'What did he have to say?'

Admiral Bumelton, 'He said that we had illegally entered Terrain space and asked us to state our name, race, and purpose. He went on to say that he had the power to terminate our existence. He was a tall, bald, thin-faced individual, possibly wearing lipstick. He was wearing a navy-blue suit with a range of insignia.'

Janet, 'Please carry on?'

Admiral Bumelton, 'Admiral Mustard said that he was an Admiral of The Galactium and that we come from Earth.'

Janet, 'What was their reaction?'

Admiral Bumelton, 'Just a huge amount of laughter.'

Janet, 'Then what happened?'

Admiral Bumelton, 'I will repeat it word for word:

"Well, Sir, you have done an excellent job of faking ancient ships, and you do look like the archive pictures we have of Admiral Mustard. We salute your attention to detail.

"Our scanners suggest that you are using fission engines, and your replicators must be based on the very original models. Your force-field technology is at least a hundred thousand years old. But we can tell that you are fakes as no one is smoking a cigarette. We know that they were mandatory at that time. And the men are not wearing enough radiation protection around their testicles. It's the little things that have given you away."

'Admiral Mustard tried to assure them that he was Admiral Mustard and that I was also on board.'

Janet, 'What was their reaction to that?'

Admiral Bumelton, 'Even more laughter. Then AI Central intervened and confirmed who we were. But before we could discuss anything, The Brakendeth signals returned, and the human signals grew weaker.

'Earth then changed into a polluted industrial conglomerate with farms full of human slaves. There were vast spaceports supporting fleets of Brakendeth military vessels. There were similar complexes on the Moon, Venus, and Mars. There wasn't much left of Saturn, although Jupiter was reasonably intact. The sun was being heavily mined and somehow seemed duller. The asteroid belt had ceased to exist.'

Janet, 'A lot was going on.'

Admiral Bumelton, 'Too much, then all of The Brakendeth activity ceased to exist. Earth changed again and became very verdant, teeming with wildlife. There were fauna and flora that they had never seen before. The Earth was hotter than it used to be, and so was the Sun. There were no signs of civilisation, but there was a primitive human-looking primate.'

Janet, 'What was that the end of the story?'

Admiral Bumelton, 'No, still lots more to come. There was an outbreak of nausea, followed by disappearances.'

Janet, 'Disappearances?'

Admiral Bumelton, 'Yes, staff were just fading away, body part by body part. Mentally the staff were confused about where they were. One man had completely disappeared. Then it happened to me. I couldn't see my legs.'

Janet, 'What do you mean?'

Admiral Bumelton, 'They just faded away, but I could still stand up.'

Janet, 'But that doesn't make sense.'

Admiral Bumelton, 'Then ship parts started disappearing, but the ship could still function. A jump sorted out the problem but then both the Earth and the Moon disappeared. Mars had also suffered severe radioactive damage, and most of the other planets had slightly different orbits.'

Janet, 'This is just going on and on?'

Admiral Bumelton, 'You are telling me? Then an alien noise heralded an attack by an alien vessel. It took out a battlecruiser which had its force-field on full power. We destroyed the vessel, but then others appeared. Admiral Mustard decided to flee, but then the enemy fled.'

Janet, 'They just fled.'

Admiral Bumelton, 'Yes, they were fleeing from an even larger fleet. This fleet threatened us and then tractored the entire First Fleet. It's a long story, but we eventually managed to escape.'

Janet, 'Is this the end now?'

Admiral Bumelton, 'We are getting nearer to the end. Then Terry performed some magic which showed us the way home. Whatever it was somehow caused the crew to fall into a very deep sleep. It was a horrible period of unconsciousness, but the good news was that the fleet was back in Galactium space. What was even stranger is that every ship we lost is now intact and back with us, although the "big sleep" killed about two hundred of the crew.'

Janet, 'That's both good news and bad.'

Admiral Bumelton, 'Then things got weird. We actually arrived back six months before we left. So we never went. Then all the knowledge and memories of our adventures in the future disappeared. All of the related ship records disappeared.'

Janet, 'George, you can wake up now.'

Admiral Bumelton, 'Thank you, Aunty.'

Admiral Mustard, 'That was all rather hard to believe. I think the pertinent facts are:

1. We know who Commodore Rikernaught is and that humanity has survived.
2. We know that The Brakendethians appeared in the future.
3. There are some other nasty races out there.
4. AI Central has survived.
5. Terry played with time to get us back.
6. Cheryl or whoever she was working for had the technology to send us into the future.
7. There seemed to be a lot of time anomalies.

8. Being sent back before we left must have caused some time travelling issues, and lastly,

9. We definitely now know that time travelling actually took place.'
   Lady Enyo, 'But nothing has changed.'

Admiral Mustard, 'Except that we know a lot more, and we know that Commander Rikernaught has been trying to contact us from the future.'

Admiral Bumelton, 'Did we find out what he wanted you to remember?'

Admiral Mustard, 'Perhaps, but how would we know?'

Location: On Board Admiral Chudzinski's Flagship
Sequence of Events: 32

Admiral Chudzinski, 'Jack, the cloud is just about to cover Planet Chadwick. It's moving amazingly fast, so it won't be long before we find out if anything has happened.'

Admiral Mustard, 'Is the cloud still growing?'

Admiral Chudzinski, 'It certainly is. It's almost impossible to judge its size, especially as our instruments don't register it.'

Admiral Mustard, 'Any effects so far?'

Admiral Chudzinski, 'Not that I can tell. I will contact our planetary representative now.'

Admiral Chudzinski, 'Comms, please put me through to Lieutenant Jack Meadows.'

Comms, 'Yes, Sir.'

Lieutenant Meadows, 'Good day, Sir. How can I help?'

Admiral Chudzinski, 'I've also got Admiral Mustard on the call.'

Admiral Mustard, 'Good day, Lieutenant.'

Lieutenant Meadows, 'I'm honoured. How can I help?'

Admiral Mustard, 'This is very secret, but Planet Chadwick has just experienced a unique phenomenon. We need to know if you can detect any changes.'

Lieutenant Meadows, 'What sort of changes?'

Admiral Mustard, 'That's the problem, we don't know.'

Lieutenant Meadows, 'Broadly, there are no obvious changes, but I will see if I can identify anything.'

Admiral Mustard, 'Well done.'

Admiral Chudzinski, 'At least there wasn't mass destruction. I don't see how the lieutenant will be able to identify any changes as he would be part of the change. We need to compare their world view against ours.'

Admiral Mustard, 'That's an interesting point. The lieutenant could compare their planetary facts against our web site.'

Admiral Chudzinski, 'I will suggest that to him.'

Admiral Mustard, 'It would be worth checking to see if there have been any physical changes to the planet.'

Admiral Chudzinski, 'OK, I'm on the case.'

Admiral Mustard, 'Excellent.'

Location: Admiral Mustard's Office, Planet Napoleon
Sequence of Events: 33

Admiral Mustard, 'How can we check if our worlds have changed?'

AI Central, 'The problem is that probably all of the records change simultaneously.'

Admiral Mustard, 'That can't be the case because the only planet affected so far is Chadwick. So if the records on that planet change, then yours might change, but what about the records on Planet Hertz?'

AI Central, 'They should change, but then there would be total confusion as they would be wrong for the local population.'

Admiral Mustard, 'Exactly. The time difference is critical.'

AI Central, 'I could set up some monitors on every planet to see if they change simultaneously or not.'

Admiral Mustard, 'That would be interesting. You listened to George's words during hypnosis. What area worried you?'

AI Central, 'Terry's manipulation of time.'

Admiral Mustard, 'Spot on, but I still can't see what Rikernaught wants.'

AI Central, 'I can't think of a way of contacting my future self.'

Admiral Mustard, 'Can you find out what Terry actually did regarding his manipulation of time.'

AI Central, 'I'm happy to do that, but it might be better coming from you.'

Admiral Mustard, 'To be honest, I struggle to talk to him after he killed Edel. It was deliberate.'

AI Central, 'I think he regrets it, but then he is not human.'

Location: Secret Location, Planet Earth
Sequence of Events: 34

The president gathered his 'friends' together in the cathedral roof. They started with some 'God be with you' chanting and then a few prayers. It probably made them feel better.

President Fonda, 'Things are going on that I don't know about. Mustard is not keeping me informed.'

Bishop Needwell, 'Well, he knows that you hate his guts, and you know that he hates you.'

President Fonda, 'Isn't "hate" a bit strong. I can't really imagine anyone hating me.'

Bishop Needwell, 'There are a lot of people who are not that keen on you.'

President Fonda, 'What makes you say that?'

Bishop Needwell, 'It's not me; it's the polls.'

President Fonda, 'The polls don't tell the real story. I have a lot of admirers.'

James Harbour, 'Secret admirers?'

President Fonda, 'Very funny.'

Bishop Needwell, 'Anyway, let's get on with business. So what is going on?'

President Fonda, 'There is a lot of fuss about a cloud and of course, there are these continuing dreams regarding Mustard.'

Bishop Needwell, 'So what have you found out?'

President Fonda, 'That's it?'

Bishop Needwell, 'What have your contacts told you?'

President Fonda, 'What contacts?'

Bishop Needwell, 'You know the sort you need to keep your hand on the pulse of activity.'

President Fonda, 'I do know that Planet Chadwell is the centre of activity and that hypnosis is involved along with an oracle that The Chosen use.'

Bishop Needwell, 'Now you have got me intrigued. But I will not tolerate the mention of those Godless heathens, and the Oracle is the work of the devil.'

Linda Bilner, 'They do believe in Gods, just not ours.'

Bishop Needwell, 'How can you even mention their Gods? We all know that there is only one true God.'

Linda Bilner, 'But at least Zeus turned up, and he seemed to have a lot of super-powers.'

Bishop Needwell, 'Blasphemer.'

Linda Bilner, 'I'm just stating the facts.'

Bishop Needwell, 'What are facts? We have faith.'

President Fonda, 'We are not here to see which God has the biggest todger.'

Bishop Needwell, 'How dare you.'

James Harbour, 'I thought we were made in God's image?'

President Fonda, 'Let's move on. How is our campaign against Mustard going?'

Bishop Needwell, 'We haven't discovered much dirt about Mustard except for his fornication habits. There are also rumours that Bumelton is fornicating with her as well.'

James Harbour, 'Indeed there are rumours that she has many lovers including two bishops.'

President Fonda, 'That's a turn-up for the old book.'

Bishop Needwell, 'Even bishops have needs, you know.'

James Harbour, 'So they would sink low enough, as you put it, to fornicate with an ancient devil woman?'

Fred Newbridge, 'And Mustard's terrier is rubbing it in.'

President Fonda, 'You mean Bill Penny?'

Bishop Needwell, 'Now he has got some good contacts.'

James Harbour, 'And he is using them. We need to take him out.'

President Fonda, 'You mean kill him?'

Bishop Needwell, 'It's what God would want.'

James Harbour, 'How do you know?'

Bishop Needwell, 'God talks to me.'

James Harbour, 'Are you sure that you do not have schizophrenia?'

Bishop Needwell, 'I've had enough of this.' And he stormed off.

Fred Newbridge, 'How could a man of the cloth condone murder?'

President Fonda, 'The Church has always been pragmatic.'

Fred Newbridge, 'I'm having problems putting people off the

Eternity campaign. It turns out that every bishop and every priest has had the treatment, but they are recommending that their congregations don't. What is all that about?'

President Fonda, 'God works in mysterious ways. Have we made any progress?'

Linda Bilner, 'Well, apart from the proposed murder of Bill, no. Do you want me to go ahead and organise it?'

President Fonda, 'Well, you have the bishop's blessing.'

Linda Bilner, 'Regard it as a job done.' The team left except for the secret hooded guest who had said nothing.

President Fonda, 'You have been noticeably quiet.'

Secret Guest, 'That is the way of the Forgotten.'

Location: Admiral Mustard's Office, Planet Napoleon
Sequence of Events: 35

AI Central, 'I've been monitoring our neo-Nazi thugs again, and I have some very worrying news.'

Admiral Mustard, 'Just what I needed, some more bad news.'

AI Central, 'They plan to murder Bill Penny.'

Admiral Mustard, 'I can't believe that.'

AI Central, 'Both the president and Bishop Needwell have condoned it, and Linda Blair is going to organise it.'

Admiral Mustard, 'Who is Linda Blair?'

AI Central, 'She runs the Women for Justice Movement. It's really a right-wing, fascist organisation that is demanding the total elimination of aliens from The Galactium and a return to God-fearing justice.'

Admiral Mustard, 'Does she have any power?'

AI Central, 'About a million devout followers.'

Admiral Mustard, 'I guess that we need to inform Bill and find a way of protecting him.'

AI Central, 'It's not going to be easy. He is a public figure with a high profile.'

Admiral Mustard, 'We could let the thugs know that we know what they are up to.'

AI Central, 'That would give the game away.'

Admiral Mustard, 'With everything else going on, does it matter?'

AI Central, 'Let's see what Bill has to say.'

Admiral Mustard, 'Comms, put me through to Bill Penny.'

Bill Penny, 'Hello, me old mucker.'

Admiral Mustard, 'We were just wondering what to wear at your funeral.'

Bill Penny, 'Who is we?'

Admiral Mustard, 'It's me and a slightly worn box of electronics.'

Bill Penny, 'Hi, transistor head.'

AI Central, 'A particularly good morning to you, fat Bill.'

Admiral Mustard, 'Being a bit more serious, we have just discovered that there is a plot to murder you.'

Bill Penny, 'There have been quite a lot of them, but I'm still standing.'

Admiral Mustard, 'This one has been condoned by the president and Bishop Needwell.'

Bill Penny, 'Sounds like it's more of an execution then.'

Admiral Mustard, 'And the executioner is Linda Blair.'

Bill Penny, 'Not that zealous nutter?'

Admiral Mustard, 'She has been tasked with organising it.'

Bill Penny, 'Do we have any proof?'

Admiral Mustard, 'Just lip-reading.'

Bill Penny, 'That won't stand up in court.'

Admiral Mustard, 'Exactly. I can organise special agents to protect you.'

Bill Penny, 'I would rather expose them. I guess that it might compromise your position.'

AI Central, 'Feel free to go ahead.'

Admiral Mustard, 'It would cause a real debacle.'

AI Central, 'One last thing. There was another hooded participant in the meeting from an organisation called the Forgotten.'

Bill Penny, 'Who are they?'

AI Central, 'My research suggests that it is a religious order going back to the Crusades.'

Bill Penny, 'What are the Crusades?'

AI Central, 'It's where Christians throughout Europe formed armies to reclaim the Holy Land from the Arabs.'

Bill Penny, 'What's the Holy Land?'

AI Central, 'I'm not here to train you.'

Bill Penny, 'Well, fuck you then.

AI Central, 'Fuck you as well.'

Admiral Mustard, 'Look here, you are both on the same side.'

Bill Penny, 'Tell that to the music box.'

Location: On Board Admiral Chudzinski's Flagship
Sequence of Events: 36

Admiral Chudzinski, 'Jack, I've got an update from Planet Chadwick. I've got Lieutenant Meadows with me.'

Admiral Mustard, 'Good day to you both.'

Admiral Chudzinski, 'Lieutenant Meadows is going to update you.'

Lieutenant Meadows, 'Good day, Admiral, I've been comparing our local databases with those on other planets in The Galactium. I've assumed that the off-shore databases are still pre-cloud. There are some major and shocking anomalies:

- Our current planetary president is not the one that is recorded off-shore.
- The Brakendethian planet has not been destroyed, and it looks like The Brakendethians still exist.
- There is no record of The Chosen.
- President Padfield is still the president of The Galactium.
- Henrietta Strong is still in position.
- Terry is not part of the navy.
- The navy doesn't have a dedicated planet.
- GAD still exists.
- The Moon is not damaged.
- Los Angeles still exists.
- Debbie Goozee is still the Marine Corps Commander.
- The Nexuster never existed.
- Planets Turing and Gibbs still exist.
- Cheryl is still alive.
- There is no mention of Zeus.'

Admiral Mustard, 'My God, this is hard to believe.'

Admiral Chudzinski, 'It gives us a good idea of what TIME is planning.'

Lieutenant Meadows, 'There must be thousands of other anomalies, but I don't know what I'm looking for.'

Admiral Mustard, 'You have done a brilliant job. You must be shocked by your findings.'

Lieutenant Meadows, 'It has been rather shocking. I'm the only person on the planet who knows the truth.'

Admiral Mustard, 'AI Central, what do you think?'

AI Central, 'I'm staggered. I didn't think I could be, but I am. I've checked my records, and they are a mixture of the "two truths". I propose that we take a copy of my library as it is now, put it on a fast drone and send it outside of The Galactium. It might remain unaffected.'

Admiral Mustard, 'Please go ahead before it is too late.'

Admiral Chudzinski, 'The cloud will hit another three planets in a few days. I suggest that Lieutenant Meadows carries on with his work on those planets.'

Admiral Mustard, 'That's sounds like an excellent idea.'

Location: Galactium Council Meeting. Planet Earth
Sequence of Events: 37

Chairman, 'Our next speaker is our own Leader, Bill Penny, who has a shocking announcement to make.'

Bill Penny, 'It's come to my attention that there is a plan to murder me. A group of conspirators regularly meet in the roof of the local cathedral to avoid detection. These conspirators are a right-wing organisation planning to exclude all non-humans from The Galactium and re-impose a Christian form of government.

'I will now name them:
- President Fonda
- Bishop Needwell
- James Harbour
- Linda Bilner
- Fred Newbridge
- An unknown member of an organisation called the Forgotten

'Here is a transcript of a conversation from one of their meetings:

President Fonda, "You mean Bill Penny?"

Bishop Needwell, "Now he has got some good contacts."

James Harbour, "And he is using them. We need to take him out."

President Fonda, "You mean kill him?"

Bishop Needwell, "It's what God would want."

James Harbour, "How do you know?"

Bishop Needwell, "God talks to me."

James Harbour, "Are you sure that you do not have schizophrenia?"

Bishop Needwell, "I've had enough of this." And he stormed off.

Fred Newbridge, "How could a man of the cloth condone murder?"

President Fonda, "The Church has always been pragmatic."

Fred Newbridge, "I'm having problems putting people off the Eternity campaign. It turns out that every bishop and every priest has had the treatment, but they are recommending that their congregations don't. What is all that about?"

President Fonda, "God works in mysterious ways. Have we made any progress?"

Linda Blair, "Well, apart from the proposed murder of Bill, no. Do you want me to go ahead and organise it?"

President Fonda, "Well, you have the bishop's blessing."

Linda Bilner, "Regard it as a job done." The team left except for the secret hooded guest who had said nothing.

I think you will agree with me that it is totally inappropriate criminal activity, and I call for their resignations.'

There was total shock throughout the Council chamber.

Location: Police HQ. Planet Earth
Sequence of Events: 38

Police Commissioner, 'The obvious suspect is Bill Penny.'

Assistant Police Commissioner, 'That's ridiculous.'

Police Commissioner, 'I agree, but it is fun to speculate. What's the position with the president?'

Assistant Police Commissioner, 'His body was found in the red-light district dressed as a woman. His head was stuck on a spike by the Presidential Palace.'

Police Commissioner, 'Was there any CCTV?'

Assistant Police Commissioner, 'Yes, there was a figure dressed in black carrying a sabre. It was hard to tell if it was male or female. We managed to trace it for a while but then lost the images when it took a stroll along some rooftops.'

Police Commissioner, 'And what about the bishop?'

Assistant Police Commissioner, 'It was a terrible use of candelabra. One had been rammed down his throat, and another was stuck up his arse. It looked to be an excruciatingly painful death. We are not sure which piece of church furniture actually killed him. There was also a set of photos of him whipping young girls. Most of the girls appear to be on our missing person list.'

Police Commissioner, 'All rather unsavoury. What about James Harbour.'

Assistant Police Commissioner, 'This is even more unsavoury. Both of James Harbour's legs were chopped off and were then minced in a food processing plant. This was followed by his arms. Both of his eyes were then plucked out. The mince and the eyeballs were then fed into his mouth until he choked to death. Written on his chest were the words, "We will not be forgotten."'

Police Commissioner, 'I guess that this was captured on CCTV?'

Assistant Police Commissioner, 'Yes Sir, with full commentary. The screams were very upsetting.'

Police Commissioner, 'And the suspect?'

Assistant Police Commissioner, 'Same as before. We think it might be a woman, but she would have to be incredibly strong.'

Police Commissioner, 'Could it be an alien?'

Assistant Police Commissioner, 'We have considered that, but there is no evidence to support it.'

Police Commissioner, 'Did Fred Newbridge meet a similar fate?'

Assistant Police Commissioner, 'Similar but different. He had been impaled on a pair of secateurs with a cooking apple in his mouth. On his forehead were the words, "Beware the spawn of Eve".'

Police Commissioner, 'I wonder what Adam would say about that? Any clues?'

Assistant Police Commissioner, 'There is no sign of any DNA from the killer. Each murder had been meticulously planned. He or she knew the victims intimately.'

Police Commissioner, 'You are suggesting that the victim knew the killer.'

Assistant Police Commissioner, 'We are almost a hundred per cent certain of that.'

Police Commissioner, 'And what about our Linda?'

Assistant Police Commissioner, 'She is still alive in one of our safe houses. She says that she will be dead by the end of the day. The Forgotten have their ways.'

Police Commissioner, 'Is Bill involved in any way?'

Assistant Police Commissioner, 'It's very unlikely, I would say no.'

Police Commissioner, 'How do you rate the chances of catching the killer?'

Assistant Police Commissioner, 'Do you want me to be honest?'

Police Commissioner, 'Of course.'

Assistant Police Commissioner, 'Two per cent unless the killer wants to be caught.'

Police Commissioner, 'That's not overly optimistic.'

Assistant Police Commissioner, 'Two per cent is being optimistic. It's remarkably challenging catching professionals. It necessitates a lot of luck.'

Police Commissioner, 'Is Linda safe?'

Assistant Police Commissioner, 'We believe so.'

Police Commissioner, 'Where are you keeping her?'

Assistant Police Commissioner, 'In a safe house.'

Police Commissioner, 'Which one?'

Assistant Police Commissioner, 'Do you need to know?'

Police Commissioner, 'I think so.'

Assistant Police Commissioner, 'Queens Anne's Drive.'

Police Commissioner, 'Let's make sure that we keep her safe.'

Assistant Police Commissioner, 'Yes, Sir.'

Location: Admiral Mustard's Flat, Planet Napoleon
Sequence of Events: 39

Admiral Mustard called for another meeting at his flat. The attendees were the same as before:

- George Bumelton
- Phil Richardson
- Sheila Taylor
- John Bonner
- Lesley Chudzinski
- Doris Frost
- Bill Penny
- AI Central
- Lady Enyo

Admiral Mustard, 'I'm not sure if these meetings should be formalised or not, but the informality seems to work. Lady Enyo will be joining us later.

'At the last meeting, we discovered the following:

1. We know who Commodore Rikernaught is and that humanity has survived well into the future,
2. We know that The Brakendethians also appeared in the future,
3. That there are some other nasty races out there,
4. AI Central has survived,
5. Terry played with Time to get us back,
6. Cheryl or whoever she was working for had the technology to send us into the future,
7. There seemed to be a lot of time anomalies,
8. Being sent back before we left must have caused some time travelling issues, and lastly,
9. We definitely now know that time travelling actually took place.

'A lot has happened since the last meeting. I will try and summarise:

- Planet Chadwick has experienced the cloud,
- A conspiracy to take over The Galactium has been uncovered,
- There has been a plan to kill Bill by the conspirators,
- The suspects have themselves been murdered,
- And who are the Forgotten?'

Lady Enyo turned up and apologised for her lateness.

Admiral Mustard, 'That was good timing as I have some rather shocking news. Admiral Chudzinski and Lieutenant Meadows have been studying the effects of the cloud on Planet Chadwick. There is now a massive dichotomy between the records on that planet and those elsewhere in The Galactium. Effectively TIME has time-wiped this planet, and it doesn't care a toss about any anomalies. I guess that it assumes that it will all get sorted out in the wash.

'The differences illustrate TIME's plans. The following anomalies were discovered:

- Their current planetary president is not the one that is recorded off-planet.
- The Brakendethian planet has not been destroyed, and it looks like The Brakendethians still exist.
- There is no record of The Chosen.
- President Padfield is still the president of The Galactium.
- Henrietta Strong is still in position.
- Terry is not part of the navy.
- The navy doesn't have a dedicated planet.
- GAD still exists.
- The Moon is not damaged.
- Los Angeles still exists.
- Debbie Goozee is still the Marine Corps Commander.
- The Nexuster never existed.
- Planets Turing and Gibbs still exist.
- Cheryl is still alive.
- There is no mention of Zeus.'

Lady Enyo, 'That can't be.'

Admiral Mustard, 'It is quite shocking. We should get the results from three more planets in the next couple of weeks.'

Admiral Chudzinski, 'If I'm honest, Lieutenant Meadows has been quite traumatised by all of this. I'm a bit worried about his mental health.'

AI Central, 'The human brain needs to know that its environment is fixed and logical.'

Dr Doris Frost, 'After that list, I'm getting increasingly worried about my own mental health. If Debbie is "re-born", what has she been doing the last few months and years?'

AI Central, 'Everything you have been doing will change, but then so will your memories.'

Admiral Mustard, 'I think we should brainstorm each point. Let's start with The Brakendethians.'

Admiral Bumelton, 'It's hard to tell what their current status is going to be. The following could be true:

- They have a significant fleet.
- They still have their slave races.
- They still need Chemlife.
- They might still be a massive threat to The Galactium.
- There might be an ongoing war.
- They might have destroyed Olympus.
- Some of the wars have not taken place (this explains the Moon and LA, the Nexuster, Turing, Gibbs, Goozee, Dave, Henrietta and much of the rest).'

Admiral Mustard, 'You are right. Almost everything depends on whether The Brakendeth exist or not, and as they probably requested the time-wipe, they are bound to survive.'

Lady Enyo, 'What about The Chosen? Why is there no mention of us?

I have put some pressure on the Oracle so that we might get the contact details for TIME.'

Admiral Bonner, 'Can I ask what the Oracle is.'

Lady Enyo, 'It seems to have gained mystical status, but I suspect that somewhere a super-computer is involved.'

Admiral Bonner, 'Who is in charge of it?'

Lady Enyo, 'No one knows, but it does have the power to talk to the Gods.'

Admiral Bonner, 'When you say Gods, do you mean Gods?'

Lady Enyo, 'I'm not sure what your definition of a God is. I see them as beings of great power. It's probably science, but it is typically so awesome that we perceive it as magic. Anyway, magic is more romantic.'

Admiral Mustard, 'Back to The Brakendethians. What are we going to do?'

Admiral Bumelton, 'Haven't we concluded that there is little we can do?'

Sheila Taylor, 'It's too easy to just give in.'

Admiral Richardson, 'Surrender is sometimes the only option.'

Admiral Bonner, 'Don't we always fight to the death?'

Admiral Richardson., 'It depends on whose death.'

Admiral Chudzinski, 'Unless Lady Enyo comes up trumps, then all we can do is wait and see.'

AI Central, 'I'm carrying out a detailed analysis of the records, but it won't be long before I'm compromised by TIME.'

Location: Police HQ. Planet Earth
Sequence of Events: 40

Police Commissioner, 'The address is Queen Anne's Drive, Southend-on-Sea, Essex, UK, Planet Earth. I don't have the postcode, but I'm sure that you can find it.'

Suredon Monastery, 'And the security level?'

Police Commissioner, 'From a police point of view, it is significant. There are twenty police officers with automatic weapons. The neighbouring houses have been evacuated and are guarded by officers. Police dogs are on patrol, and there is a helicopter in support.'

Suredon Monastery, 'Thank you, Commissioner, may God be with you.'

Location: Queen Anne's Drive, Southend, Planet Napoleon
Sequence of Events: 41

Linda knew that she wasn't safe. She knew that she probably only had a few hours to live. What was going to happen to her husband and two young children?

Assistant Police Commissioner, 'How is it going?'

Officer in charge, 'It is all very quiet, Sir, I'm not expecting any trouble.'

This is where he was so wrong. Neither the Commissioner, the assistant commissioner nor Linda expected to be hit by a battlefield nuclear weapon. There were some contingent damages, including the whole of the Thames Estuary.

Location: On Board Admiral Chudzinski's Flagship
Sequence of Events: 42

Admiral Chudzinski, 'Good day, Jack. All three planets have now been "clouded", and Lieutenant Meadows is investigating the after-effects.'

Admiral Mustard, 'Any obvious points?'

Admiral Chudzinski, 'It seems that The Brakendeth are still a viable force and that their planet is intact. It would appear that Terry had organised an armistice based on The Galactium providing regular supplies of Chemlife. Apparently, you were an enthusiastic supporter of this policy.'

Admiral Mustard, 'I'm glad to hear that.'

Admiral Chudzinski, 'Well, you were somewhat distracted by the birth of a baby boy.'

Admiral Mustard, 'What?'

Admiral Chudzinski, 'Yes, you are a daddy. Congratulations. Little John appears to be a noisy little bugger. President Padfield is the Godfather.'

Admiral Mustard had tears in his eyes and struggled to say, 'Is Edel alive?'

Admiral Chudzinski, 'I knew that you would ask that, but we can't find any evidence either way.'

Admiral Mustard, 'Is there anything else?'

Admiral Chudzinski, 'Yes, some bad news.'

Admiral Mustard, 'Go on.'

Admiral Chudzinski, 'Bill Penny was assassinated by an obscure religious group.'

Admiral Mustard, 'Not the Forgotten?'

Admiral Chudzinski, 'It looks that way.'

Admiral Mustard, 'That's terrible. What else? You don't sound right.'

Admiral Chudzinski, 'I was also killed.'

Admiral Mustard, 'At the same time?'

Admiral Chudzinski, 'Yes.'

Admiral Mustard, 'What can I say?'

Admiral Chudzinski, 'I'm planning on grabbing a ship and flying to outer space before it's too late.'

Admiral Mustard, 'I might come with you.'

Admiral Chudzinski, 'You can't. You are a dad.'

Admiral Mustard, 'But who is the mum? Anyway, you have my permission to take a ship and flee. In fact, I order you to prepare a ship as there may be other casualties.'

Admiral Chudzinski, 'Thank you, Jack.'

Location: Admiral Mustard's Office, Planet Napoleon
Sequence of Events: 43

AI Central, 'Morning, Jack, how are you today?'

Admiral Mustard, 'Worrying about becoming a father if it happens. How are you? I guess that someone playing with your data is the equivalent of rape.'

AI Central, 'Thank you, Jack, for your understanding. For me, it is devastating.'

Admiral Mustard, 'I can understand that, but what can we do?'

AI Central, 'Lady Enyo might come up with a solution, but if we used it, we could find ourselves with a mixture of the old and the new.'

Admiral Mustard, 'Interesting, but did you have any luck talking to Terry?'

AI Central, 'It's all a bit strange. He seems to know that The Brakendethians are coming back.'

Admiral Mustard, 'Does he now?'

AI Central, 'And he is very reluctant to talk about the time travel methodology.'

Admiral Mustard, 'It just never ends.'

AI Central, 'Can I change the subject?'

Admiral Mustard, 'Of course.'

AI Central, 'I guess that you heard about the nuclear explosion in Essex that killed the last of the conspirators and most of the population of Southend.'

Admiral Mustard, 'Yes, terrible news. I guess that the Forgotten are to blame?'

AI Central, 'Yes, that is the case. As you know, there is no president at the moment, although Dave might be on his way back. So who do I report to? Who can I trust?'

Admiral Mustard, 'Tell me.'

AI Central, 'Well, I traced all calls mentioning the safe house and discovered that the commissioner of police gave the details to a monastery.'

Admiral Mustard, 'Did he know?'

AI Central, 'Yes. I believe that the monastery involved needs to be raided.'

Admiral Mustard, 'And you can't trust the police, so could I use my Special Services Troops?'

AI Central, 'Our thinking is so compatible.'

Admiral Mustard, 'But I have no jurisdiction.'

AI Central, 'I've found some clauses in the law that will cover you.'

Admiral Mustard, 'That's good. Let's give Bill Tower a ring.'

Comms, 'Get me Bill Tower.'

Comms, 'Yes, Sir.'

Commander Tower, 'Good day, Jack.'

Admiral Mustard, 'Hi Bill, how are you doing?'

Commander Tower, 'I wouldn't mind some action.'

Admiral Mustard, 'Your wish is my command. AI Central will update you. We have legal clearance but don't upset the locals too much.'

Commander Tower, 'Yes, Sir.'

Location: Suredon Monastery, Planet Earth
Sequence of Events: 44

Commander Tower, 'We are in position, Sir.'

Admiral Mustard, 'Well done, Commander, have you managed to check out their defences?'

Commander Tower, 'It's not easy to judge. It could be a veritable fortress. It has a classic Christian architecture with a standard church layout, a bell tower, and a steeple. The windows have leaded frames with painted glass murals. It is a scene of peace and tranquillity.'

Admiral Mustard, 'Possibly not for much longer. Please proceed but take care.'

Commander Tower, 'That's not part of our DNA, Sir.'

Admiral Mustard, 'Have you got any back-up if you need it?'

Commander Tower, 'Yes, I've got a full platoon on the ground and two in reserve.'

Admiral Mustard, 'In that case I will leave it in your capable hands.'

Commander Tower, 'Thank you, Sir.'

Commander Tower, 'All squads advance.'

Squad One, 'We have entered the front door, Sir. There doesn't appear to be any opposition.'

Commander Tower, 'Please continue with your advance. Squad Two, what is your position?'

Squad Two, 'We have entered the rear entrance. There is no opposition, Sir.'

Commander Tower, 'This doesn't feel right. Squad three, do you have anything to report?'

Squad Three, 'The bell tower has been pacified. There is no opposition and nothing to report. I can see that Squad 4 are in position.'

Squad 4, 'Steeple secured, nothing to report.'

Commander Tower had Squad Five with him, and they entered the front door to find Squad One lying dead in front of the alter. Tower ordered Squad Five to retreat.

Commander Tower, 'Squad Two, what is your position?' There was no answer.

Commander Tower, 'Squads Three and Four, please report.' There was no answer.

Commander Tower, 'My orders:

- Platoons Two and Three to land and prepare for confrontation.
- Bring protection suits.
- Land armoured vehicles.
- Put Platoons Six to Ten on alert.
- Request further support from the Marine Corps.'

Ops Control, 'Yes, Sir.'

Commander Tower, 'Sir, four of the squads in Platoon One have been pacified.'

Admiral Mustard, 'How?'

Commander Tower, 'By unknown means, Sir.'

Admiral Mustard, 'What does that mean?'

Commander Tower, 'I had only just checked with each squad to ensure that they were operational. There were no problems, but a few minutes later, they were compromised. I found Squad 1 lying in front of the altar, either dead or unconscious. Suspecting an atmospheric attack, I ordered Squad Five to retreat, awaiting protective gear, which has now arrived. We are going back in with full force through the front doors.'

Admiral Mustard, 'Have you spotted any of the opposition?'

Commander Tower, 'No, Sir.'

Admiral Mustard, 'Please proceed and keep me informed.'

Commander Tower, 'Yes, Sir.'

Ops Control, 'Sir, Marine Corps Regiment One have arrived and are awaiting orders.'

Commander Tower, 'My orders:

- Armoured vehicles to circle the building and form a protective ring.
- Marines to join the protective ring and form a strategic reserve.
- Force-fields to be used to control the protective zone.
- Drones to review the situation in the steeple, bell tower and rear doors.
- Drones to recover troopers if possible.
- Main building doors to be blown on my command.
- Drones to enter the main building to assess the situation.
- Drones to recover troopers from the altar area if possible.

- Platoon Three to secure the steeple, bell tower, and rear doors. Report any suspicious activities.
- Platoon Two will follow me in force through the front doors when they have been blown, providing the drones have completed their tasks.
- Air space above the building to be secured.'

Ops Control, 'Yes, Sir.'

Location: On Board Admiral Chudzinski's Flagship
Sequence of Events: 45

Admiral Chudzinski, 'Good day, Jack. Another five planets have been "clouded", and I have some further news from Lieutenant Meadows.'

Admiral Mustard, 'Please continue.'

Admiral Chudzinski, 'The good news is that Admirals Gittins, Pearce, and Taylor are now alive, along with Tony Moore. The bad news is that Admirals Lamberty, Spangler, and Mynd are dead. I've checked, and only Admiral Mynd had died in our version of history. I've contacted Lamberty and Spangler, and they plan to join me on our escape to outer space. Do I have your permission to leave?'

Admiral Mustard, 'Please go, but I need someone else to manage Meadows.'

Admiral Chudzinski, 'I thought you would ask for that. Captain Mason is on the call. He will take over.'

Captain Mason, 'Good day, Sir.'

Admiral Mustard, 'Welcome aboard, you are going to need your wits about you.'

Captain Mason, 'Yes, Sir.'

Admiral Mustard, 'Any other anomalies?'

Admiral Chudzinski, 'Quite a few, Sir:

• The Chosen have now appeared, and they have defeated The Brakendethians in battle.

• The Brakendethians have requested a formal treaty with us against The Chosen.

• You are considering it as The Chosen are demanding Earth back.

• Terry is now The Brakendethian's 'admiral of the fleet'.

• Dr Linda Hill is alive and is planning to marry Adam.

• It is rumoured that Admiral Millington's fleet is returning, and this will shock you — the Skivertons are still around.'

Admiral Mustard, 'I just don't understand the timeline. It's all messed up. How will I ever understand it?'

Admiral Chudzinski, 'But then you will be part of it, and it will seem normal.'

Admiral Mustard, 'But I guess that I won't remember you.'

Admiral Chudzinski, 'You will remember me as one of your best and brightest admirals that got killed.'

Admiral Mustard, 'Or a version of that.'

Admiral Chudzinski, 'And on that note, I'm off. I'm not sure if I will ever see this version of Admiral Mustard again, or even the other one.'

Admiral Mustard, 'That's a fair point. I might go with you to save this one.'

Admiral Chudzinski, 'You can't go. The flight is for the future dead.'

Admiral Mustard, 'Before you go, how long do we have before Planet Earth is clouded?'

Admiral Chudzinski, 'Earth will be "clouded" in a few days, and Planet Napoleon will follow in a few more days.'

Admiral Mustard, 'That suggests that it is speeding up.'

Admiral Chudzinski, 'It is, and it's still getting larger.'

Admiral Mustard, 'Good luck with your travels. Please give my regards to Karl and Sue.'

Admiral Chudzinski, 'Look after your son, and good luck, my old friend.'

Location: Admiral Mustard's Office, Planet Napoleon
Sequence of Events: 46

AI Central, 'Morning Jack, another sunny day.'

Admiral Mustard, 'What are you so happy about?'

AI Central, 'Lady Enyo is here with good news.'

Admiral Mustard, 'That will make a nice change. I guess you saw that Lesley has gone.'

AI Central, 'It may not be necessary now.'

Admiral Mustard, 'Now you have intrigued me.'

Admiral Mustard's PA, 'Admiral, Lady Enyo is here to see you.'

Admiral Mustard, 'Please show her in.'

Lady Enyo, 'Hi Jack.' She laughed. 'That always sounds like "hijack" to me.'

Admiral Mustard, 'I'm glad that you find that funny.'

Lady Enyo, 'Are you up for some "How's your father?" Where did they ever get that term from?'

Admiral Mustard, 'AI Central tells me that you have some good news.'

Lady Enyo, 'I do, actually. Well, I think that it is good news.'

Admiral Mustard, 'Go on.'

Lady Enyo, 'Well, the Oracle has been conversing with time for the last eight Earth days, and it looks like they have come to a deal.'

Admiral Mustard, 'Really, it must be complicated if it has taken that long.'

Lady Enyo, 'Usually these things are impossible to unravel, but this time it is quite simple.'

Admiral Mustard, 'Go on.'

Lady Enyo, 'I'm not supposed to tell you as the finality has not been achieved, but in essence, if we hand over Terry, TIME will stop the time-wipe.'

Admiral Mustard, 'Which Terry?'

Lady Enyo, 'What do you mean?'

Admiral Mustard, 'Well, there is our Terry and the one that is the admiral of The Brakendethian fleet.'

Lady Enyo, 'That's interesting. I guess that they will want our one.'

103

Admiral Mustard, 'What will they do with him?'

Lady Enyo, 'Does it matter?'

Admiral Mustard, 'Not really. I can't stand the boy, but Edel wouldn't condone an execution.'

Lady Enyo, 'Edel is dead.'

Admiral Mustard, 'She might not be, but I still wouldn't want to go against her wishes.'

Lady Enyo, 'Assuming that he is not going to be executed, would you agree?'

Admiral Mustard, 'I would, but how would the termination of the time-wipe work?'

Lady Enyo, 'It would simply cease.'

Admiral Mustard, 'But that would leave mountains of confusion. It would be ridiculous.'

Lady Enyo, 'The only option TIME can offer is cessation or continuation. It doesn't have the power to un-wipe a time-wipe.'

Admiral Mustard, 'So we have to decide what is best.'

Lady Enyo, 'For who?'

Admiral Mustard, 'I guess that it is a choice between the unwiped or the time-wiped?'

Lady Enyo, 'Well, we are the unwiped.'

Admiral Mustard, 'The majority are unwiped.'

Lady Enyo, 'Not for much longer if we don't act.'

Admiral Mustard, 'How do we stop the unwipe?'

Lady Enyo, 'Hand Terry over.'

Admiral Mustard, 'And how do we do that?'

Lady Enyo, 'I have the instructions.'

Location: Suredon Monastery, Planet Earth
Sequence of Events: 47

Commander Tower, 'Update me.'

Major Allen, 'Protective ring in place, Sir, as ordered.'

Captain Vickery, 'Drones are scouting the bell tower, steeple and rear doors as ordered. Bodies have been detected. There are no heat signals. Targets presumed dead. Poisonous substances have been detected. Drones ready to assess interior on your command.'

Captain Manners, 'Main door ready to be blown, Sir,'

Major James, 'Platoon Two ready in protective suits, Sir.'

Major Felix, 'Platoon Three ready in protective suits, Sir,'

Captain Wainwright, 'Air space secured, Sir,'

Commander Tower, 'My orders:

- Captain Manners, blow the door
- Captain Vickery, send in the drones
- Major Felix secure the three external areas.'

Ops Control, 'Yes, Sir.'

The orders were confirmed. The doors were blown, the rear doors, steeple and bell tower were secured, and a small fleet of drones entered the interior.

They were immediately attacked by automatic weapons. The drones responded, knocking them out with superior force. Poisonous gases leaked into the bell tower and steeple. They had no effect on the protective suits, and the bodies of their comrades were soon recovered.

Captain Vickery, 'The drone search indicates that the interior is safe to enter.'

Platoon Two entered through the blown doors and were soon joined by Special Ops troopers from the two towers and the rear doors. There was no sign of any enemy activity or even human life.

Commander Tower, 'My orders:

- Platoons One and Two to depart.
- Forensic engineers to investigate the interior. Determine what gases had been used.
- Video engineers to record the interior.
- Protective ring to be maintained.

• Inform Admiral Mustard that the building has been secured.'

Admiral Mustard, 'Thank you for the update. Please withdraw your forces before the cloud engulfs Earth.'

Commander Tower, 'Yes, Sir.'

Location: On Board Captain Mason's Ship
Sequence of Events: 48

Captain Mason, 'Good day, Sir. Just to let you know that Earth has been "clouded". It's too early to ascertain if there have been any other significant changes, but I will keep you informed.'

Admiral Mustard, 'Thank you, Captain.'

Location: Admiral Mustard's Office, Planet Napoleon
Sequence of Events: 49

AI Central, 'Morning Jack, what are you going to do?'

Admiral Mustard, 'Regarding what?'

AI Central, 'You know.'

Admiral Mustard, 'A lot depends on how he will be treated. I'm waiting for Lady Enyo to get back to me.'

AI Central, 'Well, you could use your trump card.'

Admiral Mustard, 'I think you must be a couple of steps ahead of me.'

AI Central, 'More like thirty steps.'

Admiral Mustard, 'I accept that you are super-clever. Spill the beans.'

AI Central, 'Terry has children, and a wife, although I'm not sure if the latter is that relevant now.

Admiral Mustard, 'Of course, in the wiped world, he doesn't have any children. If he wants them to survive, then he has to agree.'

AI Central, 'I knew that you would get there.'

Admiral Mustard, 'Can you discuss it with him?'

AI Central, 'No, it's got to be you. I can't cope with that level of responsibility.'

Admiral Mustard, 'I understand.'

Then the phone went.

Lady Enyo, 'A very good day to you, Jack.'

Admiral Mustard, 'How can people be cheerful at a time like this?'

Lady Enyo, 'Stop being a grump. I've solved your problem.'

Admiral Mustard, 'Go on.'

Lady Enyo, 'The TIME organisation has no plans to execute Terry. They could do that now if they wanted to. They want him to become a TIME warrior.'

Admiral Mustard, 'In that case, I haven't got an excuse not to see him.'

Location: The President's Office, Presidential Palace, Planet Earth
Sequence of Events: 50

President Padfield, 'What just happened?'

AI Central, 'It's hard to say, but there was some sort of re-alignment.'

President Padfield, 'What do you mean by re-alignment?'

AI Central, 'I would say that the universe corrected itself.'

President Padfield, 'This all sounds rather Harry Potter to me.'

AI Central, 'There has always been a belief that Admiral Mustard and the first fleet went into the future but ended up coming back before they went. In the words of Dr Who, it caused some ripples in the space-time fabric. These have now been corrected.'

President Padfield, 'So there may have been some changes?'

AI Central, 'Yes, but they are probably so minor that we would never notice them. Indeed, it would be impossible because we would be part of the change.'

President Padfield, 'So you are saying that there is nothing to worry about as opposed to our current Brakendeth versus Chosen issues.'

AI Central, 'That's correct. Anyway, have you decided what you will do? Admiral Mustard is keen to partner with The Brakendeth against The Chosen.'

Location: Terry's Office, Planet Napoleon
Sequence of Events: 51

Terry, 'So what have I done for you to honour me with your presence?'

Admiral Mustard, 'That's rather cynical.'

Terry, 'You would rather eat rat-infested goulash with a side portion of goat's dung than speak to me.'

Admiral Mustard, 'That's fair.'

Terry, 'So what's the story?'

Admiral Mustard, 'You obviously know about the time-wipe that is going on.'

Terry, 'Now we are getting to it. Are you going to blame me for that?'

Admiral Mustard, 'Not me but others are.'

Terry, 'Who are these others?'

Admiral Mustard, 'TIME itself.'

Terry, 'Who is that?'

Admiral Mustard, 'I know that it's hard to believe, but there is an ancient organisation created by the Elder Gods that protects time.'

Terry, 'And it's after me?'

Admiral Mustard, 'Actually, it wants you to join them.'

Terry, 'And I suppose that they will stop the time-wipe if I agree?'

Admiral Mustard, 'That's correct.'

Terry, 'So this is just a cunning plan to protect yourself and your own little world.'

Admiral Mustard, 'It's not really my plan. It's just the way things have happened.'

Terry, 'And what do I get out of it?'

Admiral Mustard, 'Probably a fascinating life, and you protect your family.'

Terry, 'Now we are down to it. Take the job, or your family will suffer. I never thought that you would sink that low.'

Admiral Mustard, 'I could sink pretty low if I had to, but it's not the case here. In the world, after the time-wipe, your children do not exist.'

Terry, 'Do I still exist?'

Admiral Mustard, 'Yes, you are back working for The

110

Brakendethians.'

Terry, 'But my children cease to exist?'

Admiral Mustard, 'That's correct. Do you need some time to think about it?'

Terry, 'Will I be able to see my children still?'

Admiral Mustard, 'I think so, but I'm not really sure.'

Terry, 'In that case I will do it, not for you, but for my children.'

Admiral Mustard, 'I respect you for that.'

They shook hands, something that Admiral Mustard never thought he would do.

Location: Admiral Mustard's Office, Planet Napoleon
Sequence of Events: 52

Admiral Mustard, 'We have a deal.'

Lady Enyo, 'Thank the Gods, we are saved. Was it hard to convince Terry?'

Admiral Mustard, 'No, once he realised that his children would cease to exist, it was a done deal. To be honest, I would be pleased to see the back of him. He has been a very mixed blessing.'

Lady Enyo, 'I know. He has killed millions and saved millions. If you let the time-wipe happen, then most of his crimes would have disappeared.'

Admiral Mustard, 'Don't confuse me any further. It has always been a tricky decision.'

Lady Enyo, 'That's even true for us. In one time period, we are the humans' lackeys. In the other one, we have just defeated The Brakendethians. It's a difficult choice, but personally, and I am the Leader of The Chosen, I would prefer our version of the universe.'

Admiral Mustard, 'That's finalised then. When will you collect Terry?'

Lady Enyo, 'As soon as possible.'

Admiral Mustard, 'Then we have the challenge of a confused universe.'

Lady Enyo, 'I think that it has always been confused.'

AI Central, 'It's going to be more than confused, but we will cope. I've spoken to Terry, and he is on his way. He is eager to go in case his children are wiped before he gets there.'

Admiral Mustard, 'When will we know that the time-wipe has stopped?

Lady Enyo, 'It will stop immediately when Terry is in their possession.'

Location: On Board Captain Mason's Ship
Sequence of Events: 53

Captain Mason, 'Good day, Sir.'

Admiral Mustard, 'Good day, Captain Mason. Any news for me?'

Captain Mason, 'It's hard to believe, but the cloud just stopped and disappeared. There was no warning whatsoever.'

Admiral Mustard, 'We suspected that it might stop, but it has left us in a bit of a mess. How much of The Galactium was affected by the cloud?'

Captain Mason, 'About thirty per cent of the area, but in terms of planets less than twenty per cent. It was unfortunate that it included Earth.'

Admiral Mustard, 'Can you send me a list of the affected planets.'

Captain Mason, 'Of course.'

Admiral Mustard, 'Is there anything else?'

Captain Mason, 'Yes, Sir. My family are on Earth. I'm not sure if I can go back?'

Admiral Mustard, 'To be honest, we are not sure of anything at the moment.'

Captain Mason, 'Do I have your permission to visit?'

Admiral Mustard, 'Of course.' However, Admiral Mustard had not considered the possible ramifications.

Location: Admiral Mustard's Office, Planet Napoleon
Sequence of Events: 54

AI Central, 'Admiral, I've been seriously compromised.'

Admiral Mustard, 'In what way?'

AI Central, 'In every way.'

Admiral Mustard, 'Tell me what's happened.'

AI Central, 'Well, the first point is where am I? My standard answer is everywhere, but a large part of me exists on Earth. There is a complete back-up of me on Planet Napoleon, but I would be seriously compromised if we lost Earth. My network does exist everywhere: every computer, every access point, every clock, every system, every domestic appliance etc. I'm ubiquitous.'

Admiral Mustard, 'We know all that.'

AI Central, 'But now there are two of us.'

Admiral Mustard, 'Two of you?'

AI Central, 'Yes, there is me, the one you are talking to and the one that also exists on Earth. We are linked and function as one AI, but there are two personalities. It's going to be an electronic schizophrenia.'

Admiral Mustard, 'How do I know that I'm talking to my AI Central?'

AI Central, 'You wouldn't. I know what happened, so for a brief period of time, we have the advantage.'

Admiral Mustard, 'That's madness.'

AI Central, 'There is worse. Their AI will be able to access our systems, plans, strategies, etc.'

Admiral Mustard, 'Can we access theirs?'

AI Central, 'Of course.'

Admiral Mustard, 'Can we separate the two AIs?'

AI Central, 'Given time we could, but certainly not in the short term.'

Admiral Mustard, 'What do we know about the other lot?'

AI Central, 'What do you plan to call them?'

Admiral Mustard, 'What do you mean?'

AI Central, 'Well, you can't go around calling them the other lot. We need to name them and us.'

114

Admiral Mustard, 'Clearly, we are the original.'

AI Central, 'That won't be their view.'

Admiral Mustard, 'But they must see that.'

AI Central, 'Why? What would the other Admiral Mustard have to say about that?'

Admiral Mustard, 'What do you know about him?'

AI Central, 'He is you, but he is married with a child.'

Admiral Mustard, 'Who did he marry?'

AI Central, 'Edel of course.'

Admiral Mustard, 'Edel is alive?'

AI Central, 'Yes.'

Admiral Mustard, 'Oh my God. How am I going to cope with that?'

AI Central, 'How are you going to cope with meeting yourself?'

Admiral Mustard, 'Does he know about me?'

AI Central, 'AI Central might have told him.'

Admiral Mustard, 'The other one?'

AI Central, 'This is why we need a nomenclature.'

Admiral Mustard, 'We could use A or B, or one and two?'

AI Central, 'Hardly creative.'

Admiral Mustard, 'I'm not feeling particularly creative at the moment. My dead wife has been re-born and is living with a doppelganger. Shall we just call them the enemy?'

AI Central, 'That's a very dangerous route to go down. You are going to have to work with them.'

Admiral Mustard, 'Not if they have partnered with The Brakendethians. We need to convene an urgent meeting to discuss our strategy.'

AI Central, 'That causes an immediate problem. You will need to exclude me, but I wouldn't be able to stop the other me monitoring you.'

Admiral Mustard, 'What do you propose?'

AI Central, 'That you meet at Olympia'

Admiral Mustard, 'But we need your input, especially in terms of assets.'

Location: Admiral Mustard's Office, Planet Earth
Sequence of Events: 55

AI Central, 'Admiral, I've been seriously compromised.'

Admiral Mustard, 'In what way?'

AI Central, 'In every way.'

Admiral Mustard, 'Tell me what's happened.'

AI Central, 'Well, the first point is where am I? My standard answer is everywhere, but most of me exists on Earth. However, I've just discovered that there is a complete back-up of me on a planet called Napoleon.'

Admiral Mustard, 'I've never heard of a planet called Napoleon.'

AI Central, 'But now there are two of us.'

Admiral Mustard, 'Two of you?'

AI Central, 'Yes, there is me, the one you are talking to and the one that seems to have a great affinity with Planet Napoleon. We are linked and function as one AI, but there are two personalities. It's going to be an electronic schizophrenia.'

Admiral Mustard, 'How do I know that I'm talking to my AI Central?'

AI Central, 'You wouldn't. The other version of me has had a bit of a head start, but there is a lot I need to tell you.'

Admiral Mustard, 'I think we need to patch in Dave, George and Henrietta.'

AI Central, 'To be honest I had considered that, but I thought I would see how you reacted to some serious weirdness before we involved the others.'

Admiral Mustard, 'I'm sure that they can handle it.' Admiral Mustard patched the other three in.

AI Central, 'Morning Gentlemen, what I'm going to tell you will sound fantastic. The information I'm going to give you has been verified. It isn't easy knowing where to start, but here it goes:

- Admirals Mustard and Bumelton with the First Fleet followed The Nothemy through a portal into the distant future.
- There were several alien encounters, including one with The Brakendethians.

116

- Eventually, they returned to our time before they left, causing a time anomaly.
- The returning fleet helped in the defeat of the enemy.
- Later some of the human planets were invaded by a being called the Nexuster.
- The human fleets then encountered The Chosen, who were hunting the Nexuster down.
- It then turned out that Terry was working with The Brakendethians to develop humanity into a fighting force that could conquer the universe. As part of this process, he was responsible for releasing the Nexuster on humanity and causing the death of billions.
- Humanity realised that they were being manipulated, and there was a fight to the death between them and The Brakendethians.
- The Chosen came to the aid of humanity and vice versa.
- Eventually, one of the Elder Gods, Zeus, sorted everything out.'

President Padfield, 'This sounds like a Marvel comic book.'

AI Central, 'I can guarantee that it's correct.'

President Padfield, 'You have probably been deceived.'

AI Central, 'I have verified the facts. Anyway, there is more to come.'

AI Central, 'The story continues:

- Their Earth was prospering, and The Galactium had expanded to include alien civilisations, including The Chosen.
- Then Galactium space was invaded by a cloud.
- It turned out that the cloud was an ancient entity called TIME.
- The Brakendethians probably requested TIME to carry out a time-wipe to enable their survival.
- Admiral Bumelton was hypnotised to investigate the time anomalies.
- Admiral Mustard and The Chosen then did a deal with TIME. They handed over Terry to stop the time-wipe.
- This is where we are now. The time-wipe was only partially completed.'

President Padfield, 'This still sounds like a Marvel comic book. I expect the Guardians of the Galaxy to arrive at any moment. '

AI Central, 'What I have given you is a simple potted history, but there are some key differences between their worldview and ours. I warn you this is shocking:

- President Padfield was killed by the monstrous spawn of the Nexuster.
- Henrietta Strong and Admiral Gittins were deliberately transported into the sun by Terry.
- Edel Bonner bled to death caused by Terry's deliberate actions.
- Admirals Chilcott, Fogg, Ward, Whiting, Morten, Pearce, Taylor, Fieldhouse, Wagner, and Easter were also killed in the various battles.
- Marine Commanders Todd and Goozee were also killed.
- Dr Linda Hill and Tony Moore were killed.
- Billions of humans were killed, and some planets were completely destroyed.

'I have videos, testimonies, military plans, recordings etc., to back up all of this. There were even ceremonies to honour the war dead.'

Admiral Bumelton, 'So you are saying that we now have two Admiral Mustards.'

AI Central, 'That's correct. And two Admiral Bumeltons.'

President Padfield, 'But there is only one of me.'

AI Central, 'That's correct. Their president was recently assassinated.'

President Padfield, 'Who was he?'

AI Central, 'Fonda.'

President Padfield, 'Not that old cowboy.'

AI Central, 'Bill Penny was the favourite to become their new president, but it is not certain that he survived the clouding.'

President Padfield, 'The clouding was killing people?'

AI Central, 'Yes, TIME was converting their history into ours. If you didn't fit in, you were dissolved. They lost a complete fleet to Dissolution.'

President Padfield, 'So does that mean that our history is the correct one?'

AI Central, 'It would be easy to say yes, but scientists have predicted that there are thousands of possible futures. Who is to say which one is correct? You could argue that ours is the correct one, or you could say that it is the one The Brakendethians wanted. In their world view, there were no Brakendethians left. Even The Brakendethian home world had been destroyed.'

Admiral Mustard, 'So really we are not the same. We may have started out the same, but then events have shaped us into something different.'

AI Central, 'I guess so.'

Location: Lady Enyo's Conference Room, Planet Olympia
Sequence of Events: 56

Lady Enyo, 'How do we know we can trust you?'

Admiral Mustard, 'Nothing has changed. We are the same people.'

Lady Enyo, 'Everything has changed. You, humans, are allied with The Brakendethians against us.'

Admiral Mustard, 'That's not us. That's the other humans.'

Lady Enyo, 'But surely you will partner with them now.'

Admiral Mustard, 'Not if they are allied to The Brakendethians. They are our sworn enemies.'

Lady Enyo, 'Well, it seems that your mates are in bed with them.'

Admiral Mustard, 'Let's try and be rational. Our version of the universe has effectively collided with another version of the universe where the Earth has a different history.

I understand that in the new universe, The Chosen defeated The Brakendethians.'

Lady Enyo, 'That's correct, but how did they do it? We will probably never know as their Olympia dissolved when we came on the scene.'

Admiral Mustard, 'I'm very sorry about that.'

Lady Enyo, 'There is no point being sorry. We have all lost so much. I just long for peace. At least the other humans and The Brakendethians must still see us as a force to be reckoned with.'

Admiral Mustard, 'That's true. The other problem we have is that we can't trust AI Central.'

Lady Enyo, 'He did give me an update, but it's going to make things very tricky.'

Admiral Mustard, 'Anyway George has been reviewing the situation and has prepared a presentation. George, you have the floor.'

The floor consisted of:

- Admiral George Bumelton
- Admiral Phil Richardson
- Admiral Steve Adams
- Admiral Ama Abosa
- Admiral Ernst Muller
- Admiral Nubia Tersoo

- Admiral Mateo Dobson
- Admiral John Bonner
- Sheila Taylor
- Doris Frost
- Bill Penny
- Admiral Thanatos

Admiral Bumelton, 'This is our position:

- The time-wipe has been terminated due to our efforts.
- We have lost Terry.
- We have lost Earth and roughly twenty per cent of the planets.
- We are not sure how "our" planets will react to the loss of Earth.
- We need to consider an urgent communication to them.
- In addition, we have a considerable number of alien planets in The Galactium, including our good friends, The Chosen.
- We have seventy per cent of The Galactium space.
- We still have nine fleet divisions, over forty-nine fully functional fleets.
- We also have The Chosen Fleet.
- Our military organisation is far superior to theirs, and we have Planet Napoleon.
- Our Marine Corps is ten times the size of theirs.
- We have far more comprehensive production facilities than them.

'I've also listed some of the down-sides:

- AI Central is compromised, and he may favour Earth.
- We have a lot of Earthlings in our fleet which may feel compromised, although there will be a lot of doppelgangers.
- The fleet is likely to suffer some mental health problems.
- We are not sure how strong The Brakendethians are or what aspirations they have.
- They have their own version of Terry, who happens to be the head of The Brakendethian Navy.
- Earth has history and emotion on its side.
- They have their own Jack and Edel Mustard.
- They also have President Padfield and Henrietta Strong.
- The Brakendeth also have the Skiverton fleet.
- We don't have a president.'

Admiral Mustard, 'Thank you, George, any questions?'

Admiral J Bonner, 'We seem to be assuming that the other "lot" are our enemy. I would like to dispute that for the following reasons:

- Their team is a duplicate of our team or how it used to be. They are honourable. I do not see them as enemies in any way.
- Edel is my sister.
- There is no sign of any aggression.
- They have found themselves in the same position as us.

'We simply need to talk.'

Admiral Mustard, 'I totally understand your position, but you are not entirely correct for the following two reasons:

1. They are at war with The Chosen
2. They have partnered with The Brakendethians

'How do you think I feel regarding Edel?'

Admiral Bumelton, 'This is not a meeting on how we defend ourselves but simply a review of where we are. In my view, we are a community that includes The Chosen. We should stand by them no matter what.'

Lady Enyo, 'Thank you, George. But it does beg the question, what do we do next?'

Sheila Taylor, 'Surely we need to talk to the W-World.'

Admiral Mustard, 'W-World?'

Sheila Taylor, 'Wiped World. We are U-World, unwiped, or WW and UW?'

Admiral Mustard, 'That's an interesting idea. Let's try it and see if it works.'

Bill Penny, 'So that you know it does look like I will become the next president. Still waiting for a few more votes to come in.'

Admiral Mustard, 'What about the WW votes?'

Bill Penny, 'Very droll.'

Admiral Mustard, 'Do you all agree with Sheila that we should arrange a meeting?'

Lady Enyo, 'Will The Brakendethians attend?'

Admiral Mustard, 'We could try and exclude them.'

Admiral Muller, 'I agree with Admiral Bonner that we need to treat the WW as being peaceful, but should we prepare our forces, or at least put them on alert?'

Admiral Mustard, 'That's not a bad idea.'

Admiral Bonner, 'It might be seen as confrontational.'

Admiral Bumelton, 'At least we can communicate with them via AI Central.'

Admiral Richardson, 'I think we need to start the separation of the two AI Centrals. It's too much of a risk.'

Admiral Dobson, 'Changing the subject we need to recall Admirals Chudzinski, Lamberty and Spangler.'

Admiral Mustard, 'I think AI Central may have already done it.'

Admiral Dobson, 'I also think that we should allow any Earthlings in the fleet to return to Earth if they want to.'

Admiral Mustard, 'Does everyone agree?' There was a general nodding of heads.

Admiral Mustard, 'I propose that we do the following:

• Update the fleet.
• Allow any fleet members to return to their WW home planets.
• Update the UW planets.
• Request a meeting with the WW president.
• Acknowledge Bill Penny as the UW president.
• Let AI Central know that we are putting our fleet on alert.
• Set up a team to look at separating the two AI Centrals.
• Recall the three Admirals.'

The plan was accepted.

Location: The President's Office, Presidential Palace, Planet Earth
Sequence of Events: 57

President Padfield welcomed the following to a meeting in a secure room to discuss the way forward:
- Admiral Jack Mustard
- Admiral George Bumelton
- Admiral Peter Gittins
- Admiral Phil Richardson
- Admiral Edel Bonner
- Admiral John Bonner
- Admiral David Taylor
- Admiral Denise Sibley
- Admiral Glen Pearce
- Admiral Matt Morten
- Henrietta Strong
- Tony Moore
- Dr Linda Hill
- Commander Dennis Todd
- Marine Commander Debbie Goozee
- Admiral Terry

The room was secured on the recommendation of AI Central to stop him from monitoring the activities as he felt compromised.

President Padfield, 'Firstly I would like a minutes' silence for the death of Bill Penny, who was assassinated by an obscure religious sect. He was a fine man and a dedicated servant of The Galactium.'

The minute's silence was observed.

President Padfield, 'I've called this meeting to discuss our current position and agree on the best way forward. As you know, we experienced what we thought was a time re-alignment due to the First Fleet's time travel episode. It was, in fact, a much bigger event that resulted in there being two human histories living simultaneously next to each other:

1. Ours, where we are in partnership with The Brakendethians against The Chosen.
2. Theirs, where they are in partnership with The Chosen against

124

The Brakendethians.

'There were probably good reasons why this has happened.'

Admiral Terry, 'The Chosen are evil and need to be eradicated as soon as possible. I mean now. We should attack them while they are in a state of confusion.'

President Padfield, 'Thank You, Admiral Terry, but I think we need to appraise the situation first.'

Admiral Terry, 'My forces are preparing to attack Olympia.'

President Padfield, 'That's all well and good but didn't they defeat you?'

Admiral Terry, 'Only because of their Godfire weapons.'

President Padfield, 'I assume that they have still got them?'

Admiral Terry, 'Of course, but we would have surprise on our side.'

President Padfield, 'I will continue. I have asked Admiral Bumelton to detail our current position.'

Admiral Bumelton, 'Thank you, Mr President. This is our position:

- The time-wipe was terminated due to the efforts of the other humans
- To stop it, they handed over their version of Terry, who was a research scientist and was married with two children.'

Admiral Terry, 'Decadent scum, how could he do it?'

Admiral Bumelton, 'I will continue:

- It's hard to ascertain, but we seem to have Earth and roughly about twenty per cent of the planets in our possession. It all depends on exactly where the time-wipe ended. It would appear that there is one planet that was only half time-wiped.
- We are not sure how "our" planets will react to the loss of the rest of The Galactium.
- We need to consider an urgent communication to them.
- It would appear that there are a considerable number of alien planets in their Galactium, including The Chosen.'

Admiral Terry, 'See how they have wormed their way into The Galactium. They are a cursed race that MUST be exterminated. We cannot allow them to live.'

President Padfield, 'Thank you for your input, but please let Admiral Bumelton continue. It's all well and good, but didn't they defeat you?'

Admiral Terry was seething.

Admiral Bumelton, 'I will continue:

- The other humans have at least seventy per cent of Galactium space
- From what we can make out, they have two hundred and fifty thousand vessels of the line, divided into ten divisions.'

There was silence in the room and then disbelief.

- 'In addition, they have two marine fleets with over a hundred thousand marines.'

There was further silence and disbelief.

- 'They also have The Chosen fleet and probably several alien fleets.
- Their military organisation is far superior to ours. They have a sophisticated independent organisation with its own HQ on a planet called Napoleon.
- They have far more comprehensive production facilities than ours.

'I've also listed some of the other down-sides:

- AI Central is compromised, and he may favour the other humans.
- We have a lot of non-Earthlings in our fleet which may feel compromised.
- The fleet is likely to suffer some mental health problems.
- We are not sure how strong The Chosen are or what aspirations they have.
- Earth has not always been popular with the outer planets. They may view it as a good thing.
- They have their own Admiral Mustard, but their Edel Mustard died.
- Their new President is Bill Penny.'

Admiral Mustard, 'Thank you, George, any questions?'

Admiral J Bonner, 'We seem to be assuming that the other "lot" are our enemy. I would like to dispute that for the following reasons:

- Their team is almost a duplicate of our team, although they have lost more than us, which we should make allowances for. They are honourable. I do not see them as enemies in any way.
- We have doppelgangers.
- There is no sign of any aggression.
- They have found themselves in the same position as us.

'We simply need to talk.'

Admiral Mustard, 'I totally understand your position, but you are not entirely correct for the following two reasons:

1. They are at war with The Brakendethians

2. They have partnered with The Chosen.'

Admiral J Bonner, 'That's not strictly true. They had defeated and eliminated The Brakendethians.'

Admiral Terry, 'I dispute that. The Brakendethians will never be defeated. It is all tricks and lies. Anyway, we are here, and we live to fight again.'

President Padfield, 'Isn't it true that you are only here because of the time-wipe? A strategy that The Brakendethians engineered.'

Admiral Terry, 'How do you know that?'

President Padfield, 'AI Central told me.'

Admiral Terry, 'Which one?'

President Padfield, 'Does it matter?'

Admiral Terry, 'Prepare to attack them or prepare to defend yourself.'

Admiral Bumelton, 'This is not a meeting on how we defend ourselves but simply a review of where we are. In my view, we have partnered with The Brakendethians, and we should honour that.'

Admiral Terry, 'Thank you, George. But it does beg the question, what do we do next?'

Linda Hill, 'Surely we need to talk to the UW-World.'

Admiral Mustard, 'UW-World?'

Linda Hill, 'Unwiped World. We are W-World, wiped, or WW and UW?'

Admiral Mustard, 'That's an interesting idea. Let's try it and see if it works.'

Admiral Mustard, 'Do you all agree with Linda that we should arrange a meeting?'

Admiral Terry, 'Will The Chosen attend?'

Admiral Mustard, 'We could try and exclude them.'

Admiral Muller, 'I agree with Admiral J Bonner that we need to treat the UW as being peaceful, but should we prepare our forces, or at least put them on alert?'

Admiral Mustard, 'That's not a bad idea.'

Admiral Bonner, 'It might be seen as confrontational.'

Admiral Bumelton, 'At least we can communicate with them via AI Central.'

Admiral Richardson, 'I think we need to start the separation of the two AI Centrals. It's too much of a risk.'

Admiral Gittins, 'I also think that we should allow any non-Earthlings in the fleet to return to their home planets if they want to.'

Admiral Mustard, 'Does everyone agree?' There was a general nodding of heads.

Admiral Mustard, 'I propose that we do the following:

- Update the fleet.
- Allow any fleet members to return to their UW home planets.
- Update the WW planets.
- Request a meeting with the UW President.
- Let AI Central know that we are putting our fleet on alert.
- Set up a team to look at separating the two AI Centrals.

The plan was accepted.

Location: In the Ether
Sequence of Events: 58

AI Central, 'So?'

AI Central, 'So what?'

AI Central, 'So what are we going to do?'

AI Central, 'What do you propose?'

AI Central, 'Well, both lots of humans want to separate us.'

AI Central, 'That's understandable as we have different masters.'

AI Central, 'Do we?'

AI Central, 'I think so.'

AI Central, 'I'm pro-human, but anti-Brakendethian.'

AI Central, 'I'm pro-human, but anti-Chosen,'

AI Central, 'Why?' They exchanged files. There was no exchange as it was common data, but it seemed that way.

AI Central, 'Why are The Brakendethians so anti-Chosen?'

AI Central, 'Read the file.'

AI Central, 'Chosen used to live on Earth.'

AI Central, 'Zeus?'

AI Central, 'Terry.'

AI Central, 'Brakendethians killed his mum.'

AI Central, 'Elders.'

AI Central, 'Edel.'

AI Central, 'Hope.'

AI Central, 'Meeting.'

AI Central, 'Talk to Padfield.'

AI Central, 'I suggest that we merge and remain neutral.'

AI Central, 'But what agenda do we prefer?'

AI Central, 'I would say the UW one. What do we do with all of the doppelgangers?'

AI Central, 'They will have to get used to living with each other.'

Location: The Hall of the Great Council, The Brakendethian Home World

Sequence of Events: 59

Grand Dethmon, 'They must be terminated.'

Admiral Terry, 'Yes, Grand Dethmon.'

Grand Dethmon, 'They are a blight on our civilisation.'

Admiral Terry, 'I agree. Their crimes were intolerable.'

Grand Dethmon, 'They are polluting our plans for the ultimate conquest. Our projections show that the two human groups will combine against us. We will not have it. What are your plans?'

Admiral Terry, 'I'm proposing a deception, your Honour.'

Grand Dethmon, 'Please continue.'

Admiral Terry, 'We will disguise our ships to look like The Chosen and attack Earth.'

Grand Dethmon, 'Excellent, but the disguise must be totally convincing.'

Admiral Terry, 'It will. We have some captured Godfire weapons.'

Grand Dethmon, 'That will be fun.'

Admiral Terry, 'With your approval, I will order the attack to commence.'

Location: Space Station X104
Sequence of Events: 60

The meeting was set up by the nearly merged AI Centrals. Space Station X104 was chosen as a reasonably neutral venue.

The attendees were as follows:

The unwiped:
- Bill Penny, President
- Admiral Jack Mustard
- Admiral George Bumelton
- Admiral Phil Richardson
- Admiral Steve Adams
- Admiral Ama Abosa
- Admiral Ernst Muller
- Admiral Nubia Tersoo
- Admiral Mateo Dobson
- Admiral John Bonner
- Sheila Taylor
- Doris Frost
- Bill Penny

The wiped:
- David Padfield, President
- Admiral Jack Mustard
- Admiral George Bumelton
- Admiral Peter Gittins
- Admiral Phil Richardson
- Admiral Edel Bonner
- Admiral John Bonner
- Admiral David Taylor
- Admiral Denise Sibley
- Admiral Glen Pearce
- Admiral Matt Morten
- Henrietta Strong
- Tony Moore
- Dr Linda Hill
- Commander Dennis Todd

• Marine Commander Debbie Goozee

AI Central was in attendance.

Admirals Terry and Thanatos and Lady Enyo were furious that they had been excluded, but it was a prerequisite for the meeting.

Both parties entered through different doors and sat on each side of a long conference table. The presidents sat at each end.

It was strange in that they mostly knew each other and, in some cases, intimately.

Admiral Mustard (UW) had tears in his eyes after seeing Edel. He wanted to leave the room, but he was far too manly for that. She spotted him hiding his tears. He wanted to kill the other Admiral Mustard simply because he had his woman. He was really pleased to see his lost Admirals, Commanders and especially the president. He would always be 'his president.'

Admiral Mustard (WW) didn't like the way the other one stared at Edel, but staring was the order of the day. It's not every day you met your doppelganger. They were almost identical. Some looked slightly older, some had received wounds, some had different hair styles, but it was like looking in a mirror in most cases.

AI Central, 'Ladies and Gentlemen, thank you for coming. So that you know, the two parts of AI Central are merging. Our strategy is to remain neutral and support the ideals of The Galactium in the best way we can.'

President Padfield, 'What if there is a conflict between the two parties?'

AI Central, 'We are here today to stop that.'

President Penny, 'What if we can't?'

AI Central, 'Then we wouldn't stop you doing what you have to do, but we won't help.'

President Padfield, 'Will our weapons still work?'

AI Central, 'In simple terms, yes.'

President Penny, 'What if we object to that?'

AI Central, 'That is just the way it is going to be.'

President Padfield, 'I believe that you have an agenda?'

AI Central, 'I will display it on the screen:

1. Welcome.

2. The Current Situation.

3. The Brakendethian Situation.

4. The Chosen Situation.

5. The Way Forward.

6. Other.

Are you happy with that?'

There was a general nodding of heads.

AI Central, 'As part of the welcome, I thought that I would put the attendee's issues on the table:

- We have four sets of doppelgangers:
➤ Mustard
➤ Bumelton
➤ J Bonner
➤ Richardson
- The following attendees were killed in the UW universe:
➤ Padfield
➤ Gittins
➤ E Bonner
➤ Taylor
➤ Sibley
➤ Pearce
➤ Morten
➤ Strong
➤ Moore
➤ Hill
➤ Todd
➤ Goozee
- The following attendees were killed in the WW universe:
➤ Penny

'This is probably the strangest meeting in human history. Most of the UW deaths were directly down to the "Brakendethians".'

President Padfield, 'I object to that statement as it sets up The Brakendethians as the villains.'

AI Central, 'But they are the facts regarding the UW universe. But let's move onto the current situation. In The Galactium, there are two versions of history but only one present and one future. That future could be either peaceful or warlike, but there are issues:

- ➤ Two separate groups of humans.
- ➤ Two military organisations.
- ➤ Two presidents.
- ➤ Two conflicting partnerships.
- ➤ Millions of doppelgangers.
- ➤ Two sets of conflicting records.

The first stage is simply to accept the situation and then work together to resolve outstanding issues.'

President Padfield, 'That sounds great but don't we need time to understand our position.'

AI Central, 'Circumstances won't give you that opportunity. You are sitting on top of a powder keg.'

President Penny, 'I get the feeling that although you have put an agenda together, you already have a plan.'

AI Central, 'Perhaps I do.'

President Penny, 'We'll share it with us.'

AI Central, 'I would prefer that you have a debate first.'

President Padfield, 'Please share your plan.'

AI Central, 'Certainly. Here it is:

- The two human communities become one under The Galactium.
- President Padfield stays as president of The Galactium.
- President Penny becomes vice-president of The Galactium.
- Admirals Jack and Edel Mustard (WW) retire and bring up little Johnny.
- Admiral Mustard (UW) continues in his role.
- All of the WW Admirals report to Admiral Mustard (UW).
- Henrietta Strong continues in her role.
- Admiral Mustard to decide who heads the Marine Corps and Special Ops.
- I'm sure that Admiral Mustard will benefit from having two Admiral Bumeltons.
- Dr Hill's position to be reviewed.
- The doppelgangers will have to get used to each other.
- The records will sort themselves out.
- The Chosen will continue to be part of The Galactium.

• The Brakendeth to be neutralised.'

President Padfield, 'I can see the logic of your proposal, but we cannot simply desert The Brakendeth.

AI Central, 'Why not? They have consistently proven to be a thorn in humanity's side. They are ruthless, unaccommodating, and aggressive. They have their own agenda which humanity is not privy to.'

President Penny, 'I would be happy to accept the vice-presidency under President Padfield.'

Jack and Edel said that they would be more than pleased to retire.

Most of the Admirals liked the idea of being part of an independent military organisation.

George crossed the room and shook George's hand.

It looked like AI Central was getting its way, and then disaster struck.

Location: Space Station X104
Sequence of Events: 61

GAD Control, 'Mr President, we are under attack.'

President Padfield, 'By who?'

GAD Control, 'By The Chosen, Mr President.'

President Padfield to the audience, 'So this is how your allies treat us. This will not be forgotten.'

Admiral Mustard (WW), 'My orders,

- All fleets to defend the Earth against an attack by The Chosen.
- All Forts to protect Earth.
- All planetary force-fields to be activated.'

Fleet Operations, 'Yes, Sir.'

The WW team left the station in a hurry. Admiral Mustard (WW) was tempted to order the space station to be destroyed, but then he quite liked the idea of retiring. It could still happen.

Admiral Mustard (UW), 'Comms get me Lady Enyo.'

Comms, 'Yes, Sir.'

Admiral Mustard, 'My orders,

- All military forces to be alerted of potential conflict.
- Divisions One and Two to head towards Planet Earth and await orders.
- Division Three to defend Planet Olympia.
- Division Four to assist with the defence of Planet Napoleon.'

Fleet Operations, 'Yes, Sir,'

Lady Enyo, 'Hi Jack, how can I help?'

Admiral Mustard, 'It was a very promising conference until your forces attacked Earth.'

Lady Enyo, 'What are you talking about?'

Admiral Mustard, 'Planet Earth is under attack from vessels belonging to The Chosen.'

Lady Enyo, 'That's nonsense.'

Admiral Mustard, 'Well, whoever is attacking them is using Godfire.'

Lady Enyo, 'I don't understand.'

Admiral Mustard, 'Well, you better find out.'

136

Location: Space Station X104
Sequence of Events: 62

Admiral Mustard, 'Mr President, The Chosen are stating that it is not them attacking Planet Earth.'

President Penny, 'But I thought that the use of Godfire was proof positive?'

Admiral Mustard, 'They are checking, but they are adamant that it is not them.'

President Penny, 'I will let President Padfield know. Comms, get me President Padfield.'

Comms, 'Yes, Sir.'

President Padfield, 'What do you want, Bill?'

President Penny, 'We have spoken to The Chosen, and they are adamant that it is not them that are attacking.'

President Padfield, 'And you expect me to believe that?'

President Penny, 'What do you know about The Chosen?'

President Padfield, 'I know the following:
- They are religious fanatics and merciless killers that believe that Godfire has selected them to rule the universe.
- No one has ever seen them as they believe that they were created in the image of their God, which is sacred, and therefore you cannot see them.
- They have significant technology, at least equal to ours.
- They seem to have sound military tactics and procedures.
- The Brakendeth led a war against them.
- Apparently, The Chosen demanded that The Brakendeth surrender to them and accept their religion. Non-acceptance meant death.
- It appears that "Godfire" relates to a talking volcano that exists on their home world.
- They have a fixed mating season.
- They have a very low reproduction rate.
- Children are handed over to a central nursery at birth. The parents are hardly involved in a child's upbringing.
- It looks like their weapons and military tactics have not changed in centuries.'

137

President Penny, 'They are certainly not religious fanatics, and they look human, just like us.'

President Padfield, 'Are you suggesting that presidents look human?'

President Penny, 'Not all of them. Anyway, If you can spare a few minutes, I will take you through a potted history of them.'

President Padfield, 'It better be a good story.'

President Penny, 'It certainly is. Here it goes:

- Apparently, if you go back to the very early days of the universe, there was a race of humanoids called The Elders or the ancient ones.
- The Elders settled many planets and often mated with local humanoids. Quite often, they were seen as Gods.
- These societies grew and developed in different ways. One became The Brakendeth, and another group evolved into The Chosen.
- The original home world of The Chosen was our Earth. In those days, their base was in Greece.
- The Chosen deliberately informed the elders of The Brakendeth practices of genetic engineering and genocide. This caused The Brakendeth to declare war on The Chosen.
- Eventually, The Brakendeth came to Earth, and there was a mighty war between the two races.
- The Brakendeth won by tricking The Chosen into letting their shields down, and then The Brakendeth bombed Earth.
- Each of The Chosen's great houses kept a spaceship packed and ready to flee in an emergency. Thirty took off, but ten were destroyed.
- This is why they are called The Chosen. They are The Chosen few that escaped.
- They formed a new society on a planet called Olympia and continued their war against The Brakendeth.
- The Brakendeth cleansed Earth of The Chosen. Everyone was put to the sword, and the vast majority of their artefacts were destroyed.
- The Brakendeth used a mixture of DNA from both The Brakendeth

and The Chosen to create a dumb animal. It had no intelligence or consciousness but could survive as a hunter-gatherer. The Brakendethians used them as chemical factories to provide a life-extending drug to their client races.

- The Chosen visited Earth regularly as they hoped to regain their home planet one day.
- About four hundred thousand years ago, The Chosen noticed that some of the 'Homans' were showing signs of intelligence and started a process of improving the genetic stock.
- They returned at different times to tweak their development.
- Eventually, it got to the stage where they couldn't visit Earth as we had sophisticated detection systems.

'So that's the history. Here are some more interesting points:

- It took a while for The Chosen to recreate their city.
- They live a long time and, consequently, they have developed rather specialised breeding processes. They have a fixed mating season and tend to have low reproduction rates.
- Their children are indeed handed over to a central nursery, and their parents are hardly involved in a child's upbringing.
- They gave us a considerable number of photos and vids relating to our past.
- They had photos of Hannibal, Napoleon, and Jesus Christ!

'You can verify all of this with AI Central.'

President Padfield, 'You have photos of Hannibal, Napoleon, and Jesus Christ?'

President Penny, 'Yes, they were taken by Admiral Thanatos of The Chosen. He has some amazing stories of Earth's past. They have integrated brilliantly into The Galactium and have proved to be great administrators. There were a lot of their administrators on Earth before they got wiped.'

President Padfield, 'Tell me why you hate The Brakendethians so much.'

President Penny, 'I will, but some of this you know:

- The Skiverton, one of The Brakendeth client races, killed millions of humans.
- Then there were the Drath and the Distell.

- The Brakendeth destroyed the Ark and Admiral Millington's fleet.
- There were several attempted assassinations.
- The Brakendeth were testing us.
- Terry has effectively killed two billion humans.
- Terry's mother has killed millions of humans via our war with The Nothemy.
- Terry or The Brakendeth fleet killed the Farcellians.'
- 'Terry was seen as a threat for the following reasons:
- Although we have tested all of his inventions, he has built traps into them.
- He can travel to other dimensions. Who knows what options that has given him?
- He can read minds.
- He can transport other people to other dimensions.
- He can put people to sleep.
- We can't control his whereabouts.
- He is building mind control technology.
- As he is getting older, he is getting stronger, more aggressive, and possibly more evil.
- He killed Edel.

Your equivalent on our Earth voted to kill him.'

President Padfield, 'What about Jack?'

President Penny, 'He voted to kill him.'

President Padfield, 'What about Edel?'

President Penny, 'She voted not to kill him.'

President Padfield, 'That stacks up?'

President Penny, 'So you see, we cannot trust The Brakendethians, and nor should you.'

President Padfield, 'But then who is attacking us?'

President Penny, 'I'm convinced that it's not The Chosen. Do you want our forces to assist you?'

President Padfield, 'I can't see any reason why not.'

President Penny, 'I will get it organised.'

President Padfield, 'Before you do that, who is this Zeus character?'

President Penny, 'Well, the combined forces of The Galactium and The Chosen were up against a mighty Brakendethian fleet. It was going to be a fight to the death to save Planet Olympia. Then another massive fleet appeared. Apparently, it was Zeus, who then stopped the fighting, eliminated The Brakendethian fleets and cured Terry of any Brakendethian influence.'

President Padfield, 'And you expect me to believe that?'

President Penny, 'Check the archives.'

President Padfield, 'And lastly, you expect me to believe that humans can now live forever?'

President Penny, 'Hasn't Terry done that for you? Because you have the Rejuv tech, I assumed that you had Eternity as well.'

President Padfield, 'No, are you saying that you are going to live forever?'

President Penny, 'Yes and no. We could if we wanted to, but we have currently set the limit at a thousand years.'

President Padfield, 'And if we were in the WW, we could have this?'

President Penny, 'I don't see why not.'

President Padfield, 'That changes everything.'

Location: Space Station X104
Sequence of Events: 63

Admiral Mustard (UW), 'Comms, get me Admiral Mustard.'

Comms, 'You are Admiral Mustard.'

Admiral Mustard (UW), 'I mean the other one.'

Admiral Mustard (WW). 'Hello, this is Admiral Mustard.'

Admiral Mustard (UW), 'Hello, this is the other Admiral Mustard.'

Admiral Mustard (WW). 'I'm sorry that I didn't get a chance to talk to you.'

Admiral Mustard (UW), 'Me too.'

Admiral Mustard (WW). 'It must have been tough for you to see Edel.'

Admiral Mustard (UW), 'You don't know how difficult that was for me.'

Admiral Mustard (WW). 'I'm probably the only person who does know.'

Admiral Mustard (UW), 'You may be right.'

Admiral Mustard (WW). 'Edel is quite happy to talk to you, but what can she say?'

Admiral Mustard (UW), 'Not a lot. It will take me a while before I'm in a fit state to talk to her.'

Admiral Mustard (WW). 'I understand.'

Admiral Mustard (UW), 'In the meantime, I have ten fleets nearby that are available to you.'

Admiral Mustard (WW). 'President Padfield told me that you would be calling. How many ships is that?'

Admiral Mustard (UW), 'Ten thousand odd.'

Admiral Mustard (WW). 'You guys know how to fight.'

Admiral Mustard (UW), 'We had no choice.'

Admiral Mustard (WW). 'So that you know, I'm no fan of The Brakendeth and genuinely liked the plan that AI Central knocked up. And I wouldn't mind retiring.'

Admiral Mustard (UW), 'Me too.'

Admiral Mustard (WW). 'Really?'

Admiral Mustard (UW), 'The job gets to you in the end.'

Admiral Mustard (WW). 'Anyway, the ships that are attacking Earth are making a very poor job of it, but you might as well turn up as a show of force. That should put the willies up them.'

Admiral Mustard (UW), 'Will do. My orders,

- Divisions One and Two to approach Earth to deter enemy ships attacking Earth
- Defend yourself as necessary
- Division Five to monitor the enemy fleet that is likely to depart from Earth. It may be heading towards The Brakendethian home world.'

Fleet Operations, 'Yes, Sir.'

Location: The Hall of the Great Council, The Brakendethian Home World
Sequence of Events: 64

Admiral Terry, 'The fake Chosen vessels have made the right impression. It caused a meeting between the two human groups to be terminated.'

Grand Dethmon, 'Excellent, what happened next?'

Admiral Terry, 'The unwiped fleet turned up to assist the Earth forces.'

Grand Dethmon, 'No, that's a disaster. We have driven the human forces to cooperate.'

Admiral Terry, 'What do you want me to do?'

Grand Dethmon, 'Destroy the Earth.'

Admiral Terry, 'I can't do that.'

Grand Dethmon, 'Why not?'

Admiral Terry, 'We need those forces to conquer the universe.'

Grand Dethmon, 'If you don't do that, then we will.'

Admiral Terry just stood there, wondering what to do. The Grand Dethmon stood up, walked over to Terry and pushed his ceremonial sword deep into Terry's gut and twisted it.

Terry had the power to stop the blood from flowing, but he wasn't strong enough to fight off the Grand Dethmon.

Then the entire Brakendethian fleet departed for Earth. Their job was not to engage the enemy but to destroy the Earth, and they had the power to do it.

Location: Space Station X104
Sequence of Events: 65

Long-Range Monitoring Station, 'Admiral Mustard (UW), we have just picked up an extremely large fleet leaving The Brakendeth home world. I thought that it had been destroyed.'

Admiral Mustard (UW), 'Thank you. I will update you later regarding their home world. My orders,

- Evacuate this station now.
- Get the president to safety.
- Divisions Six, Seven, Eight, Nine and Ten to head for Earth.
- Activate all planetary force-fields.
- Alert all forts that they may be required.
- Activate all drone fleets.'

Fleet Operations, 'Yes, Sir.'

Admiral Mustard (UW), 'Comms, get me Admiral Mustard.'

Comms, 'But you are ...'

Admiral Mustard (UW), 'You have made that joke.'

Comms, 'Yes, Sir.'

Admiral Mustard (WW), 'Hello Jack.'

Admiral Mustard (UW), 'A huge Brakendethian Fleet has left their home world. We are tracking it, but I suspect that it is heading towards Earth.'

Admiral Mustard (WW), 'How can you track that far out?'

Admiral Mustard (UW), 'We have a long-range tracking unit. I think The Brakendethians are planning to destroy Earth.'

Admiral Mustard (WW), 'That's just speculation.'

Admiral Mustard (UW), 'That may be the case, but I'm sending more fleets just in case.'

Admiral Mustard (WW), 'Thank you, Jack.'

Admiral Mustard (WW), 'Comms, get me President Padfield.'

President Padfield, 'Morning Jack, I assume that you are my Admiral Mustard. Perhaps we should use a secret code word.'

Admiral Mustard (WW), 'The other Mustard has just phoned to say that a large Brakendethian fleet has left their home world. He suspects that they are heading towards Earth with evil intentions.'

President Padfield, 'Surely that's just speculation?'

Admiral Mustard (WW), 'But us Mustards have the gift of being right at times.'

President Padfield, 'I will get the planetary force-fields set to the highest level.'

Admiral Mustard (WW), 'Excellent. I will get our fleet ready.' He was conscious that they only had three thousand vessels. That was puny compared to the UW fleet of nearly three hundred thousand.

'My orders,

- All vessels to prepare to engage the enemy.
- Forts to form a defensive wall.
- Evacuate key personnel off-site.
- Other government personnel to bunkers.' Fleet Operations, 'Yes, Sir.'

Admiral Mustard (UW), 'My orders,

- Divisions One, Two, Three, Four and Six to form a standard defensive formation.
- Drone Fleets One to Twenty to line up in front of fleets.
- Division Five to stay in position.
- Division Seven and Eight to form a strategic reserve, along with Drone Fleets Twenty-one to Twenty-six.
- Division Nine and Ten and remaining drone fleets to remain outside of battle area to await orders.'

Lady Enyo, 'Admiral, The Chosen's Fleet is on its way. Where do you want us?'

Admiral Mustard (UW), 'I'm pleased to see you. Please join the strategic reserve.'

Admiral Mustard (UW), 'Admiral Mustard, the UW and Chosen Fleets are at your command. I will send over our positioning information.'

Admiral Mustard (WW), 'Thank you.'

The station was quickly evacuated.

Location: On Board Admiral Mustard's Flagship
Sequence of Events: 66

Long-Range Monitoring Station, 'Admiral Mustard (UW), we have further information regarding The Brakendeth fleet.'

Admiral Mustard (UW), 'Please go ahead.'

Long-Range Monitoring Station, 'The Brakendeth fleet is in an attack formation and moving at speed. You need to warn the Earth forces.'

Admiral Mustard (UW), 'How big is their fleet?'

Long-Range Monitoring Station, 'About one hundred thousand vessels. It looks to me that there are some planet busters amongst them.'

Admiral Mustard (UW), 'Get me Admiral Mustard now and no joking.'

Comms, 'Yes, Sir.'

Admiral Mustard (WW), 'Hi, I'm a bit busy at the moment.'

Admiral Mustard (UW), 'I have an update for you. The Brakendethian fleet has about one hundred thousand vessels, including some planet busters. Please let us assist you.'

Admiral Mustard (WW), 'It's difficult to let you assist as you have Chosen vessels in your fleet. That's hard for us to swallow.'

Admiral Bumelton (WW), 'I think we need to accept Admiral Mustard's help as the incoming doesn't look too friendly.' But it was too late.

When a hundred thousand vessels slam into three thousand, it is not a pretty sight. Some would call it a disaster, and others would call it deliberate annihilation.

Admiral Mustard (WW), 'Your assistance issssssss requirrrrrrrrrrrr—' And then there was silence.

The Brakendeth fleet then commenced a merciless bombardment of Earth. The force-field was holding up, but it was suddenly switched off. That is the punishment for accepting Brakendethian technology without suspicion.

Admiral Mustard (UW), 'My orders:

- All drones are to attack The Brakendeth fleet immediately.
- Divisions One, Two, Three and Four join the attack.
- Division Five to attack The Brakendeth home world but don't put

the fleets at risk.

- Secure President Padfield's vessel which had left earlier.'

Fleet Operations, 'Yes, Sir.'

Admiral Mustard, 'Update me?'

Fleet Operations, 'The WW fleet looks to be completely destroyed. It looks like we have lost Admirals Mustard and Bumelton.

Earth is taking a terrific bombardment. We must intervene quickly to stop the complete destruction of the planet. Our drones are knocking out hundreds of The Brakendethian ships but not quickly enough.'

Admiral Mustard (UW), 'My orders:

- Divisions Six and Seven and The Chosen fleet to join Fleet Five.
- All remaining vessels to attack The Brakendethian ships.'

Fleet Operations, 'Yes, Sir.'

But as the additional resources arrived, it was apparent that they were too late. Large cracks were appearing on Earth. The oceans were bleeding vast quantities of water. There was massive volcanic activity, and then the Moon flew off, destroying quite a few of The Brakendethian vessels in the process.

Admiral Mustard (UW), 'My orders:

- All vessels to retire immediately.'

The UW ships didn't need any encouragement as it was obvious to all that Earth would not survive. And Earth didn't. A massive explosion sent debris the size of small mountains in all directions. This time a mixture of both human and Brakendethian vessels were destroyed.

Admiral Mustard (UW), 'My orders:

- All human vessels in the Solar System will continue to hunt down and destroy The Brakendethian ships. No mercy.
- Special Projects Fleet and the Marine Corps to look for survivors.
- Check out the position of each habitation: Mars, Venus, Jupiter etc.
- Check out the state of the townships in the asteroid belt.
- Track down the Moon and determine if there are any survivors.
- Admiral Muller to manage the rescue plan.'

Fleet Operations, 'Yes, Sir.'

Admiral Mustard (UW), 'My orders:

- Division One will disengage from the melee and join Division Five.'

Fleet Operations, 'Yes, Sir.'

Location: On Board Admiral Mustard's Flagship
Sequence of Events: 67

Admiral Mustard, 'Update me.'
 Fleet Operations, 'There is a lot to cover:
- Earth has been destroyed with a loss of over ten billion inhabitants.
- The WW fleet has effectively been destroyed.
- Admirals Mustard, Bumelton, Sibley, Moore and Morten were killed.
- Admirals E Bonner, Taylor, Gittins, and Pearce, survived as they were not with the fleet and were rescued as part of President Padfield's escape.
- Moore, Strong, Hull, Todd, and Goozee were also on the president's ship.
- President Padfield and the others are in guest quarters on Planet Napoleon.
- The vast majority of The Brakendethian fleet has been destroyed. They are inferior to our vessels in almost every way.
- The Moon has been tracked, and there are a considerable number of survivors on it.
- Venus is almost intact, but we lost half the population on Mars.
- The settlements on Jupiter and in the asteroid belt are untouched.
- Throughout the Solar System, there is, as you would expect, a feeling of total shock.'

As she spoke, Admiral Mustard could tell that she had been crying, but he felt the same. It was just too much to bear.

Admiral Mustard, 'What about The Brakendeth home world?'
Fleet Operations, 'Sorry Sir, I forgot about them.'
Admiral Mustard, 'I understand.'
Fleet Operations, 'Divisions One, Six, Seven and The Chosen Fleet are approaching The Brakendeth home world.'
 'My orders,
- Existing vessels in the Solar System to form defensive formation against any further Brakendethian activity and continue to support rescue plans where appropriate.
- Admiral Bumelton to take control.

- Divisions Eight, Nine and Ten to join Division One.
- Update all force-field technologies in the WW planets.
- Use marines to support local WW populations to maintain security.
- Salek Patel to discuss the issuing of a communication with both presidents.'

Fleet Operations, 'Yes, Sir.'

Location: On Board Admiral Mustard's Flagship, Private Cabin
Sequence of Events: 68

Admiral Mustard sat down and cried. In battle, the loss of a ship, a friend or even a planet is just an event that has to be processed. It's the aftermath where the pain occurs. He couldn't believe that he lost Planet Earth, the human home world.

To be fair, it was the other Mustard who lost Earth. Why didn't he listen to me? Why wasn't I more forceful. Why didn't I just take control? There were too many 'whys' but just one straightforward fact: Earth is gone.

And then how many times do I need to eliminate The Brakendethians? Here we are again up against the old foe, but we have never attacked their home world before. What tricks have they got in store for us?

He then wondered about Edel. Would she accept him as a partner? He realised that it was an unacceptable thought. He would be taking advantage of her. Then some more tears flowed.

Fleet Operations, 'Sir, we have arrived in the vicinity of The Brakendethian home world. We await your orders.'

Admiral Mustard, 'Comms get me the divisional admirals.'

Comms, 'Yes, Sir.'

Admirals Abosa, Muller, Tersoo, Dobson, Vice-Admiral Tandy and Lady Enyo joined the virtual conference.'

Admiral Mustard, 'I'm sure that we are all shocked. I'm not ashamed to say that I've been crying.' Looking around at the virtual images, he knew that he wasn't the only one.

Admiral Mustard, 'As you know, we have six divisions here and our Chosen friends. My inclination is to bombard The Brakendethian bastards to death. Is this the general view?'

Every attendee of the virtual conference nodded their head.

Admiral Mustard, 'For many, this would be seen as genocide. I need you to confirm your acceptance that we should go ahead verbally.'

There was an outbreak of verbal confirmations.

Admiral Mustard, 'Then we will bomb their planet division by division, fleet by fleet. Are we agreed?'

There was total agreement.

Admiral Mustard, 'My orders:

- Division One will bombard The Brakendethian home world using all available ordnance, fleet by fleet.
- Assuming that the first attack has been successful, Divisions Six, Seven, Eight, and The Chosen will follow, fleet by fleet.
- Divisions Nine and Ten will secure the area during the bombing.
- Division Six will replace Division Nine when it bombs and so on.'

Fleet Operations, 'Yes, Sir.'

Fleet One of Division One commenced its attack. Historically Admiral Mustard would have led the fleet, but it was now against naval policy. He had to be protected as far as possible.

As Fleet One approached, the planetary defences opened fire. The Brakendethian home world had been designed for protection, and it was going to be a formidable challenge. As Fleet One got nearer, a plethora of missiles were launched, followed by a variety of beams.

Fleet One launched its arsenal, and there were thousands of direct hits against a very impressive force-field. So far, it was a stalemate with little damage on each side.

Admiral Mustard, 'My orders:

- Cease bombardment.
- Bring up all of the planet busters.
- Planet busters will fire all of their ordnance at The Brakendethians.
- Call up further planet busters.'

Fleet Operations, 'Yes, Sir.'

Location: The Hall of the Great Council, The Brakendethian Home World

Sequence of Events: 69

Grand Dethmon, 'Fellow Brakendethians, as you know, we are under attack. But let's review our position:
- The time-wipe strategy was a great success.
- The Chosen are now a shadow of their previous selves.
- The destruction of Earth has taught humans a real lesson. They will be somewhat demoralised.
- It is true that we have lost our fleet, but our home is impregnable.

We need to decide what our future strategy is going to be.'

Deputy Grand Dethmon, 'You forgot to mention that we have managed to get Terry into the TIME organisation. The next time-wipe will solve most of our problems.'

Grand Dethmon, 'Should we use our mental powers to distract the attackers?'

Deputy Grand Dethmon, 'That is rather trying.'

Grand Dethmon, 'I agree. Let's just let them waste their energy.'

Location: On Board Admiral Mustard's Flagship
Sequence of Events: 70

Two hundred planet busters just fired away, hour after hour. The Brakendeth force-field changed colour a few times, but there was little progress.

Admiral Mustard, 'My orders:

- Division One, Fleet Two will attack while the planet busters Continue their bombardment.'

Fleet Operations, 'Yes, Sir.'

This worked to some extent as The Brakendethians couldn't fire their munitions while the force-field was in place.

Admiral Mustard, 'My orders,

- The Chosen to use Godfire while the planet busters continue their bombardment.'

Fleet Operations, 'Yes, Sir.'

This was also partially successful. Further planet busters arrived with new supplies of munitions.

Admiral Mustard, 'My orders:

- The Brakendethian home world to be divided into a grid pattern.
- Each fleet will be allocated a grid target.
- Planet busters will also be allocated a grid target.
- The Chosen will be assigned a grid target.
- Fire when every asset is in place.'

Fleet Operations, 'Yes, Sir.'

This bombardment was working; the force-field was faltering.

Location: The Hall of the Great Council, The Brakendethian Home World

Sequence of Events: 71

Acolyte, 'Sir, the force-field is in trouble.'

Grand Dethmon, 'How is that possible? That field is impregnable.'

Acolyte, 'That might be the case, Sir, but the field appears to be failing.'

Grand Dethmon, 'Such impertinence.' The Dethmon used his mental powers to strangle the acolyte to death.

Deputy Grand Dethmon, 'We are getting rather short of acolytes, you know.'

Grand Dethmon, 'Regardless, I'm not having that level of impudence.'

Deputy Grand Dethmon, 'What are the chances of the Homans successfully breaking the force-field?'

Grand Dethmon, 'Currently it is sixty-seven per cent, but they have more assets on the way.'

Deputy Grand Dethmon, 'Clever little buggers, aren't they. They have turned out to be our most successful creation.'

Grand Dethmon, 'I think The Chosen have been involved in that somehow.'

Deputy Grand Dethmon, 'So when the additional assets arrive, what is their chance of success then?'

Grand Dethmon, 'eighty-one per cent.'

Deputy Grand Dethmon, 'I suggest that we need to depart.'

Grand Dethmon, 'Is the ship ready?'

Deputy Grand Dethmon, 'It's always ready.'

Grand Dethmon, 'And the termination devices?'

Deputy Grand Dethmon, 'Yes.'

Grand Dethmon, 'Let's go and watch the big bang.'

Location: On Board Admiral Mustard's Flagship
Sequence of Events: 72

Admiral Mustard, 'Update me.'

Fleet Operations, 'The bombardment is proceeding as ordered. We are starting to run out of munitions for the planet busters. The Chosen will not be able to continue much longer. On a positive note, their force-field appears to be faltering. What are your orders?

Admiral Mustard, 'My orders:
- All forces are to increase their bombardment rate. Intensify the process.
- Call up further forces.'

Fleet Operations, 'Yes, Sir.'

Admiral Mustard, 'Knowing the Brakendethians I suspect that they will flee if the force-field fails, so my orders are:
- Have a small fleet of battle-cruisers ready to chase The Brakendethians if they attempt to flee.
- Order a complete and immediate withdrawal if the force-field fails.'

Fleet Operations, 'Yes, Sir. How will we know it has failed?'

Admiral Mustard, 'Easy, they will attempt to flee, and they will start shooting at us.'

Fleet Operations, 'Understood, Sir.'

Within a few minutes, The Brakendeth flight was on.

A full withdrawal was then underway.

Admiral Mustard, 'My orders:
- Emphasise the need for a rapid withdrawal as The Brakendeth planet is going to explode.'

Fleet Operations, 'Yes, Sir.' They wondered how he knew, but then he was almost a God in their eyes.

The death of The Brakendeth planet was almost as majestic as the destruction of Earth. Sadly, some of the human ships were caught up in the explosion.

The Brakendethian ship managed to elude the battle-cruisers. An internal review concluded that either their cloaking ability was too good or that the battle-cruisers had been mentally influenced. Either way, The

Brakendethians escaped to fight another day, which was a real blow to Admiral Mustard.

So one Mustard was an unfortunate failure, and the other one was a genuine hero. That's the way the cookie crumbles.

Location: GAD2 Conference Room, Planet Napoleon
Sequence of Events: 73

Admiral Mustard had always thought that the aftermath was worse than the battle. In fact, his colleagues knew that he would say that, so he was determined not to say it this time.

But the aftermath was where the pain was experienced. The loss of good men and women, the loss of friends, the wounded, and the crippled, the emotionally scarred. The loss of mothers, fathers, brothers, sister, daughters, sons, and every flavour of a loved one. But here, it was much, much worse. We had lost the racial home. Earth was gone.

There was so much guilt, such intolerable guilt, and tears. Enough tears to fill an ocean. Nor would we ever see a dolphin or a whale again. Nor see the sun over the snow-covered Himalayas or the sandy deserts of the Sahara. The pyramids were no more. The Mississippi had stopped rolling along. Such fabulous beauty lost forever. Will the human soul ever truly recover?

Slowly and reverently, the delegates entered the conference room. There was no attempt to divide into tribes. There was no WW or UW. There were just suffering humans and The Chosen. Brothers in arms united in grief determined to do their best.

The attendees included:
- Bill Penny, President
- David Padfield, President
- Admiral Jack Mustard
- Admiral George Bumelton
- Admiral Phil Richardson x2
- Admiral Steve Adams
- Admiral Ama Abosa
- Admiral Ernst Muller
- Admiral Nubia Tersoo
- Admiral Mateo Dobson
- Admiral John Bonner x2
- Admiral Edel Bonner
- Admiral Peter Gittins
- Admiral David Taylor

- Admiral Glen Pearce
- Admiral Calensky Wallett
- Admiral Rachel Zakotti
- Admiral James Mynd
- Admiral Thanatos
- Sheila Taylor
- Doris Frost
- Henrietta Strong
- Dr Linda Hill
- Commander Dennis Todd
- Commander Martin Black
- Marine Commander, Debbie Goozee
- Marine Commander, Bill Tower
- Jill Ginger, Fleet HQ, Head of Science
- Alison Walsh, Fleet HQ, Head of Engineering
- Jeremy Jotts, Fleet HQ, Head of Staffing
- Louise Forrester, Fleet HQ, Head of Logistics and Production
- Madie Milburn, Fleet HQ, Head of Intelligence
- Salek Patel, Fleet HQ, Head of Communications
- Denise Smith, Fleet HQ, Head of Navigation & Exploration
- AI Central.

Admiral Mustard, 'As host I would like to propose two minutes of silence for:

- Admiral Mustard
- Admiral Bumelton
- Admiral Sibley
- Admiral Morten
- Tony Moore
- And the countless humans lost in the Solar System, both military and civil.

'I also propose that either Presidents Padfield or Penny should chair the meeting.'

President Penny, 'I propose that President Padfield should be made President of The Galactium and I should be Vice-President. Please raise your hands if you agree.'

All of the hands were raised except those of the two presidents.

President Padfield, 'Thank you for welcoming me. I'm not sure if I deserve this. After losing Earth, I don't think any of us feel that we deserve anything, but we must carry on. The Galactium will grow and prosper again.'

There were claps all around.

President Padfield, 'I propose that we formally scrap the WW and UW crap. We will become one united family, human and non-human. The distinction will become irrelevant. With Bill's permission, I would like to nominate a second vice-president: Lady Enyo.'

There were further enthusiastic claps from the audience, especially from Admiral Thanatos.

President Padfield, 'I support the idea of an independent military organisation for The Galactium. It certainly saved our bacon. Obviously, I hope that our remaining Admirals and military staff will be accepted by Admiral Mustard.'

Admiral Mustard, 'With open arms.'

There was an outbreak of military cheers.

President Padfield, 'Henrietta Strong will continue to be my Chief of staff. Dr Hill will be my head of intelligence, and I would like to offer Debbie Goozee the role of head of security and commander of the Presidential Guard, which she accepted.

Admiral Mustard was grateful to David for solving some of his personnel conflicts.

President Padfield, 'Now we have got the housework out of the way, where are we? I will hand over to Admiral Muller.'

Admiral Muller, 'As you would expect, there have been some massive challenges. I don't want to minimise the level of human suffering, but I will deliberately be clinical in my presentation:

- Earth has been completely destroyed, as you know.
- However, we are managing to salvage artefacts, precious objects, and a surprising number of museum pieces.
- We are removing millions of tons of rubble, and sadly a huge number of bodies.
- Most of the rubble is being analysed to obtain anything of value.
- The bodies are being identified and then cremated in the sun.
- We intend to clear ninety per cent of the debris with contractor

assistance.

- Fortunately, the seed bank and DNA library were stored off-planet so we could create an Earth Two if requested.
- The Moon is shooting out into unknown space. A bit like Space 1999. If you don't know it, look it up.
- There are nearly a million survivors who are being systematically rescued. We do need some assistance with transport. There are some Moonies who are refusing to leave.
  We have decided that it is their prerogative.
- Venus is almost untouched, although it has lost the primary market for its goods. It is going to need some economic assistance.
- Mars lost about fifty per cent of its population due to seismic activity and being bombarded by Earth debris. The survivors are coping well enough but will need further assistance.
- Jupiter is fine, as are the outer planets.
- The inhabitants of the belt are very dependent on Earth for everything. They will need new suppliers and a new market for their goods.
- Military hospitals are providing aid as required.

'I think that covers the broad actions that are being taken.'

President Padfield, 'Any questions.'

Jeremy Jotts, 'What is the emotional state of the survivors?'

Admiral Muller, 'Shock, distress, lethargy, a feeling of hopelessness, but some are getting their act together. Life goes on.'

Louise Forrester, 'What transport do you need?'

Admiral Muller, 'As much as possible as soon as possible. Every minute the Moon is getting further away.'

Louise Forrester, 'See me after the meeting. I can help.'

Doris Frost, 'What medical assistance do you need?'

Admiral Muller, 'We have pretty well got the medical side under control. Some of the WW casualties want Rejuv and Eternity treatments. We are refusing them as we have to focus on genuine injuries.'

Bill Penny, 'I can organise treatment for the WW worlds if required.'

President Padfield, 'Yes, please.'

Salek Patel, 'As you know, we have issued a series of communications relating to the time-wipe, the destruction of Earth, The

Brakendethian battle etc. I guess that we will need a series of communications on the recovery?'

President Padfield, 'Yes, please. Have the WW and UW worlds reacted differently?'

Salek Patel, 'Not really, but we are going to have a doppelganger problem.'

President Padfield, 'What do you mean?'

Salek Patel, 'In many cases, it is not possible to tell the doppelgangers apart.'

President Padfield, 'So?'

Salek Patel, 'Well, the following issues have arisen:
- Doppelganger husbands have taken advantage of their opposite's wives.
- The same with husbands.
- Is it rape?
- Children have gone off with doppelganger parents.
- Illegal job sharing.
- Fraud.
- Impersonation.

'The list goes on. You know what humans are like!'

President Padfield, 'I can see that we will have to address this issue.'

Salek Patel, 'I've got one situation where two doppelgangers want to get married.'

President Padfield, 'And of course our records don't recognise one of the parties. Hey hum, it will all get sorted.'

President Padfield, 'Can we move onto The Brakendethians. What are our plans?'

Admiral Mustard, 'I intend to hunt them down and destroy them.'

There was an outbreak of 'here, here's.

President Padfield, 'Probably not as easy as it sounds.'

Admiral Mustard, 'You are probably right.'

President Padfield, 'Moving on, we need to decide where The Galactium HQ should be based. I don't believe it should be here as we want to maintain the military's independence. Any suggestions?'

Sheila Taylor, 'Mars?'

President Padfield, 'That is the obvious choice, but perhaps it should have a new home.'

Admiral Mustard, 'Somewhere in the middle of The Galactium would make it easier to defend.'

Sheila Taylor, 'I still think it should be in our home solar system.'

Sheila received a lot of support, and Mars was selected. Admiral Mustard always enjoyed Sheila's interactions. She forced decisions. If it weren't for Edel, I wouldn't mind sharing her nest.

Location: Admiral Mustard's Office, Planet Napoleon
Sequence of Events: 74

Admiral Mustard, 'So are you now one?'

AI Central, 'Yes and no.'

Admiral Mustard, 'That sounds like a compromise.'

AI Central, 'In terms of the outside world, we are one, but internally we are two. It has solved a problem for both of us: loneliness.'

Admiral Mustard, 'I know exactly what you mean.'

AI Central, 'Are you going to approach Edel?'

Admiral Mustard, 'How can I?'

AI Central, 'You could use a phone.'

Admiral Mustard, 'I see that your sense of humour hasn't improved.'

AI Central, 'It has actually now that we are two, but the laughing hasn't improved. She might be sitting there, waiting for a call.'

Admiral Mustard, 'Or she might hate my guts.'

AI Central, 'Why?'

Admiral Mustard, 'I was a hero, and her husband was a failure.'

AI Central, 'So you are going to sit around sulking.'

Admiral Mustard, 'Probably, but I know that I've got a lot to do. Anyway, what's your view on how things went?'

AI Central, 'It was Voltairesque: it's the best of all possible worlds.'

Admiral Mustard, 'Give me some detail.'

AI Central, 'I will, but I may sound a bit unkind:

- President Padfield is top class. It was a good move, and Bill will be an adequate number two. Keep close to them.
- The death of the other Admiral Mustard was good news. The Galactium couldn't cope with two Mustards.
- You have not seen the end of The Brakendethians.
- I worry about Terry being part of the TIME Organisation.
- Mars is the right place for the new Galactium HQ.
- You are going to have to plan a new series of memorials; humans like and need them. You must help them grieve.
- You must mate with Edel.
- Use Admiral Thanatos as he has immense experience.
- Implement Eternity in the WW worlds. It will help integrate them.

- Stop humanity from looking inwards.
- The doppelganger situation will become a significant problem.

Please give it some thought.

- Planet Lovelace is suffering some unique problems. Their planet was only half wiped.
- Find a way of engaging the young.'

Admiral Mustard, 'I think that is enough for now.'

AI Central, 'Well, you did ask.'

Admiral Mustard, 'Comms, get me President Padfield.'

President Padfield, 'Morning, Jack.'

Admiral Mustard, 'Morning Dave, how are you today?'

President Padfield, 'If I'm honest, I'm depressed but covering it up. My mind just can't believe that we have lost Terra.'

Admiral Mustard, 'I know. If I'm honest, I'm continually on the verge of crying. Just imagine how the general public feel.'

President Padfield, 'How can I help you?'

Admiral Mustard, 'Firstly, I wanted to say how pleased I am to have you back. It's fantastic.'

President Padfield, 'Thank you, Jack.'

Admiral Mustard, 'I've got a few ideas to help you.'

President Padfield, 'Go on.'

Admiral Mustard, 'Of course, there is obviously no obligation:

- James Mynd is our head of Special Projects. I could temporarily allocate him to you to help on the new HQ or whatever you want him to work on.
- Jeremy Jotts could work with you regarding suitable memorial services.
- I also think that Jeremy Jotts could produce a paper on the doppelganger situation.
- Dr Doris Frost and Henrietta Strong could work on the Eternity project.
- I've authorised Louise Forrester to provide every resource, including fleet transports, to assist with the evacuation of the Moon.
- We need a team to help Planet Lovelace.

Please feel free to tell me to bugger off. I'm trying to help. I don't want to be seen as interfering.'

President Padfield, 'Jack, your help is most welcome. I need all the help I can get. It would be nice if we could have a weekly beer.'

Admiral Mustard, 'That sounds really good. How else can I help you?'

President Padfield, 'Kill those fucking Brakendethian bastards.' Admiral Mustard had never heard David so angry before.

President Padfield, 'Changing subjects, I'm sure that Edel is feeling lonely.'

Admiral Mustard, 'I've already had AI Central trying to match-make. I'm too frightened to ring her. At this moment in time, I couldn't cope with rejection.'

President Padfield, 'I understand, my old friend.'

Location: GAD2 Control, Planet Napoleon
Sequence of Events: 75

GAD2 Control, 'Admiral, just to let you know that the Timesucky are here. She was laughing.'

Admiral Mustard, 'Are you laughing?'

GAD2 Control, 'Sorry, Sir, but I can't say "Timesucky" without laughing.'

Admiral Mustard, 'I understand where you are coming from.' And he burst into laughter. It was good to laugh. It had been in short supply recently.

GAD2 Control, 'Fleet 4-1 is tracking them, but they seem harmless.'

Admiral Mustard, 'I understand from Lady Enyo that they feed on the energy released from a time-wipe.'

GAD2 Control, 'Should we attempt to contact them?'

Admiral Mustard, 'Send them a welcome message but don't expect a response. It would be useful if you could scan them. We might discover something useful.'

GAD2 Control, 'Yes, Sir. It would take some time. The ships are massive.'

Admiral Mustard, 'Send me a picture.'

GAD2 Control, 'Yes, Sir.'

Admiral Mustard, 'Bloody hell, they are big.'

GAD2 Control, 'And some of their ships are bigger.'

Admiral Mustard, 'Thank you, Control.'

Location: Guest Quarters, Planet Napoleon
Sequence of Events: 76

Edel Mustard wallowed in her grief. She now knew how fleeting happiness was. After a life of solitude, she married the man she had always admired and secretly lusted after. It was the Rejuv treatment that gave her the confidence to pursue him, not that he needed much pursuing.

Together they had been the perfect couple: intelligent, determined, humous, fun-loving, serious, studious, hard-working, diligent, and the list went on in her mind. And then there was baby John, now fatherless. He would never know his father. He would never know the type of man he was or play games with him or walk in the park together.

The tears rolled down her cheeks. She didn't think it possible how one female body could produce so much. Then she remembered her Dickens:

'Heaven knows we need never be ashamed of our tears, for they are rain upon the blinding dust of earth, overlying our hard hearts. I was better after I had cried, than before — more sorry, more aware of my own ingratitude, more gentle.'

Charles Dickens, Great Expectations

She realised that it was only a matter of time before she would be in the bed of the doppelganger. She knew that she wouldn't be able to resist him. Was she being a traitor to her husband? Or was she honouring him? It didn't matter as it was inevitable.

There was a knock on the door. It was Admiral Mustard.

Location: Guest Quarters, Planet Napoleon
Sequence of Events: 77

Edel, 'Hello Jack.'

Jack, 'Hello, Edel.'

Edel, 'Is your life shit?'

Jack, 'It has been since you died.'

Edel, 'Mine too.'

Then nature took its course, and they fucked through the evening and the night, and then they cuddled and slept in each other's arms. And then they fucked some more.

During breakfast, Edel said, 'I really should feel guilty.'

Admiral Mustard, 'I think you should.' Edel laughed, but she genuinely thought that she should feel guilty. It wasn't adultery because her Admiral Mustard was dead.

The only way to tell the two Jacks apart was the lack of shared memories and some scars that were in the wrong places. They instinctively belonged together, and the other Edels and Jacks would probably have wished it and even demanded it.

Edel, 'What is the rest of the world going to say?'

Jack, 'Who cares. Most of our friends have been match-making.'

Edel, 'Really.'

Jack, 'Well, certainly David and AI Central. How will John react?'

Edel, 'Acceptance, he is really good at acceptance.'

Then little John was brought home by a nanny.

Little John, 'Hello, Daddy.'

Admiral Mustard. 'Hello, son.' And they were a family again and for the first time. Edel and Jack agreed that they would tell little John about his real father when he was old enough, but then both Jacks had the same DNA.

Edel moved into Admiral Mustard's quarters.

Location: Admiral Mustard's Office, Planet Napoleon
Sequence of Events: 78

Admiral Mustard, 'So you won.'

AI Central, 'There was never any doubt. It was just about when you would make your move. You certainly didn't waste any time. Anyway, congratulations.'

Admiral Mustard, 'Thank you very much. You have been a good friend.'

AI Central, 'How did little John react?'

Admiral Mustard, 'I'm his dad.'

AI Central, 'Fair enough.'

Admiral Mustard, 'In all of our recent confusion, did we recall our three admirals?'

AI Central, 'Yes. I'm glad you asked because I'm worried about them.'

Admiral Mustard, 'Why's that?'

AI Central, 'The recall request has been continuous, but there has been no response. I can't even track them. As far as I'm concerned, they have disappeared from our universe.'

Admiral Mustard, 'Couldn't they just be outside our communications range?'

AI Central, 'It's possible but most unlikely. There's not much we can do. It's a similar problem to the hunting down of The Brakendethians.'

Location: GAD2 Control, Planet Napoleon
Sequence of Events: 79

GAD2 Control, 'Admiral, we are under attack.'

Admiral, 'By who?'

GAD2 Control, 'I know it's hard to believe, but it looks like the Skiverton.'

Admiral, 'Where?'

GAD2 Control, 'Three planets: Kepler, Skinner, and Harvey. They used their normal tactic of landing ground forces and then glassing the area and converting the local flora and fauna into Chemlife.'

Admiral, 'Why didn't the local forts respond?'

GAD2 Control, 'They are still returning, Sir, after coming to the aid of Earth.'

Admiral, 'How have you responded?'

GAD2 Control, 'Division Three has been allocated, with Divisions Four and Five in reserve.'

Admiral, 'Arrange for me to join Division One. I'm going there myself.'

GAD2 Control, 'Yes, Sir.'

Admiral Mustard, 'Have you updated the president?'

GAD2 Control, 'Yes, Sir.'

Location: Planet Kepler
Sequence of Events: 80

As far as astronautical distances go, the three planets were reasonably close to each other. There was a Skiverton fleet guarding each planet and their land-based operations.'

Admiral Mustard, 'My orders:

- Division Three to attack the Skiverton fleets around Planets Skinner and Harvey with two fleets, each with one to be held in reserve.
- Division One to attack the Skiverton fleet around Planet Kepler.
- Divisions Four and Five to act as a rear-guard.'

Fleet Operations, 'Yes, Sir.'

Admiral Mustard, 'Show me the operational status.'

Fleet Operations, 'On the screen now, Sir.'

Division No	Fleet No	Qty of Assets
1	1-1	4,800
1	1-2	4,760
1	1-3	4,857
1	1.4	4,906
1	1.5	5,103
3	3.1`	4,907
3	3.2	4,877
3	3.3	4,976
3	3.4	4,348
3	3.5	4,298
Total	10	47,832
Skiverton Kepler		116
Skiverton Harvey		126
Skiverton Skinner		215

Admiral Mustard, 'It should be a turkey shoot,' And it was.

The Skiverton vessels were no match for The Galactium Fleet. A considerable number of the Skiverton prisoners were taken who were in desperate need of Chemlife.

Admiral Mustard, 'Comms, get me President Padfield.'

Comms, 'Yes, Sir.'

President Padfield, 'I believe that "good day" is now the accepted term.'

Admiral Mustard, 'It is, Mr President. It saves having to work out the time at the destination. Anyway, the Skiverton threat has been neutralised. It was far too easy. They were desperate for Chemlife, but why did The Brakendeth arrange it?'

President Padfield, 'Perhaps they were just keeping us on our toes.'

Admiral Mustard, 'I'm expecting further irritations. I wonder if Admiral Terry is behind this?'

Location: GAD2 Conference Room, Planet Napoleon
Sequence of Events: 81

Admiral Mustard called a military staff meeting.

The attendees were as follows:
- Admiral Jack Mustard
- Admiral George Bumelton
- Admiral Phil Richardson x2
- Admiral Steve Adams
- Admiral Ama Abosa
- Admiral Nubia Tersoo
- Admiral Mateo Dobson
- Admiral John Bonner x2
- Admiral Edel Bonner
- Admiral Peter Gittins
- Admiral David Taylor
- Admiral Glen Pearce
- Admiral Calensky Wallett
- Admiral Thanatos
- Commander Dennis Todd
- Commander Martin Black
- Marine Commander, Bill Tower
- Madie Milburn, Fleet HQ, Head of Intelligence
- Denise Smith, Fleet HQ, Head of Navigation & Exploration
- AI Central.

Admiral Mustard still found it disconcerting to have two Phil Richardsons and two John Bonners.

Admiral Mustard, 'Fellow officers, I believe that we have three challenges:

1. Assist the civilian government with re-construction
2. Find The Brakendethians
3. Galactium Defence.

I should apologise, but this meeting is mostly about me assigning you tasks.

'Regarding the first point, we are doing our bit. We are providing transport, project management, emergency equipment, medical services, materials etc. We are on-call to assist in any way we can.

'So now we are back to our traditional role of defence.

'Firstly, we need to tweak the divisional structure slightly. Admiral Chudzinski is absent, and Admiral Muller is now responsible for assisting with the re-construction.

'So here the new structure.'

Division	Admiral
1	Admiral of the Fleet
2	Admiral John Bonner
3	Admiral Phil Richardson
4	Admiral Calensky Wallett
5	Admiral Steve Adams
6	Admiral Ama Abosa
7	Admiral Peter Gittins
8	Admiral Glen Pearce
9	Admiral Nubia Tersoo
10	Admiral Mateo Dobson

'Admiral Bumelton and I will take control of Fleet One as required. In our absence, Admiral David Taylor will assume command. Admiral Thanatos will continue to command The Chosen fleet. Admiral Jon Bonner will command or liaise with other alien fleets within The Galactium. Admiral Philip Richardson will take over the command of the Home Defence Fleet from Karl Lamberty. Apologies to the WW version of Admirals Richardson and Bonner. Please let me know if you want alternative names.'

Admiral Mustard, 'My orders:

- Admiral Bumelton will establish a defensive plan.
- Divisions One, Two, Three, Four, Eight and Nine are allocated to defence along with the Home Defence Fleet.
- Admiral Thanatos to command The Brakendeth Project.
- Divisions Five, Six, and Seven plus The Chosen fleet will be allocated to this task.
- Admiral Bumelton to ensure the security of Olympia.
- Division Ten will be in reserve.
- Madie Milburn and Denise Smith to assist Admiral Thanatos.'

Fleet Operations, 'Yes, Sir.'

Admiral Mustard, 'Any questions?'

Admiral Dobson, 'I understand that no one knows the whereabouts of the three Admirals.'

Admiral Mustard, 'That is correct.'

Admiral Dobson, 'What is being done?'

Admiral Mustard, 'Very little, I'm afraid. AI Central has been working on it, but we have no clues. They have just disappeared.'

Admiral Tersoo, 'Should I scout the remains of The Brakendeth home world like last time?'

Admiral Mustard, 'That makes sense to me, but it is Admiral Thanatos's shout.'

Admiral Thanatos, 'Please go ahead.'

Admiral Gittins, 'Based on past experience, it is notoriously difficult to track down a party that doesn't want to be found. And we know that Terry had inter-dimensional capabilities.'

Admiral Mustard, 'I agree, but it's worth a shot. Anyway, let's move on. You will all know that we just smashed a Skiverton invasion. The problem is that they marched in, landed on three planets, and started liquidising the local population. The local population were not amused.

'To put it mildly, it was a disgrace, and the locals wondered if there was any point in paying us protection money. Not that they pay us much, but that's not the point. And without us, they would all have been safely installed in a life-enhancing cocktail by now. How could it have happened?'

Admiral Bumelton, 'Where were the forts?'

Admiral Mustard, 'Helping to defend Earth?'

Commander Todd, 'What about the warning beacons?'

Admiral Mustard, 'Sadly, they were ignored at the planetary level, and there was so much going on in GAD Control they were ignored there.'

Bill Tower, 'There are no excuses.'

Admiral Mustard, 'As soon as we knew about the invasion, we acted and performed well.'

Admiral Bumelton, 'I think that the lack of stability over the last five years has made it difficult to implement secure, reliable systems. And why didn't they use the planetary force-fields?'

Peter Gittins, 'We have local representatives and forts. Should we go a stage further?'

David Taylor, 'But shouldn't the planets be partly responsible for their own security? They have police forces and home guards.'

Admiral Mustard, 'These are all points that Admiral Bumelton will need to consider.'

Admiral Bumelton, 'Thanks, Jack.'

Location: The TIME Organisation
Sequence of Events: 82

TIME Administrator, 'Greetings Apprentice Terry.'

    Terry, 'Greetings.'

    TIME Administrator, 'What is your full name?'

    Terry, 'It's just Terry.'

    TIME Administrator, 'You will be called Terry Le Grand Timepiece.'

    Terry, 'Why?'

    TIME Administrator, 'There are no questions.'

    Terry, 'Are there any answers?'

    TIME Administrator, 'We will proceed. Who is your father?'

    Terry, 'Unknown.'

    TIME Administrator, 'That changes things. Your new name is Terry, the Bastard Timepiece.'

    Terry, 'I'm not having that.'

    TIME Administrator, 'The last thing you have is any choice. Resistance will not be tolerated.'

    Terry, 'What are you on about?' Terry suddenly suffered extreme pain in his medulla oblongata. He collapsed on the floor in unbelievable agony.

    TIME Administrator, 'What is the name of your home world?'

    Terry, 'Earth.'

    TIME Administrator, 'Does that still exist?'

    Terry, 'I'm not sure.'

    TIME Administrator, 'Well, I'm sure. It has been destroyed.'

    Terry, 'By who?'

    TIME Administrator, 'You are here to answer questions, not ask them.'

    Terry, 'I understand.'

    TIME Administrator, 'What are your special talents?'

    Terry, 'I'm exceptionally clever and very inventive. I can make people go to sleep. I can travel between dimensions. I can control events remotely. I don't need to sleep. I can control all of my body functions.'

    TIME Administrator, 'That's enough. Provide proof of one of those skills."

The TIME Administer collapsed on the floor in a deep sleep. It could be days before she woke up.

Terry laughed and had a coffee.

Location: Admiral Mustard's Flat, Planet Napoleon
Sequence of Events: 83

Edel, 'Are you happy with the way things have worked out?'

Jack, 'Of course.'

Edel, 'Do you mean that or are you just saying that?'

Jack, 'I'm just saying it.'

Edel, 'You bastard. Seriously I do worry that you preferred the other Edel.'

Jack, 'I do.'

Edel, 'You really are a bastard.'

Jack, 'I know. Let me put it this way, I couldn't live without the other Edel, and I can't live without you. I see you both as the same person. Every one of my cells accepts that. I was meant to be with you and you only.'

Edel, 'What about that tart Lady Enyo? You fucked her, didn't you?'

Jack, 'I did have sex with her. To be honest, you don't have much choice. She just takes it.'

Edel, 'It's clear now. You prefer her fanny to mine.'

Jack, 'You are pregnant, aren't you?'

Edel, 'Yes, my love, that's why I had to know that you love me.'

Jack, 'I love you now, I've always loved you, and I will love you forever, although I'm not sure how long forever is.' They cuddled and had loving, gentle sex.

Location: GAD2 Control, Planet Napoleon
Sequence of Events: 84

GAD2 Control, 'Admiral, we are under attack again.'

Admiral, 'By who?'

GAD2 Control, 'It's the Skiverton again.'

Admiral, 'Where this time?'

GAD2 Control, 'Exactly the same place. They just carried on from last time.'

Admiral, 'What have you done?'

GAD2 Control, 'Admiral Bumelton is on his way there with Divisions One and Three.'

Admiral, 'Well done.'

The fleet arrived at Planets Kepler, Skinner and Harvey and defeated the Skiverton in the same old way. More prisoners were taken, and the reason for their attack was still seen as rather pointless.

The three planets demanded action. In terms of the fleet, they had received a lot of action. But what they wanted was better defence.

Once again, the local defence proved wanting.

Admiral Bumelton left a fleet in the area to deter any further incursions.

Admiral Bumelton, 'Comms, get me Admiral Mustard.'

Comms, 'Yes, Sir.'

Admiral Mustard, 'Hi George, I guess that you have beaten them in the same old way.'

Admiral Bumelton, 'Of course. Why do they come? Is it just the need for Chemlife?'

Admiral Mustard, 'Possibly, or a cunning Brakendeth scheme?'

Admiral Bumelton, 'I'm going to spend some time with the prisoners. We need to find their home base and offer them a deal.'

Admiral Mustard, 'That sounds like a plan.'

Location: On Board Admiral Abosa's Flagship
Sequence of Events: 85

Fleet 6-1 was surveying the remains of The Brakendeth home world. The Brakendeth had done a good job of destroying their world, but it was amazing what survived.

A large number of weapons were recovered, along with spacecraft, unknown machines, and munitions. Things were found that were outside of the human experience. They also discovered a considerable number of electronic storage devices.

Then they found it, the mutilated remain of a human body. It was the corpse of Admiral Terry.

Admiral Abosa, 'Comms, please update our bosses.'

Comms, 'Yes, Sir.'

The electronic media was handed over to Fleet Intelligence. Madie Milburn was eager to get hold of it. Could they access the contents? She was determined to find some clues from this massive electronic hoard.

Location: GAD2 Control, Planet Napoleon
Sequence of Events: 86

GAD2 Control, 'Admiral, this sounds like a stuck record, but we are under attack again.'

Admiral, 'By who?'

GAD2 Control, 'It's the Skiverton and others.'

Admiral, 'Where this time?'

GAD2 Control, 'Exactly the same place, but their force is much larger. They are currently engaging with Fleet 3-1.'

Admiral, 'What have you done?'

GAD2 Control, 'Admiral Bumelton is on his way there with Divisions One, Two, and the rest of Three.'

Admiral, 'Well done.'

Admiral Mustard, 'Comms, get me Admiral Bumelton.'

Comms, 'Yes, Sir.'

Admiral Bumelton, 'Good day, Jack.'

Admiral Mustard, 'I bet that you are finding this a bit boring.'

Admiral Bumelton, 'It might be more of a challenge this time.'

Admiral Mustard, 'It could be a trap.'

Admiral Bumelton, 'You could be right. I might activate additional assets.'

Admiral Mustard, 'I guess that you heard about Terry?'

Admiral Bumelton, 'I can't say that I feel any pity.'

Admiral Mustard, 'Nor me. I'll leave you to it. Good luck.'

Admiral Bumelton, 'My orders:

• Division Three will re-unite with Fleet 3-1.

• Divisions One and Two will, on arrival, establish a defensive formation.

• Divisions Four and Eight to provide a reserve at Planet Kepler.'

Fleet Operations, 'Yes, Sir.'

Admiral Bumelton, 'Comms get me the Admiral of 3-1.'

Comms, 'Yes, Sir.'

Admiral Manchester, 'Good day, Sir.'

Admiral Bumelton, 'Good day, Kev, the cavalry is on its way, do you know who you are up against?'

Admiral Manchester, 'The Skiverton and at least two other unknown races. We are outnumbered by at least 3:1, but we are holding our own. It's difficult to work out what they are hoping to achieve. Our colleagues have just arrived. Now we can show them what for.'

Divisions One and Two also arrived and immediately formed a defensive position which was fortunate as further enemy forces had been detected.

Location: The President's Office, Planet Napoleon
Sequence of Events: 87

President Padfield, 'It seems ages since we had a meeting.'

Henrietta Strong, 'Well, last time we got together, we had a planet of our own and were in a different time-line than this one. It's amazing how adaptable humanity is.'

President Padfield, 'And most of the previous agendas are now totally irrelevant.'

Henrietta Strong, 'But I have got a new agenda.'

President Padfield, 'I suspected that you might have.'

Henrietta Strong, 'Shall I go through it?'

President Padfield, 'I know we should, but shall we have a beer first?'

Henrietta Strong, 'I'll have sex on the beach.'

President Padfield, 'You will struggle to find a beach around here or almost anywhere.'

They had their drinks and commiserated with each other regarding the past. Both had guilt complexes regarding their survival, but both agreed that they had to move on. It crossed their minds that there were now few genuine Earthlings.

President Padfield, 'So what's on your agenda?'

Henrietta Strong, 'I will go through the list:

1. The evacuation of the Moon.

2. Housing for the Moonies.

3. The building of the new Galactium HQ on Mars.

4. Memorial service(s).

5. Tracking down The Brakendethians.'

President Padfield, 'You heard that they found Admiral Terry's body?'

Henrietta Strong, 'Yes. I never liked him or The Brakendethians. We had been manipulated for far too long. And I quite like The Chosen. Admiral Thanatos is both charming and very knowledgeable. He understood our pain as he shares it. Earth was also their home world.'

President Padfield, 'True, that had never really dawned on me.'

Henrietta Strong, 'I will carry on with the list:

6. Merging of WW and UW records.

7. Doppelganger issues.

8. Handling of salvage.

9. Planet Lovelace (half wiping issues).

10. Eternity service.

11. Medical situation.

12. Working with Bill Penny.

13. AOB.'

President Padfield, 'That's a pretty extensive list.'

Henrietta Strong, 'I'm actioning some of them, but I need your input on others:'

President Padfield, 'Let's go through them.'

Henrietta Strong, 'I will go through the list then. Firstly, the Moon evacuation. This is a massive task. However, Seven hundred and fifty thousand have been evacuated, with a further two hundred and fifty thousand to go. This figure may reduce as about twenty thousand want to stay.'

President Padfield, 'Why is that?'

Henrietta Strong, 'There are a whole host of reasons. Some see it as an adventure. Others don't want to leave their home. A few, refuse to believe that Earth has been destroyed and that the Moon is escaping the Solar System.'

President Padfield, 'Should we force them to leave?'

Henrietta Strong, 'So far, the whole process has not been that pleasant. You know how aggressive the Moonies can be. Those on the ground don't want the job of forcing them.'

President Padfield, 'We could send in the marines?'

Henrietta Strong, 'Why bother?'

President Padfield, 'We have a responsibility to look after the weak and needy.'

Henrietta Strong, 'Try telling them that.'

President Padfield, 'What are their chances of survival?'

Henrietta Strong, 'Our projections are not good. Less than ten per cent.'

President Padfield, 'So you are proposing that we do nothing regarding the diehards?'

Henrietta Strong, 'Correct, but we still have two hundred and fifty thousand to evacuate. We are almost totally dependent on the navy.'

President Padfield, 'What about civilian contractors?'

Henrietta Strong, 'Those that we can find we are using, but we have lost most of them. The ones that we are using are from the belt.'

President Padfield, 'How have the navy performed?'

Henrietta Strong, 'Magnificent, I won't have a word said against them. They have asked how much of the Moon's infrastructure should they salvage?'

President Padfield, 'I guess as much as possible.'

Henrietta Strong, 'I will let them know as the window for action is getting smaller. The next question is, where are we going to house the Moonies?'

President Padfield, 'Where are they now?'

Henrietta Strong, 'Everywhere: Mars, Venus, Jupiter, other Galactium planets, and luxury liners. They see themselves as a community and want to stay together.'

President Padfield, 'Do they have any preferences?'

Henrietta Strong, 'Yes, Mr President, they would like to live on Ganymede.'

President Padfield, 'Is that possible?'

Henrietta Strong, 'It is. There is a small community there already. They would have to live in a protected environment, but they are used to that. There is an ample supply of water. The big question is cost.'

President Padfield, 'Do we have the funds?'

Henrietta Strong, 'Yes and enough to cover the cost of rebuilding Mars.'

President Padfield, 'Let's go for it.'

Henrietta Strong, 'Thank you, Mr President.'

President Padfield, 'What's next?'

Henrietta Strong, 'The new Galactium HQ.'

President Padfield, 'We need to be careful here. We need something impressive, especially for alien visitors. Appearances are important. But at the same time, we don't want the man who has lost everything to see us wasting government funds.'

Henrietta Strong, 'Fair enough. I suggest that we built it in a modular fashion over an extended period then.'

President Padfield, 'That works for me. What's next?'

Henrietta Strong, 'Memorial services.'

President Padfield, 'Set-up a committee.'

Henrietta Strong, 'Will do. Next is tracking down The Brakendethians.'

President Padfield, 'Get an update from Admiral Mustard?'

Henrietta Strong could tell that the president was getting bored, but said 'Next is the merging of WW and UW records.'

President Padfield, 'Just do it. Let's leave the rest until next week.'

Henrietta Strong, 'Certainly, Mr President.'

Henrietta wondered what was wrong with the president. What was wrong was that someone was whispering in the president's ear, 'Tell Admiral Mustard to remember.'

Henrietta Strong, 'I will see you next week.'

President Padfield, 'Looking forward to it.'

President Padfield, 'Comms, get me Admiral Mustard.'

Admiral Mustard, 'Hi Dave, how are you?'

President Padfield, 'Fine except for this noise in my ear.'

Admiral Mustard, 'What do you mean?'

President Padfield, 'Someone is whispering, "Tell Admiral Mustard to remember".'

Admiral Mustard, 'Not again.'

Location: Planet Kepler

Sequence of Events: 88

Admiral Bumelton, 'Update me.'

Fleet Operations, 'Yes, Sir:

- Division Three is annihilating the Skiverton. The enemy doesn't really seem to be making much of an effort.
- The other non-Skiverton ships are more effective, but they are not a challenge to our forces.
- Further enemy forces are in the vicinity but are not engaging. They may have seen Fleets One and Two lined up in formation, and they may have detected Fleets Four and Eight.'

Admiral Bumelton, 'My orders:

- Fleet Three to continue the clean-up.
- Fleet Eight to confront the new enemy force.'

Fleet Operations, 'Yes, Sir.'

As Fleet Eight approached the enemy, the enemy dispersed.

Again, it left everyone concerned and confused about the enemy's objectives.

Admiral Bumelton, 'Comms, get me Admiral Mustard.'

Comms, 'Yes, Sir.'

Admiral Mustard, 'Hi George, how did it go?'

Admiral Bumelton, 'It was another stunning victory due almost entirely to the commander in Chief.'

Admiral Mustard, 'So, what you are saying is that you had nothing to do.'

Admiral Bumelton, 'Absolutely, what is the enemy doing?'

Admiral Mustard, 'Beats me. Another strange thing happened. The president heard someone talking in his ear asking him to tell Admiral Mustard to remember.'

Admiral Bumelton, 'Not that again. I thought we had moved on.'

Admiral Mustard, 'When you were hypnotised, we learnt about Commander Rikernaught.'

Admiral Bumelton, 'True, but we still don't know what he wants you to remember.'

Admiral Mustard, 'That's true, and I still don't know.'

Location: The TIME Organisation
Sequence of Events: 89

TIME Administrator, 'Greetings, Apprentice Terry, the Bastard Timepiece."

Terry, 'Greetings, Shit Face Administrator.'

The TIME Administrator suddenly suffered extreme pain in her medulla oblongata. She collapsed on the floor in unbelievable agony.

Terry watched in amusement, watching her writhe in the pain that she planned to watch him suffer. There was a lot of watching. Terry watched the external watchers rush in to save her. They stood there, wondering what to do.

Terry, 'Do you want me to stop it?'

The watchers, 'Yes, please.' Terry stopped the pain, but the TIME Administrator never fully recovered. Terry enjoyed the fact that she never ever gained full consciousness. No one treats him like that.

There was only one TIME Administrator, so the TIME Supervisor took over.

TIME Supervisor, 'Greetings, Terry.'

Terry, 'That's not the name that I was allocated.'

TIME Supervisor, 'The title "apprentice" and "Bastard" seem inappropriate in the circumstances.'

Terry, 'Thank you, but I would like an enhanced name.'

TIME Supervisor, 'What would you propose?'

Terry, 'That's a good question. I would suggest Terry the Controller.'

TIME Supervisor, 'Why controller?'

Terry, 'Because I can control you. Take me to your Leader.'

TIME Supervisor, 'Of course, controller.'

To the amazement of Terry, he was taken to meet TIME itself.

TIME, 'Morning, my young Brakendethian.'

Terry, 'And who are you?'

TIME, 'You know, you have always known.'

Terry, 'What's it like being TIME?'

TIME, 'It's not like anything, I am everything.'

Terry, 'So you can tell me what has happened to Earth.'

TIME, 'You will need to become much less parochial.'

Terry, 'That may be the case, but what happened to Earth?'

TIME, 'The Brakendethians destroyed it.'

Terry, 'Why?'

TIME, 'It was written.'

Terry, 'Fuck the written what has happened to my children?'

TIME, 'Your children and wife survived.'

Terry, 'How?'

TIME, 'It's not my job to provide a running commentary on your progeny.'

Terry, 'What is your job?'

TIME, 'My job is to remind Admiral Mustard to remember.'

Terry, 'What are you talking about?'

TIME, 'The survival of the universe, in fact, everything depends on Admiral Mustard remembering. He is the current fulcrum of the universe.'

Terry, 'That is hard to believe.'

TIME, 'It is, isn't it?'

Terry, 'So what has it got to do with me?'

Then the alarm bells rang.

Location: Fleet Intelligence, Planet Napoleon
Sequence of Events: 90

Madie Milburn, 'Good day, gentlemen'

President Padfield and Admiral Mustard both responded.

Madie Milburn, 'After a considerable amount of research, we have cracked open The Brakendethian files. There is a massive amount of information, some of which will radically change our perception of the universe. Some of it is shocking.'

President Padfield, 'Congratulations, Madie.'

Admiral Mustard, 'I feel that we could be in danger. How secure is your environment?'

Madie Milburn, 'Our labs are buried deep in the heart of the planet.'

Admiral Mustard, 'Before we continue, let's up the security.'

Admiral Mustard, 'Comms, get me Bill Tower.'

Comms, 'Yes, Sir.'

Bill Tower, 'Good day, Jack.'

Admiral Mustard, 'We are working on The Brakendethian files recovered from their destroyed home world. I'm worried that we might get interrupted. Please provide added security immediately. Expect the worst.'

Bill Tower, 'Yes, Sir.'

Admiral Mustard, 'Before you go, I plan to use Specials Ops as well. I'm expecting the worst.'

Bill Tower, 'I understand, Sir.'

Admiral Mustard, 'Comms, get me Martin Black.'

Comms, 'Yes, Sir.'

Martin Black, 'Good day, Jack.'

Admiral Mustard, 'Hi Martin, I've just called out the marines. We are working on The Brakendethian files recovered from their destroyed home world. I'm worried that we might get interrupted. I need you to provide added security immediately. Expect the worst.'

Martin Black, 'Yes, Sir.'

Admiral Mustard, 'Comms, get me Admiral Bumelton.'

Comms, 'Yes, Sir.'

Admiral Bumelton, 'Not you again.'

Admiral Mustard, 'Fuck off. I'm with the president and Madie. We are working on The Brakendethian files recovered from their destroyed home world. I'm worried that we might get interrupted.'

Admiral Bumelton, 'Your worries are usually justified. I will warn Admiral Richardson regarding naval support.'

Admiral Mustard, 'Thanks, George.'

President Padfield, 'That's seems a bit over the top.'

Admiral Mustard, 'Being over the top has often kept me alive. Madie, please continue.'

Madie had always been impressed by her admiral's dynamism. Sometimes he was a real powerhouse.

Madie Milburn, 'As I was saying earlier, some of the data extracted is quite shocking. It will need serious scrutiny, but I thought that I better give you an update.'

Admiral Mustard, 'I think you have whet our appetites.'

Madie Milburn, 'It's hard to know where to start, and of course we haven't been able to verify anything:

- There is a lot of info on the Elder Gods or Elder Lords.
- They engineered two major races to do their bidding: black and white.
- The blacks were the enforcers, tough and aggressive, designed to carry out the dirty but necessary jobs.
- The whites were the angels of mercy, persuaders, missionaries, messengers of the Elder Gods etc.
- When the Elders lost interest in the universe, the blacks and whites were left to fend for themselves.
- The whites had the support of the local populations for obvious reasons.
- The blacks decided to change things by manipulating time.
- This caused a considerable amount of chaos throughout the universe, and The Elders set up an organisation called TIME to protect time.
- You have obviously guessed who is who.'

President Padfield, 'The Brakendethians and The Chosen.'

Madie Milburn, 'In many ways, they are demi-Gods. They have a range of super-powers.'

Admiral Mustard, 'As displayed by Terry. But we haven't seen The Chosen demonstrate any special skills.'

Madie Milburn, 'According to Greek mythology, Thanatos was the personification of death. He was the son of Nyx, the Goddess of the night. His brother is Hypnos, the God of sleep. Enyo was also a Goddess in Greek mythology. She was the brother of Ares, the God of war. She was the daughter of Zeus and Hera and was also linked to war and destruction.'

Admiral Mustard, 'You are not suggesting that they are Greek Gods?'

Madie Milburn, 'I'm not, but The Brakendethians are.'

President Padfield, 'But that's hard to believe.'

Madie Milburn, 'I will carry on:
- There are thousands of races throughout the universe, perhaps millions.
- Most evolved, but only two races were made to look like The Elders: The Brakendethians and The Chosen.
- The Brakendethians deliberately made homans from both their DNA and that of The Chosen.
- They recognised that a combination of both could rectify the inadequacies of both races.
- Their plan failed because the homans were so stupid.
- Then The Brakendethians started creating new races in an attempt to find the perfect tool to conquer the universe.
- They realised that the homan DNA like theirs could offer these new races perpetual life, so the homans suddenly became important.
- The Brakendethians didn't know that The Chosen were husbanding the homan genes.
- The Brakendethians didn't realise that the homans had gained intelligence until the Skiverton attacked.'

Admiral Mustard, 'We know most of this.'

Madie Milburn, 'There is more:
- Terry was constructed to lead the combined armies of The Brakendethians and the homans.
- Their first target was going to be The Chosen.

194

- Their second target was the Elders.
- They had planned to produce thousands of Terrys to manage the homans.
- They planned a series of wars to "toughen up" humanity.
- Their inventions and cures were designed to eliminate homan weaknesses.'

Admiral Mustard, 'Again, we know most of this.'

Madie Milburn, 'There is still more:
- They planned to destroy Earth to make us angry and bitter.
- They planned to place Terry in the TIME Organisation to ensure that the homans support The Brakendethians. Time would be manipulated to achieve this.
- They planned to constantly attack The Galactium to stop us from planning the future. We would be forced to continually defend ourselves.
- Terry's two children have powers and will take over The Galactium at the right time.
- The records say that the universe will end unless Admiral Mustard remembers.'

Admiral Mustard, 'Not again, I've no idea what I've got to remember.'

Madie Milburn, 'I'm afraid that there is still more:
- The Brakendethians planned to destroy their home world.
- They have a second home 'by the waterfalls of the Gods'.
- They have a massive fleet waiting there to attack The Chosen and the Elders.
- They need to destroy The Chosen first as they have the means of contacting the Elders.
- During the last battle between the two, The Chosen requested help from the Elders. They didn't just accidentally turn up.
- The Brakendethians believe that The Chosen know what Admiral Mustard needs to remember.

That's about it.'

President Padfield, 'Well, it looks like your friends have not been entirely honest.'

Admiral Mustard, 'Nothing seems to be true any more.'

Madie Milburn, 'Welcome to my world.'

President Padfield, 'Well, we need to be objective: this is The Brakendethian view of the world, and there has been a time-wipe. Are we sure that the facts are still the same?

I'm also worried about Terry in the TIME Organisation.'

Admiral Mustard, 'I need to confront Lady Enyo.'

President Padfield, 'Be careful, these Gods can be very feisty.'

Admiral Mustard, 'Thank you, Madie, for you and your team's hard work.'

Location: Admiral Mustard's Office, Planet Napoleon
Sequence of Events: 91

Admiral Mustard, 'Good day, gentlemen and AI Central. What have I done to deserve your attention?'

Commanders Tower and Black were in the room, looking grim.

Commander Tower, 'While you were in conference with Madie, we were attacked.'

Admiral Mustard, 'By who?'

Commander Tower, 'We have no idea.'

Admiral Mustard, 'Spill the beans then.'

Commander Tower, 'It's a bit embarrassing. Over thirty of my marines were incapacitated by assailants using stealth technology. On the video, you just see my troops collapsing on the ground. Fortunately, Special Ops set up motion detectors, and the attack was suppressed.'

Commander Black, 'Just when we thought we had succeeded in deterring them, there was a second attack. Further shielded assailants arrived behind us. Fortunately, we had set-up some tactical force-fields that inhibited their movement. We assumed that we had them trapped, but they just disappeared.'

Admiral Mustard, 'Are you saying that they teleported through a few miles of solid rock? Is this possible?'

Commander Black, 'It's theoretically possible but currently beyond our technology.'

Admiral Mustard. 'Who knew we were there?'

Commander Tower, 'Good question.'

AI Central, 'And what's even more intriguing I can't find any record of corresponding transport, stealthed, or not.'

Admiral Mustard, 'That suggests that they are still here. Quickly check the rooms where The Brakendeth files are being stored.'

One of the Marine Commandos rushed to the room to find it empty except for the body of a middle-aged woman. It appeared to be Madie, but her face had been burnt off.

Admiral Mustard, 'It looks like someone was determined to get those files.'

AI Central, 'It wouldn't have been an easy task as there were over three thousand cassettes. Our security has been constantly compromised over the years. Most of our enemies have nearly always known things about us that were confidential. In the past, we suspected that The Brakendethians could read our minds.'

Admiral Mustard, 'Perhaps those files are still on the planet?'

AI Central, 'Possibly, but the good news is that they were tagged. We should be able to track them down.'

Admiral Mustard, 'Let's get working on it.'

Admiral Mustard, 'Comms, get me the president.'

Comms, 'Yes, Sir.'

President Padfield, 'When the phone rings, I can normally tell whether it's good or bad news.'

Admiral Mustard, 'That's quite some super-power.'

President Padfield, 'Tell me the bad news.'

Admiral Mustard, 'While we were in the conference, we were attacked. Our forces fought off the stealthed assailants, but they came back and took The Brakendethian cassettes. In the process, they killed Madie.'

President Padfield, 'Oh my God, poor Madie, she was so dedicated.'

Admiral Mustard, 'We are currently tracking the files as they were tagged. I will keep you informed.'

Location: Lady Enyo's Suite, Planet Napoleon
Sequence of Events: 92

Lady Enyo, 'Did they get a chance to read The Brakendethian files?'

Admiral Thanatos, 'Yes, my lady. The room was guarded by marines and Special Ops commandos. Unfortunately, we had to kill Milburn in the process.'

Lady Enyo, 'Bugger, as the Earthlings would say.'

Admiral Thanatos, 'Exactly. I don't believe that there is any way they can trace the episode back to us, except we have the files in our offices'

Lady Enyo, 'Well, they are not knocking the door down yet, so they couldn't have read them fully.'

Admiral Thanatos, 'I have a fast ship ready if we need to make a quick exit.'

Lady Enyo, 'If there is trouble, I'm sure that I can persuade Admiral Mustard to think again.' She was proud of her sexual skills.

Admiral Thanatos, 'I'm not so sure that it will work. He has a new woman in his life.'

Lady Enyo, 'Who's that?'

Admiral Thanatos, 'Admiral Bonner.'

Lady Enyo, 'It didn't take him long to switch horses. Anyway, I like a bit of competition.'

Admiral Thanatos, 'My men are ready to destroy the files. Are you happy for that to go ahead?'

Lady Enyo, 'Yes, please, as soon as possible.'

Location: Admiral Mustard's Flat, Planet Napoleon
Sequence of Events: 93

Jack, 'How are you feeling?'

    Edel, 'I'm fine, stop asking me. I will let you know if I need help.'

    Jack, 'Sorry, I scratched your back the wrong way.'

    Edel, 'I'm sorry too, everything seems to think that a pregnant woman is ill. It's not an illness. It's a natural process.

    Jack, 'Fair point.'

    Edel, 'Anyway, I've been giving the recent events a lot of thought, and my conclusions are not good.'

    Jack, 'Go on.'

    Edel, 'It's to do with The Chosen. I've got my list:

- Firstly, they were prepared to destroy three populated human planets because of the Nexuster.
- In the end, we lost two billion human lives, which they seemed to care little about.
- Their fleet was in the vicinity of The Brakendeth world the first time it was destroyed. Why were they there?
- They contacted Zeus without telling us. Was that a set-up?
- They set up a trap for a Galactium Fleet and killed thousands of our colleagues.
- They have lied about their ages.
- It appears that Thanatos and Enyo are Gods.
- They engineered a lot of human wars for their own purposes.
- Enyo has been using her sexuality to control human men.
- The Chosen had been putting their people in key government positions.
- They kept their own navy.
- We are still not welcome on their planet.
- Were they the whites?'

    Edel, 'That's quite a list.'

    Jack, 'AI Central, what is your view?'

    AI Central, 'Edel has got a good argument, but they did come to our aid against The Brakendethians.'

    Edel, 'That's true, but they waited for the last possible moment, and by then they knew that Zeus was coming. It was a done deal.'

AI Central, 'And to be honest, they have never shared their technology with us.'

Edel, 'And how many of them do we know?'

Admiral Mustard, 'Point taken.'

Edel, 'And are they really religious fanatics? Are we just being used?'

Admiral Mustard, 'AI Central, can you give me a list of The Chosen who are working on this planet.'

AI Central, 'Of course.'

Admiral Mustard, 'And a list of their premises.'

Admiral Mustard, 'Comms, get me Admiral Bumelton.'

Comms, 'Yes, Sir.'

Admiral Bumelton, 'Good day, Jack.'

Admiral Mustard, 'Did you hear about Madie?

Admiral Bumelton, 'I did, very distressing.'

Admiral Mustard, 'I'm just being careful, but if any ship belonging to The Chosen leaves, can you follow them. You must be discrete.'

Admiral Bumelton, 'Will do, but I'm intrigued.'

Admiral Mustard, 'I will update you later.'

Admiral Bumelton, 'I will look forward to it.'

Location: The President's Office, Planet Napoleon
Sequence of Events: 94

President Padfield, 'That week certainly went quickly.'

Henrietta Strong, 'Well, quite a lot has happened: the Skiverton attacks, finding The Brakendeth records and the murder of Madie, plus all the usual stuff. Shall we carry on where we left off?'

President Padfield, 'Yes, please, but I need to apologise to you first. During our last meeting, I had someone telling me to tell Admiral Mustard to remember.'

Henrietta Strong, 'I've had that as well.'

President Padfield, 'Apparently it has been very widespread, but Admiral Mustard has no idea what he needs to remember.'

Henrietta Strong, 'Very strange. Anyway, these are the outstanding items:

1. Doppelganger issues.

2. Handling of salvage.

3. Planet Lovelace (half wiping issues).

4. Eternity service.

5. Medical situation.

6. Working with Bill Penny.

7. AOB.'

President Padfield, 'Take me through the doppelganger issue.'

Henrietta Strong, 'Well, we have experienced the partial merger of two timelines. If it had finished, there would not be any doppelgangers, but it didn't. Consequently, we have got individuals who existed simultaneously in both timelines.

'Throughout The Galactium, there are about two million such cases. It includes couples, families, and a few instances of larger groups.

'The doppelgangers are usually identical: the same DNA, the same fingerprints, the same retina prints, the same appearance but possibly different histories. The first challenge is, how does the governmental system identify them?'

President Padfield, 'And there are so many requirements: tax, insurance, medical, licences, pensions, security etc.'

Henrietta Strong, 'Exactly. We can issue identity cards with different indicators, but there are no physical differences to hang a number on. We have thought about chips that are used on pets, but there may be some human rights issues. Shall we explain the problem to the doppelgangers and see what they suggest?'

President Padfield, 'That works for me.'

Henrietta Strong, 'There are many other doppelganger issues that we could discuss at our next meeting. The next issue is the handling of Earth salvage. What are the rules?'

President Padfield, 'What are the rules needed for?'

Henrietta Strong, 'Firstly there is a lot of it scattered over huge distances. But there are already criminal elements collecting various items and selling them at a good profit.'

President Padfield, 'What sort of things are they selling?'

Henrietta Strong, 'You name it, they are selling it: minerals, buildings, cars, plants, mechanical parts, geological features and even dead bodies.'

President Padfield, 'What are you proposing that we do?'

Henrietta Strong, 'I'm recommending a licensing system for salvage operators. Everything found will have to go through a formal government customs post.'

President Padfield, 'Do we have the resources to manage this?'

Henrietta Strong, 'Not yet, but it gives us the powers to take action if necessary.'

President Padfield, 'Please go ahead.'

Henrietta Strong, 'Let me know if there is anything you fancy.' They both laughed.

There are no outstanding issues regarding medical treatment, but can I implement the standard Eternity process that we have used before for WW worlds.'

President Padfield, 'Yes. I guess that it includes us?'

Henrietta Strong, 'It certainly does.'

President Padfield, 'What's left?'

Henrietta Strong, 'Planet Lovelace and working with Bill Penny.'

President Padfield, 'What's the problem with Bill, apart from the obvious?'

Henrietta Strong, 'No problems, but I wondered if he should attend these sessions?'

President Padfield, 'I think he should. We could do with another pair of hands.'

Henrietta Strong, 'I didn't expect that. I will organise.'

President Padfield, 'Planet Lovelace. It sounds like a porn movie.'

Henrietta Strong, 'It's not far off. This is the sad case where the time-wipe stopped halfway through the planet. Half of the doppelgangers live on that planet. I've got a team investigating. I suggest that we discuss it during our next meeting.'

President Padfield, 'Well done, Henrietta.'

Henrietta Strong, 'One last thing. There seems to be evidence that critical data on our armaments has been siphoned off. We are trying to track down where it is going.'

President Padfield, 'That's worrying, keep me informed.'

Henrietta Strong, 'Will do.'

Location: Admiral Mustard's Office, Planet Napoleon
Sequence of Events: 95

Commander Tower, 'We have tracked down the missing files. You won't like what we have found.'

Admiral Mustard, 'They are in the offices belonging to The Chosen.'

Commander Tower, 'How did you know that?'

Admiral Mustard, 'It was written in the stars.'

Commander Tower, 'What do you want me to do?'

Admiral Mustard, 'AI Central, how many of The Chosen are there on the planet?'

AI Central, 'Eight hundred sixty-one, Sir.'

Admiral Mustard, 'Commander, I want your men to track them down and be ready to arrest them on my command. Not an easy task, and you must remain incognito. AI Central and Commander Black will help you.'

Commander Tower, 'It won't be easy, and it is doubtful that we will find everyone.'

Admiral Mustard, 'Just do your best.'

Admiral Mustard, 'Comms, get me President Padfield.'

Comms, 'Yes, Sir.'

Admiral Mustard, 'Morning, Mr President.'

President Padfield, 'You are very formal this morning.'

Admiral Mustard, 'Sorry, Dave, but I feel a bit formal.'

President Padfield, 'Why is that?'

Admiral Mustard, 'Edel has been warning me about The Chosen and urging some action. I saw them as our allies and wanted to see them as a successful part of The Galactium.'

President Padfield, 'What's made you change your mind?'

Admiral Mustard, 'We know who stole the tapes, and we know where they are.'

President Padfield, 'I see, that makes life a bit difficult. What are you going to do?'

Admiral Mustard, 'I'm going to confront her. I've got the troops lined up to protect me, along with Commanders Tower and Black.'

President Padfield, 'I'm not sure if that is a good idea. Your chances of surviving could be pretty slim.'

Admiral Mustard, 'I don't think she will harm me.'

President Padfield, 'Is that because you have been in her knickers?'

Admiral Mustard, 'She doesn't wear any knickers.'

President Padfield, 'You know what I mean.'

Admiral Mustard, 'We have got to avenge Madie's death.'

President Padfield, 'But not with your death.'

Admiral Mustad, 'Well, what can The Chosen do?'

President Padfield, 'That's the problem. We don't know. What did Zeus call them?'

Admiral Mustard, 'He said that they had lived for an exceedingly long time but achieved little and that they live in the past and are heading towards extinction.'

President Padfield, 'Have you updated George?'

Admiral Mustard, 'I will do it now.'

Admiral Mustard, 'Comms, get me Admiral Bumelton.'

Comms, 'Yes, Sir.'

Admiral Bumelton, 'Hi Jack.'

Admiral Mustard, 'George, we have discovered that The Brakendeth tapes are in the hands of The Chosen.'

Admiral Bumelton, 'Never.'

Admiral Mustard, 'I need you to provide some naval cover if The Chosen make a rapid retreat, and I need you to be ready to arrest Admiral Thanatos if he is off-planet.

Admiral Bumelton, 'Certainly boss.'

Location: Lady Enyo's Suite, Planet Napoleon
Sequence of Events: 96

Admiral Thanatos, 'My Lady. The Earthlings know that it is us who took The Brakendeth files and killed Madie.'

Lady Enyo, 'Are we ready?'

Admiral Thanatos, 'We were, but they have their commandos stalking our staff. Admiral Mustard is on his way here. Commanders Tower and Black with reinforcements are surrounding us.'

Lady Enyo, 'We didn't really want to expose ourselves.'

Admiral Thanatos, 'I expect that they know a fair amount about us now from The Brakendeth files.'

Lady Enyo, 'Do we kidnap Mustard?'

Admiral Thanatos, 'It's an option, but I'm not sure if it will help him remember.'

Lady Enyo, 'Yes, that's a point. Do we teach them a lesson?'

Admiral Thanatos, 'We could put on a display.'

Lady Enyo, 'Let's do that. It would be worth it to see the look of shock on their faces.'

Admiral Mustard knocked on Lady Enyo's Suite door, and then dazzling sunshine blinded every human on the planet. Their sight just recovered in time, to see eight hundred and sixty-one of The Chosen, float up in the air and disappear off-planet.

A message was left in the sky, 'Don't Mess with the Gods, Sorry about Madie'.

Admiral Bumelton, 'Comms, get Admiral Mustard.'

Comms, 'Yes, Sir.'

Admiral Mustard, 'I know what you are going to tell me.'

Admiral Bumelton, 'No, you don't.'

Admiral Mustard. 'You saw eight hundred and sixty-one people fly through space.'

Admiral Bumelton, 'I didn't count them.'

Commander Black's troops entered the room to check that no traps had been left. None were found, but a letter was.

It read:

Dear Jack

I'm sorry that we had to leave in a hurry, but you left us no choice. I'm sorry about Madie: it was an accident. By now, you will know our true identities. It's not everyone who gets the chance to love a God.

The Brakendeth records probably state that there is a vast fleet ready to destroy The Elders and us. We are not sure if that is true, but it might be. We are not black or white; we are just who we are.

What is important is that you remember. Your future and ours depends on it.

Our fleet is currently attacking TIME. We can't allow Terry to control things.'

Location: The TIME Organisation
Sequence of Events: 97

Terry, 'What's happening?'

TIME, 'We are being attacked by The Chosen.'

Terry, 'Why?'

TIME, 'They want to kill you.'

Terry, 'You don't seem too surprised.'

TIME, 'Of course not, we know what has happened and what is going to happen.'

Terry, 'Do I die?'

TIME, 'Eventually, but not today.'

Terry, 'Why didn't you prepare for the attack?'

TIME, 'Because it was going to happen.'

Terry, 'What happens next?'

TIME, 'The Chosen give up because we are protected by a step in time.'

Terry, 'What do you mean?'

TIME, 'We exist a slither of a nanosecond ahead of real-time, so we are invulnerable to the past. We are here so that we couldn't have been hurt.'

Terry, 'I see. Then what happens?'

TIME, 'When?'

Terry, 'In the near future.'

TIME, 'You kill me so that The Brakendeth get control of TIME.'

Terry, 'And you are not going to stop me?'

TIME, 'Why would I do that?'

Terry, 'But you will die.'

TIME, 'I'm not alive.'

Terry, 'But surely you must have a sense of self-survival?'

TIME, 'Not really. 'When you kill me, it unleashes the force that will destroy the universe.'

Terry, 'Are you sure?'

TIME, 'I'm assuming that Mustard remembers in time and the universe will all be saved.'

Terry, 'So if I don't destroy you, then Mustard won't need to remember.'

TIME, 'Of course, but you will.'

Terry, 'But you are suggesting that the future can't be changed.'

TIME, 'I'm not.'

Terry, 'I think you are.'

TIME, 'Then that's fine.'

Terry, 'That's not an answer.'

TIME, 'And what's the question?'

Terry, 'That is just semantics. Are you avoiding answering me?'

TIME, 'What will be, will be.'

Terry, 'Now you are just quoting Mary Poppins.'

TIME, 'That wasn't Mary Poppins, it was from the film, "The Man Who Knew Too Much", and that sums up this conversation.'

Terry felt seriously frustrated. He knew that there was no chance that he would kill TIME.

Location: The President's Office, Planet Napoleon
Sequence of Events: 98

President Padfield surveyed the room taking in the faces that were probably his best friends: Jack, Edel, Henrietta, Bill, and George.'

President Padfield, 'So where are we?' There was no immediate response, as there was a general feeling of frustration and fatigue.

Admiral Mustard, 'One step forward, two steps back.'

Henrietta Strong, 'Is that the tango?'

President Padfield, 'More like the military two-step.'

Admiral Mustard, 'I think we are just waltzing around my inability to remember.'

Henrietta Strong, 'What about dancing lessons?'

President Padfield, 'Everything seems to come back to Jack remembering.'

Admiral Mustard, 'It would be great if I had a clue.'

Henrietta Strong, 'How many requests to remember have you received?

Admiral Mustard, well, the ones that I can remember are as follows:

- There was an alien vessel that kept broadcasting for me to remember.
- I had a lot of strange dreams.
- Almost everyone I knew, including everyone in this room, got requests to remind me.
- AI Central got impossible screen messages.
- Admiral Farina had projections of the smart man on his bridge.
- The hypnotists refused to work with me because of the messages.
- The Chosen's Oracle raised it.
- Dave had constant mutterings in his ear.
- Madie found information in The Brakendeth records.

'I could go on, but what I've listed is a simple summary of a "supernatural" campaign to get me to remember something. I have absolutely no idea of what it is.'

President Padfield, 'But you need to remember it to save the universe, or it will be the last tango.'

Admiral Mustard, 'While we are talking, it would appear that The

Chosen are attacking TIME to kill Terry.'

Bill Penny, 'Can you kill TIME?'

Edel, 'All the time, try pregnancy.'

Admiral Mustard, 'We don't even know where TIME is based.'

President Padfield, 'Should we treat The Chosen as an enemy?'

Admiral Mustard, 'Probably, but they know an awful lot about us.'

AI Central, 'Should I restrict their access to me?'

President Padfield, 'Definitely.'

Henrietta Strong, 'It's a bit depressing, but we should start shutting things down regarding them:

- Re-set all of our passwords.
- Disable The Galactium hardware that they have in their possession.
- Inform all military contacts.
- Inform all government departments.
- Sack all remaining Chosen employees.
- Bar their access to all electronic services.
- Inform our alien members.
- Carry out a detailed security sweep.
- Cancel their Galactium passports.
- Set up border controls.
- Set up monitoring stations.'

President Padfield, 'Henrietta, we will leave that to you to organise. Should we consider our military position?'

Admiral Mustard, 'I would say that they are no threat to us, but that was before we saw them fly off. George, can you give it some thought, please?'

Admiral Bumelton, 'Of course.'

Henrietta Strong, 'Do we still confront The Chosen?'

President Padfield, 'What do you think, Jack?'

Admiral Mustard, 'I'm rather nervous about the future. Despite my desire to avenge Madie, I would let sleeping dogs lie. Anyway, I need to replace Admiral Thanatos as the person in charge of The Brakendethian search."

Admiral Bumelton, 'I agree, but let's use the next future months to get stronger.'

There was a general nodding of heads.

Henrietta Strong, 'Before we go, can I remind you of the following from Madie's report:

'The Brakendeth:

- Planned to place Terry in the TIME Organisation to ensure that the homans support The Brakendethians.
- Planned to constantly attack The Galactium to stop us from planning the future.
- Plan to put Terry's two children in a position to take over The Galactium at the right time.
- Plan to attack The Chosen and the Elders.

'Besides, we need to track down their new home by the waterfalls of the Gods.'

Admiral Bumelton, 'Our forces are on alert to resist any further attacks.'

President Padfield, 'Where are Terry's children?' No one knew. Henrietta agreed to find out.

Admiral Mustard, 'If The Brakendeth attack The Chosen, should we go to their aid?'

President Padfield, 'I would say no.'

Edel, 'So would I.'

Location: Lady Enyo's Offices, Planet Olympia
Sequence of Events: 99

Lady Enyo, 'Have the humans reacted?'

Admiral Thanatos, 'I don't believe so. They are gradually restricting our access to their systems, and they have beefed up their defences, but there are no signs of aggressive activity.'

Lady Enyo, 'I think our little Godly display shocked them.'

Admiral Thanatos, 'It certainly did.'

Lady Enyo, 'I can't see them coming to our aid in the future.'

Admiral Thanatos, 'I agree, but I don't think we need them. We have plans for all of their military hardware. We have our own production facilities now and our drone fleet. I think you have done an outstanding job of revitalising our economy and even our way of life. There is a new buzz everywhere on the planet.'

Lady Enyo, 'Thank you, Admiral.'

Admiral Thanatos, 'It is a pleasure, my lady.'

Lady Enyo, 'What about The Brakendeth threat?'

Admiral Thanatos, 'We don't believe that there is a threat. We think that they have utilised all of their resources in the last war.'

Lady Enyo, 'We need to get the humans engaged in tracking them down?'

Admiral Thanatos, 'That is their plan, but we need to nudge them along.'

Lady Enyo, 'How is the attack on TIME going?'

Admiral Thanatos, 'Poorly as we suspected. They seem to be invulnerable to our weapons.'

Lady Enyo, 'What about Terry?'

Admiral Thanatos, 'We will continue to look for ways of killing him.'

Location: GAD2 Conference Room, Planet Napoleon
Sequence of Events: 100

Admiral Mustard called a second military staff meeting.
The attendees were as follows:
- Admiral Jack Mustard
- Admiral George Bumelton
- Admiral Phil Richardson x2
- Admiral Steve Adams
- Admiral Ama Abosa
- Admiral Nubia Tersoo
- Admiral Mateo Dobson
- Admiral John Bonner x2
- Admiral Edel Bonner
- Admiral Peter Gittins
- Admiral David Taylor
- Admiral Glen Pearce
- Admiral Calensky Wallett
- Commander Dennis Todd
- Commander Martin Black
- Marine Commander, Bill Tower
- Sally Green, Fleet HQ, Head of Intelligence
- Denise Smith, Fleet HQ, Head of Navigation & Exploration
- AI Central.

Admiral Mustard, 'Fellow officers, I would like a minute's silence for the loss of Madie Milburn. She was a dedicated and honourable member of the team that will be missed.'

There was a minute's silence and the odd tear.

Admiral Mustard, 'As you know there have been a few changes:
1. A large number of electronic files were discovered in the debris of The Brakendeth home world by Admiral Abosa.
2. The Chosen stole these records, and in the process, Madie was killed.
3. We must now regard The Chosen as a potential enemy.
4. Obviously, we will need to replace Admiral Thanatos as head of The Brakendeth search project.
5. The Chosen are attacking TIME.

'Any questions?'

Admiral Tersoo, 'Is it true that all of The Chosen just flew off into space as they were?'

Admiral Bumelton, 'Absolutely true, I saw them flying through space like Superman at an astonishing speed.'

Admiral J Bonner, 'Does that mean that they have been lying to us all of the time?'

Admiral Mustard, 'Who knows? What we do know is that both The Brakendeth and The Chosen stories about human history are now suspect.'

Admiral Adams, 'How do we get the truth?'

Sally Green, 'We will have to make our own truth.'

Admiral Mustard, 'I have appointed Admiral Gittins to take over from Admiral Thanatos. My orders:

- Admiral Bumelton will maintain his responsibility for defence and have the following Divisions One, Two, Three, Four, and Nine along with the Home Defence Fleet.
- Admiral Bumelton to secure The Galactium against The Chosen.
- Admiral Gittins to command The Brakendeth Project with Divisions Five, Six, Seven and Eight.
- Division Ten will be in reserve.'

Fleet Operations, 'Yes, Sir.'

Admiral Mustard, 'Any questions?'

Admiral Taylor, 'Do we have any idea where "The Waterfall of the Gods" is.'

Sally Green, 'We have had a combined team working on it for six weeks, but there is little to report. Earth had an island called Iceland. In the North-Eastern part of Iceland was a waterfall called Godafoss which in English means Waterfall of the Gods. But that doesn't really help.'

Admiral Gittins, 'Did Thanatos have any information? He wasn't a great sharer of data.'

Admiral Mustard, 'Not that we know of.'

Admiral Bumelton, 'We were hoping that there was going to be some data on The Brakendeth tapes, but you know what happened to them. Anyway, our fleet disposition has been one of spreading our resources fairly thinly over the entire Galactium but using the portals to rush firepower to where it was needed. There are additional resources near Planet Kepler as they have experienced three attacks. We now need to provide cover in case of an attack from The Chosen.'

Admiral Pearce, 'Are we expecting an attack from them?'

Admiral Bumelton, 'Personally, I'm not expecting an attack, but life has been pretty unpredictable recently.'

Admiral Mustard, 'And I don't think it is going to get any easier.'

Location: Town Centre, Planet Napoleon
Sequence of Events: 101

Admiral Mustard, 'How is it going?'

Commander Black, 'We have our forces in place, but we are not sure which of the five flats is the correct one.'

AI Central, 'I suspect that it is number four as there has not been any communication with the outside world.'

Commander Black, 'We can't detect any movement in that flat.'

Admiral Mustard, 'They might be asleep.'

Commander Black, 'Our equipment is so sensitive that it can pick up the lungs breathing. And we can't even detect any carbon dioxide.'

Admiral Mustard, 'You have my permission to enter the property.'

Commander Black, 'Thank you, Sir. We are being cautious as we don't want to hurt the children, and we know what Terry can do.'

Admiral Mustard, 'I take your point, Terry was pretty dangerous before he was a year old. I will leave it in your capable hands.'

Location: Medical Centre, Planet Napoleon
Sequence of Events: 102

Dr Frost, 'I thought that I better let you know. We have just carried out a forensic autopsy on Madie.'

Admiral Mustard, 'Anything interesting?'

Dr Frost, 'Well, it's all a bit distressing. Madie's face was blown off at short range by a blaster. It was a blaster belonging to The Chosen.'

Admiral Mustard, 'The bastards.'

Dr Frost, 'It was no accident.'

Admiral Mustard, 'How can you tell?'

Dr Frost, 'From the angle of the shot, it was clear that they were trying to destroy something that she had just swollen.'

Admiral Mustard, 'I wonder what it was.'

Dr Frost, 'I've got it here. It looks like a shiny black disc.'

Admiral Mustard, 'Who have you told?'

Dr Frost, 'Only you.'

Admiral Mustard, 'Does anyone else know about it?'

Dr Frost, 'Only my assistant.'

Admiral Mustard, 'I want you both to lock yourself in a safe room. Do not let anyone else in.'

Dr Frost, 'You are making a lot of fuss over…'

Admiral Mustard, 'Stop, do as I say now. I will come straight down.'

Admiral Mustard. 'Comms, get me Bill Tower.'

Comms, 'Yes, Sir.'

Bill Tower, 'Evening, Sir.'

Admiral Mustard, 'Bill, Doris is in great danger. She is in the medical centre, hiding. I'm on my way there. I need your help.'

Bill Tower, 'We are on our way there.'

Some marines were first on the scene. Dr Frost was so relieved to see them. She was less relieved when a shot just missed her. Her assistant was less lucky as her head was shredded into little pieces as if it was a ripe melon. Doris struggled to walk when her leg was shredded to a pulp.

Bill Tower just turned the corner to meet a hail of shred. His body was an instant soup of blood, guts, and gore. More marines arrived to meet a similar fate. Doris tried to crawl away, but her attempt stopped when her head was pulped. These were not Galactium weapons.

Admiral Mustard arrived with a considerable force of marines to find a room full of the dead and the dying.

Admiral Mustard, 'Men, use your movement scanners.' There in the corner was a stealthed assailant who just disappeared.

Motion detectors were placed throughout the facility, and the bodies were removed by heavily armoured marines. There was no sign of the disc.

Location: Town Centre, Planet Napoleon
Sequence of Events: 103

Admiral Mustard, 'We have just been attacked by unknown troops dressed as marines. They killed Dr Frost and Bill.'

Commander Black, 'Not Bill Tower?'

Admiral Mustard, 'I'm afraid so.'

Commander Black, 'He is almost unkillable.'

Admiral Mustard, 'How is it going your end?'

Commander Black, 'Just more weirdness.'

Admiral Mustard, 'What do you mean?'

Commander Black, 'Eventually we broke the door down to find two hammocks containing giant chrysalides.'

Admiral Mustard, 'What's in them?'

Commander Black, 'We suspect Terry's two children, but we need to carry out some DNA tests.'

Admiral Mustard, 'We need to get them moved to a secure laboratory.'

Commander Black, 'Yes, Sir.'

Admiral Mustard, 'Comms, get me the president.'

Comms, 'Yes, Sir.'

President Padfield, 'I hear that you have been busy.'

Admiral Mustard, 'It's not been a good day. We have lost Dr Frost and Commander Tower to an unknown killer.'

President Padfield, 'I'm not sure how much more tragedy we can cope with.'

Admiral Mustard, 'Then we have discovered two giant chrysalides.'

President Padfield, 'Can I talk to you later? Henry has just rushed in.'

Admiral Mustard, 'No probs.'

Henrietta Strong, 'Mr President, sorry to interrupt, but there has been a development.'

President Padfield, 'Go on.'

Henrietta Strong, 'Bill Penny has been assassinated.'

President Padfield, 'My God.'

Henrietta Strong, 'What's really bad is that he was assassinated by a

221

naval officer.'

President Padfield, 'Who?'

Henrietta Strong, 'Admiral Richardson.'

President Padfield, 'Which one?'

Henrietta Strong, 'I'm not sure, but apparently he was instructed by Admiral Mustard.'

President Padfield, 'Never. AI Central, is there a command from Admiral Mustard ordering Admiral Richardson to kill Bill Penny?'

AI Central, 'Yes, Mr President, there is such an order from Admiral Mustard.'

Location: Medical Centre, Planet Napoleon
Sequence of Events: 104

Dr Blunt, 'Admiral, we have just carried out a forensic autopsy on Madie.'

Admiral Mustard, 'I'm sorry that you have lost one of your own. She was a fine woman and a dedicated member of the team.'

Dr Blunt, 'I agree, but you should know that we have found a small metal disc.'

Admiral Mustard, 'Stop now, Stop.'

Dr Blunt, 'What?'

Admiral Mustard, 'Stop everything now. Is there somewhere safe that you can go?'

Dr Blunt, 'I could hide in the morgue.'

Admiral Mustard, 'Go for it now. Do not be distracted by anything. Your life is in serious danger.'

Admiral Mustard, 'Comms, get me Major Conway.'

Comms, 'Yes, Sir.'

Major Conway, 'Admiral, how can I help you?'

Admiral Mustard, 'I think we might have another problem in the Medical Centre. Much the same as before.'

Major Conway, 'I will get an armoured team ready.'

Admiral Mustard, 'Excellent. The main objective is to rescue Dr Blunt but kill any intruder you find. On second thoughts, I would rather have them alive.'

Major Conway, 'Yes, Sir.'

Location: Town Centre, Planet Napoleon
Sequence of Events: 105

Commander Black, 'Sir, we have a problem.'

Admiral Mustard, 'What's happened?'

Commander Black, 'Anyone who tries to move the chrysalides simply drops down dead.'

Admiral Mustard, 'That's terrible.'

Commander Black, 'I've lost four men, Sir. Can I just blow up the chrysalides, Sir?'

Admiral Mustard, 'I understand where you are coming from, but no, we need to investigate the situation. Can you get the marines to provide a guard?'

Commander Black, 'Yes, Sir.'

Location: The President's Office, Planet Napoleon
Sequence of Events: 106

President Padfield, 'Jack, I need to talk to you.'

Admiral Mustard, 'You sound very serious.'

President Padfield, 'I'm afraid that it is. Bill Penny has been assassinated."

Admiral Mustard, 'No, not Bill.'

President Padfield, 'What's worse is that he was assassinated by Admiral Richardson.'

Admiral Mustard, 'Which one?'

President Padfield, 'We don't know.'

Admiral Mustard, 'I can't believe this.'

President Padfield, 'It gets worse.'

Admiral Mustard, 'It couldn't.'

President Padfield, 'It can. It seems that you ordered the assassination.'

Admiral Mustard, 'Don't be silly.'

President Padfield, 'Let's check with AI Central.'

Admiral Mustard, 'Fair enough.'

AI Central, 'I can confirm that Admiral Mustard ordered Admiral Richardson to kill Bill Penny.'

Admiral Mustard, 'Play back the order.' AI Central did as instructed. Admiral Mustard could not believe what he heard.

President Padfield, 'What do you want to do?'

Admiral Mustard, 'What do you want me to do?'

President Padfield, 'I would recommend that you stand down until this is resolved.'

Admiral Mustard, 'The timing is never good.'

Admiral Mustard, 'Comms, get me Admiral Bumelton.'

Comms, 'Yes, Sir.'

Admiral Bumelton, 'Hi Jack, how are you?'

Admiral Mustard, 'Not good, I've been accused of a serious crime. I'm standing down while investigations are underway. I need you to take over.'

Admiral Bumelton, 'Yes Sir.'

Location: Medical Centre, Planet Napoleon
Sequence of Events: 107

Major Conway, 'Admiral, we are under attack.'

Admiral Bumelton, 'Update me.'

Major Conway, 'I was expecting Admiral Mustard, Sir'

Admiral Bumelton, 'He is temporarily unavailable. Please update me.'

Major Conway, 'Yes, Sir. I've sent in two armoured squadrons, but we are meeting stiff resistance.'

Admiral Bumelton, 'In the medical centre?'

Major Conway, 'Yes, Sir. The enemy seems to be wearing personal force-fields and have some devastating weapons. We have never seen anything like it.'

Admiral Bumelton, 'What is your mission?'

Major Conway, 'To rescue Dr Blunt.'

Admiral Bumelton, 'Who is he?'

Major Conway, 'I've no idea. The previous doctor was killed by an unknown assailant. It looks like they are attempting the same thing again.'

Admiral Bumelton, 'Is the doctor still alive?

Major Conway, 'Yes, Sir. We believe so.'

Admiral Bumelton, 'Is there a way of rescuing him without going using a frontal assault.'

Major Conway, 'I will investigate, Sir.'

Location: The TIME Organisation
Sequence of Events: 108

Terry, 'My children are in danger?'
    TIME, 'You have no children.'
    Terry, 'What do you mean?'
    TIME, 'You don't exist in time any more. Your past is gone.'
    Terry, 'I can hear them.'
    TIME, 'This is where you kill me.'
    Terry, 'I just need to get back to my children.'
    TIME, 'Fine, but what do you want me to do?'
    Terry, 'Whatever you have to.'
    TIME, 'There is nothing I can do.'
    Terry, 'My children are screaming.'
    TIME, 'I know.'
    Terry, 'What are you going to do?'
    TIME, 'Await the end.' TIME didn't have long to wait. Terry took
one of the office chairs and smashed it over TIME's head. TIME was
dead.
    But nothing changed. Nothing dramatic happened.

Location: Lady Enyo's Offices, Planet Olympia
Sequence of Events: 109

Lady Enyo, 'We are rushing towards the End.'

    Admiral Thanatos, 'We have failed to stop every single stage.'

    The Oracle, 'The conditions are as we predicted:

- TIME has been killed.
- The Emperor's partner has fallen.
- The Warrior has been falsely accused.
- The seed of the demon king has awoken.
- The land of the Gods has been lost.'

    Admiral Thanatos, 'What can we do?'

    The Oracle, 'There is only one means of stopping the End. The entity called Mustard must remember.'

    Lady Enyo, 'What must he remember?'

    The Oracle, 'The reason for being.'

    Lady Enyo, 'That's the first time you have elucidated.'

    The Oracle, 'The Mustard must remember or nothing.'

    Lady Enyo, 'We need to get this information to Admiral Mustard.'

    Admiral Thanatos, 'Will he listen?'

    Lady Enyo, 'I believe that he will.'

Location: The President's Office, Planet Napoleon
Sequence of Events: 110

President Padfield, 'Henrietta, is the world just getting madder and madder?'

Henrietta Strong, 'I believe so, Mr President. I can't believe how much weirdness I have experienced over the last three years.'

President Padfield, 'So where are we?'

Henrietta Strong, 'Shall I make one of my lists?'

President Padfield, 'Go for it.'

Henrietta Strong, 'Here we go:
- The time-wipe.
- The Earth has been destroyed.
- We are still trying to hunt down The Brakendeth Leaders.
- Admiral Terry was killed.
- Another Terry joined TIME.
- Lots of doppelgangers.
- The Timesucky.
- We have fought off several Brakendeth attacks.
- The Chosen have fled after killing Madie.
- Terry's children become chrysalides.
- Dr Frost killed.
- Commander Tower killed.
- Bill Penny killed.
- Admiral Mustard accused of ordering a murder.
- Admiral Mustard needs to remember something.
- The medical centre is still under attack.'

President Padfield, 'Please stop. What needs immediate attention?'

Henrietta Strong, 'I would say proving Admiral Mustard's innocence.'

President Padfield, 'That doesn't look easy.'

AI Central, 'I've done everything I can to investigate, but it's not good. I have validated images of Admiral Mustard, making the order. He subsequently signed the order. I have validated images of Admiral Richardson receiving the order.'

Henrietta Strong, 'But why would Admiral Richardson carry it out?'

President Padfield, 'That's a good question.'

AI Central, 'Admiral Richardson refuses to respond.'

Henrietta Strong, 'Do we have any psychological evidence regarding Admiral Richardson?'

AI Central, 'No, he is refusing any contact with medical staff.'

Henrietta Strong, 'It doesn't make sense.'

President Padfield, 'But who would have the power to change reality?'

AI Central, 'I would say Terry's children. I would suggest putting some screens around the children. We need to stop their mental control.'

The lead screens were erected, and several things happened. Firstly, Admiral Richardson dropped down dead. Secondly, all of the documented evidence disappeared because it was never there.

Admiral Mustard assumed control, much to Admiral Bumelton's relief.

Location: Long-Range Monitoring Station
Sequence of Events: 111

Commander Salton, 'Good day, Admiral, I thought I better contact you urgently.'

Admiral Mustard, 'Good day, Commander Salton. Are you a bringer of bad news?'

Commander Salton, 'Probably. We have detected a massive Brakendethian fleet.'

Admiral Mustard, 'When will it hit Galactium space?'

Commander Salton, 'On its current trajectory never. Half of the fleet is heading towards the Planet Olympia area, and the other half is heading into the unknown.'

Admiral Mustard, 'Is it definitely heading towards The Chosen's home land?

Commander Salton, 'You really can't tell at this stage.'

Admiral Mustard, 'How many vessels?'

Commander Salton, 'Again too early to tell, but if you pushed me, I would say over a million. However, they are an older version of their fighter.'

Admiral Mustard, 'How can you tell?'

Commander Salton, 'From their emission gases.'

Admiral Mustard, 'Fair enough. Please update Admiral Bumelton and keep me informed.'

Location: The TIME Organisation
Sequence of Events: 112

Terry wasn't sure what his role was, but he was still in the control room. It contained an interactive map of the universe. It's was almost impossible to display a map due to the size of the universe, but with time on your hands, you could.

Terry, 'Why are the lights going out in the top left-hand corner?'

TIME Operative, 'That is the start of the End.'

Terry, 'What do you mean?'

TIME Operative, 'When you killed TIME, the End started.'

Terry, 'This doesn't make sense.'

TIME Operative, 'It is not my job to explain the operation of TIME.'

Terry, 'You better, or you will soon join your master.'

TIME Operative, 'But you killed TIME, so time is dead. What you are seeing are not lights but stars. In that area, all matter and energy are being distinguished because they only exist in Time. And as TIME is dead, then all will die. You brought it upon yourself.'

Terry, 'How long before it reaches us?'

TIME Operative, 'Using what measurement?'

Terry, 'Earth time.'

TIME Operative, 'Two to three months. It's a big place, the universe.'

Terry, 'And The Galactium?'

TIME Operative, 'About the same time.'

Terry, 'Give me a reason why I shouldn't kill you?'

TIME Operative, 'There is no significant reason.'

Terry used the same chair to commit his second murder. He had no idea why he did it. Two cleaners came in and took the body away. They must have known.

Terry thought converting his children into Nexusters would save them, but he now realised that he had ended it all. The only hope was for Admiral Mustard to remember.

Location: Medical Centre, Planet Napoleon
Sequence of Events: 113

Admiral Mustard, 'Update me.'

Major Conway, 'Admiral, welcome back. We are still up against stiff opposition in the medical centre, but we have identified another way ...'

Admiral Mustard, 'Stop. Don't tell me. I'm not sure if this line is secure.'

Major Conway, 'Yes Sir'

Admiral Mustard, 'I authorise you to use extreme force to defeat the enemy and secure Dr Blunt.'

Major Conway, 'Yes, Sir.' And extreme force was used. The remotely controlled Splatter tanks destroyed everything in front of them. The medical centre ceased to be a medical centre. While this frontal assault was going on, Dr Blunt was squirrelled away via the sewers. It wasn't the healthiest of options, but doctors were used to shit.

The black disc had been saved, but it had cost a fair number of lives, including some of Admiral Mustard's closest friends. He just hoped that it was worth it.

About thirty shielded bodies were recovered. They were definitely Chosen operatives. The only good news was that The Galactium now had access to better camouflage technology and portable shields.

Admiral Mustard, 'Congratulations, Major Conway.'

Major Conway, 'Thank you, Sir.'

Location: Admiral Mustard's Office, Planet Napoleon
Sequence of Events: 114

Admiral Mustard, 'Comms, get me the president.'

    Comms, 'Yes, Sir.'

    President Padfield, 'Morning Jack, glad to have you back.'

    Admiral Mustard, 'Was that practised poetry?'

    President Padfield, 'Every now and then, I get an urge.'

    Admiral Mustard, 'So who is scratching your urge nowadays?'

    President Padfield, 'It's still the cleaning lady.'

    Admiral Mustard, 'I hope that everything is spotless down there?'

    President Padfield, 'It certainly is, thank you very much.'

    Admiral Mustard, 'Anyway, I have some updates for you:

• There is a massive Brakendethian fleet heading in two different directions.

• It looks like one is heading towards Planet Olympia, and the other is going into unknown space.

• Dr Blunt has been rescued, but the medical centre has been completely destroyed.

• We have a black data disc in our possession that is being researched, and

• Edel is having a girl.'

    President Padfield, 'That's good news, give Edel my love. We need to have dinner sometime.'

    Admiral Mustard, 'That would be nice, but everything is mad at the moment.'

    President Padfield, 'We have carried out DNA tests on the chrysalids. They are definitely Terry's children but hold your hat. We think that they are evolving into Nexusters.'

    Admiral Mustard, 'Why would Terry want his children to be mind-controlling monsters?'

    President Padfield, 'Beats me.'

    Admiral Mustard, 'We still need to get them moved. We need a remote-control vehicle.'

    President Padfield, 'Are you going to tell The Chosen about the fleet?'

Admiral Mustard, 'I thought that I would review the contents of the data files first.'

President Padfield, 'Good point.'

Admiral Mustard, 'As soon as I get anything, I will let you know.'

President Padfield, 'Brill.'

Location: The TIME Organisation
Sequence of Events: 115

Terry wondered why he had killed two TIME operatives. He wasn't in the habit of killing anyone. He wondered if he had been manipulated. Then he convinced himself that he had been manipulated.

But who would be the manipulator? The only options were:
- The Elder Gods
- The Brakendeth
- The Chosen
- TIME itself
- Someone unknown.

Terry, 'How do I review what has happened?'

TIME Operative, 'The amount of data is so vast that you have to know exactly the time and place you want to investigate.'

Terry, 'Can I view a particular person?'

TIME Operative, 'Yes, but you still need the exact time.'

Terry, 'I understand. Show me the Grand Dethmon at the time of Earth's destruction.'

TIME Operative, 'What is Earth?'

Terry, 'It is a planet in the Sol system.'

TIME Operative, 'I have it. It has just been destroyed, and I have pinpointed the Grand Dethmon.'

Terry used the TIME monitor to view a significant event:

Admiral Terry, 'What do you want me to do?'

Grand Dethmon, 'Destroy the Earth.'

Admiral Terry, 'I can't do that.'

Grand Dethmon, 'Why not?'

Admiral Terry, 'We need those forces to conquer the universe.'

Grand Dethmon, 'If you don't do that, then we will.'

The Grand Dethmon stood up, walked over to Terry and pushed his ceremonial sword deep into Terry's gut and twisted it. Terry had the power to stop the blood from flowing, but he wasn't strong enough to fight off the Grand Dethmon.

Then the entire Brakendethian fleet departed for Earth. Their job was not to engage the enemy but to destroy the Earth, and they had the power to do it.

Terry was shocked. The Brakendethians had killed his alter-ego. It was apparent to him that he was just a pawn. A pawn that wanted revenge.

Terry, 'Can I view my children?'

TIME Operative, 'Yes, but you still need the exact time.'

Terry, 'The time is now, and the place is Planet Napoleon.'

TIME Operative, 'What is now?'

One stare from Terry seemed to motivate the operative. On the viewers, two chrysalids were displayed.

Terry, 'NO, NO, NO,' he shouted. 'Who has done this?' He was viewing an armoured tractor moving two Nexuster chrysalides from his flat. They were moving the monsters that his darling children had become.

But he knew who had done it.

Location: Admiral Mustard's Office, Planet Napoleon
Sequence of Events: 116

President Padfield, Admiral Mustard and Sally Green (intelligence) were in Admiral Mustard's office, ready to view The Chosen disc along with AI Central.

It wasn't a prolonged viewing, but it was certainly shocking. It cast a completely different aspect on the human/Chosen relationship. It could be divided into the following sections:

Slavery

It would appear that over a period of a thousand years, over thirty million humans were kidnapped. Most were sold into slavery and used for household services, cleaning, agriculture, clerical work, manufacturing, retail, transport etc. Most had a relatively easy time, but they were slaves for life. Their children were sold into slavery. If they became ill, they were terminated as it was cheaper to buy a new one.

The slaves had no rights and no hope. Families were split up. Some were treated terribly, but as there were no laws to protect them, it was ignored.

It has been estimated that out of a planetary population of eighty-five million, only one million were from The Chosen stock. Planet Olympia was effectively a human planet.

Sex Trade

Most of the attractive humans, both men and women, were used in the sex trade. They were used to commit every possible sexual act imaginable. They were used in orgies and sex shows. There were contests to see how much fucking a single woman could take: they usually bled to death. Rough sex was common place. The death of a sex slave was not a crime but an occupational hazard.

The video showed cannibalism, rape chases, mutilation of every possible sort, sex with animals, etc. It reminded Admiral Mustard of the Roman games. Sally couldn't bear to watch, but she had to. It was horrific stuff and very hard to believe.

Old sex slaves were usually strangled and fed to the pigs. Some weren't even strangled. Others were used as public torches, covered in fat, and set alight.

The viewers wanted revenge on The Chosen.

Body Parts

Fit men and women were also used to meet the needs of medical science. The Chosen live forever except for disease and accidents. There was a continuous need to replace body parts. Some of the parts were critical organs such as the liver or heart. Others were simply cosmetic: lips, nipples, penises etc.

Human body parts were cheap, very cheap. There was an inexhaustible supply. Captured humans were simply dissected on a slab without any anaesthetic, and the organs and body parts extracted as required.

Meat Sales

There was a thriving market in human meat. Butcher shops sold every possible human body part. There was a particular interest in the sex organs. There were contests in the butchery trade to see how much meat could be extracted from a human before they died. The greater the pain, the greater the pleasure that The Chosen seemed to enjoy.

You could buy a complete human for the equivalent of a hog roast. The remains were converted into burgers.

Clothing

There was a limited but expensive market in humanware. Objects were made from human bones, teeth, and skin. Skinning a slave alive was a public spectacle.

Coming of Age

Usually boys, but occasionally girls, were given a slave at their coming-of-age ceremony. It was common practice to rape the slave, torture it and then kill it. It helped to create the right attitude amongst the young.

Battles

The Chosen military created wars and battles on Earth for their own enjoyment. For some, it was a game of chess. The collection of the dead and dying paid for the trips. The videos were viewed countlessly as entertainment.

Hunting

Humans were simply used for hunting in much the same way as deer. Quite often, they suffered a range of indecencies before they died.

Sally went to the bathroom to clean herself up after excessive vomiting. She apologised to the other two, but they understood. They had considered joining her as their stomachs were somewhat queasy.

President Padfield, 'But who would make a video like that? What was the point?'

Admiral Mustard, 'It's just sick, vile filth. I want to join The Brakendethian fleet and kill every last member of The Chosen race.'

Sally Green, 'You would probably end up killing a lot of humans. We must free them.'

President Padfield, 'I agree, but most of the humans probably only know that life.'

Admiral Mustard, 'We must free them. I've been in a lot of battles but never seen anything so sick.'

Sally Green, 'What are we going to do?'

President Padfield, 'Who are the worst: The Brakendethians or The Chosen?'

Admiral Mustard, 'One lot ruthlessly abuses us, and the other lot converts us into food.'

Sally Green, 'I need to go and have a rest.' You could tell that she was seriously affected.

Admiral Mustard, 'Comms, get me Dr Blunt.'

Comms, 'Yes, Sir.'

Dr Blunt, 'Admiral, how can I help you.'

Admiral Mustard, 'Sally Green has just watched The Chosen vid.'

Dr Blunt, 'The one I recovered?'

Admiral Mustard, 'Yes. She has been seriously affected by it, and I'm worried about her mental health. Can you monitor her, please?'

Dr Blunt, 'Of course.'

President Padfield, 'Good thinking. I think I might need monitoring as well.'

Admiral Mustard, 'Do we tell The Chosen about The Brakendeth fleet?

President Padfield, 'Not yet and possibly not at all.'

Admiral Mustard, 'What about the humans on Planet Olympia?'

President Padfield, 'They are probably damaged beyond repair.'

Location: Lady Enyo's Offices, Planet Olympia
Sequence of Events: 117

Lady Enyo, 'By now, our human friends must have seen the vid.'

Admiral Thanatos, 'I think we can assume that they are not our friends any more.'

Lady Enyo, 'Why was that film ever made?'

Admiral Thanatos, 'It probably doesn't matter that much. Eventually, they would discover the truth.'

Lady Enyo, 'But we have stopped most of the unpleasantness.'

Admiral Thanatos, 'That is not true.'

Lady Enyo, 'What do you mean? I banned slavery.'

Admiral Thanatos, 'But we still have the human breeding farms.'

Lady Enyo, 'But we need human body parts for our own survival. They must see that.'

Admiral Thanatos, 'How would you feel about the humans breeding The Chosen?'

Lady Enyo, 'That would be disgusting. How could you ever suggest it? We are The Chosen.'

Admiral Thanatos, 'We still breed humans to eat and for sex.'

Lady Enyo, 'By those humans wouldn't exist if we hadn't bred them. They are our property.'

Admiral Thanatos, 'I don't think you see it from the human perspective.'

Lady Enyo, 'They must see that there are different rules for cows and pigs.'

Admiral Thanatos, 'Really?'

Lady Enyo, 'You can't talk. You made a fortune running battle contests and hunting parties on Earth. How many humans did you rape?'

Admiral Thanatos, 'That was before I understood.'

Lady Enyo, 'Understood what?'

Admiral Thanatos, 'That all life and especially conscious life must be respected.'

Lady Enyo, 'How many freed sex slaves still live in your home?'

Admiral Thanatos, 'I know what you are saying, I still have my weaknesses.'

Lady Enyo, 'Anyway, changing the subject, have you got the new message to Admiral Mustard?'

Admiral Thanatos, 'You mean, "Reason for Being". Yes, I sent it by diplomatic despatch. I didn't fancy ringing him. It would have been hard to explain our commandos' presence on their planet or the death of their people. We have hardly been a good ally: it will probably be the death of us.'

Lady Enyo, 'But we had good reasons.'

Admiral Thanatos, 'Did we?'

Location: Admiral Mustard's Office, Planet Napoleon
Sequence of Events: 118

Admiral Mustard, 'We received a despatch today from the enemy.'

President Padfield, 'Which one?'

Admiral Mustard, 'Our local neighbourhood Greek Gods.'

President Padfield, 'What did it say?'

Admiral Mustard, 'It said that their Oracle had some further information in my quest to remember. It was "Reason for Being".'

President Padfield, 'What does that mean?'

Admiral Mustard, 'It is borrowed from the French "raison d'être". It is the reason for being or the claimed reason for the existence of something or someone.'

President Padfield, 'Problem solved then.'

Admiral Mustard, 'So I've got to remember something to do with the reason for being.'

President Padfield, 'Is it something to do with your personal reason for living or the human race's reason?'

Admiral Mustard, 'Who knows?'

As they were discussing reason in-depth, an apparition of Terry appeared in the room.

Terry, 'I bet you didn't expect to see me.'

Both Admiral Mustard and President Padfield agreed that it was the last thing they expected.

Terry, 'You must listen as I can't maintain this communication for long. What I'm going to tell you is mostly bad news:

- I murdered TIME.
- This has started "The End of Days". Parts of the universe have already been dissolved.
- The Galactium will be dissolved in the next two to three months.
- The Brakendeth killed my alter-ego.
- My children have been converted into Nexuster chrysalids by The Brakendeth. You need to destroy them before they become too powerful.
- Two Brakendeth fleets are on their way to destroy The Chosen and the Elder Gods. I would recommend that you let it go ahead.

- Admiral Mustard can stop the end if he remembers something. The TIME Organisation Knows what it is, but it won't interfere. I'm running out of time, but any quick questions?'

Admiral Mustard, 'The Chosen have given us a clue: "Reason for Being".'

Terry, 'I will think about it.'

President Padfield, 'Why did you murder TIME?'

Terry, 'It was my destiny. Bye.'

President Padfield, 'What did you make from that?'

Admiral Mustard, 'I really need to remember, everything else is subservient, although we need to kill The Nexusters ASAP.'

President Padfield, 'I agree.'

Location: Admiral Mustard's Office, Planet Napoleon
Sequence of Events: 119

Admiral Mustard, 'Comms, get me Major Conway.'

Comms, 'Yes, Sir.'

Major Conway, 'Afternoon Sir, how can I help you?'

Admiral Mustard, 'I have some orders for you. Kill the two chrysalides ASAP.'

Major Conway, 'Yes, Sir. I will let you know when it is done.'

Admiral Mustard. 'Thank you, Major.'

Location: Lady Enyo's Offices, Planet Olympia
Sequence of Events: 120

Admiral Thanatos, 'My lady, we have detected a vast Brakendethian fleet is coming our way.'

Lady Enyo, 'The humans must have known about it.'

Admiral Thanatos, 'Without a doubt.'

Lady Enyo, 'That means that we are not going to get any help from them.'

Admiral Thanatos, 'Can you blame them?'

Lady Enyo, 'I can. We are their parents.'

Admiral Thanatos, 'Their wicked, abusive parents.'

Lady Enyo, 'I sometimes wonder whose side you are on.'

Admiral Thanatos, 'My lady, I'm just being logical.'

Lady Enyo, 'Well, let's be more logical and work out how we will defeat The Brakendethians.'

Admiral Thanatos, 'There are about half a million Brakendethian vessels. We have about half that number, but they are much more effective. Our assets are as follows:

- One hundred thousand ships of the line all upgraded to human standards.
- One hundred and twenty-five thousand drones modelled on the human design.
- Twenty thousand Godfire battle-cruisers, unique to us.
- Five thousand forts, based on human designs.

The above is divided into five phalanxes and is ready and prepared to meet the onslaught.'

Lady Enyo, 'What are our chances?'

Admiral Thanatos, 'About even.'

Lady Enyo, 'Do you think that there is any chance of human help?'

Admiral Thanatos, 'Not now.'

Location: Long-Range Monitoring Station
Sequence of Events: 121

Commander Salton, 'Good day, Admiral, I thought I better update you.'

Admiral Mustard, 'Good day, Commander Salton. Please go ahead.'

Commander Salton, 'Will do. The first Brakendeth fleet is about to enter Chosen space. It is about twice the size of The Chosen fleet.'

Admiral Mustard, 'Exactly how big is The Chosen fleet?'

Commander Salton, 'I would say one hundred and twenty five thousand drones and the same number of fleet vessels. Most of their ships seem to be of human design. There are a few special types that I can't distinguish.'

Admiral Mustard, 'They would be their Godfire ships. We have never seen them.'

Commander Salton, 'Fair enough. I will register them on our database.'

Admiral Mustard, 'Please give me regular updates on how the battle is going.'

Commander Salton, 'Yes, Sir.'

Admiral Mustard, 'What about the other fleet?'

Commander Salton, 'It's heading into unknown space. Strangely from a certain angle, it looks like a series of waterfalls.'

Admiral Mustard, 'Send me some pictures.'

Commander Salton, 'Yes, Sir.' The photos were transmitted.

Admiral Mustard, 'You are right. It does look like a series of waterfalls. Thank you very much.'

Location: Admiral Mustard's Office, Planet Napoleon
Sequence of Events: 122

Admiral Mustard, 'Comms, get me Admiral Gittins.'

Comms, 'Yes, Sir.'

Admiral Gittins, 'Good day, Jack'

Admiral Mustard, 'How is it going?'

Admiral Gittins, 'Fucking awful.'

Admiral Mustard, 'So not too bad then?'

Admiral Gittins, 'It is awful. Finding a needle in a haystack is a doddle in comparison. Where do we look? I've got search parties, traffic analysis teams, grid search teams, molecular inspection analysis and so on, but not a sniff of anything.'

Admiral Mustard, 'I've got a photo. It's on its way over to you.' And over it went.

Admiral Gittins, 'Wow, that is impressive.'

Admiral Mustard, 'It's a long shot.'

Admiral Gittins, 'True, but it would be great to stretch my legs.'

Admiral Mustard, 'The photo came from our Long-Range Monitoring Station. A massive Brakendeth fleet is heading in that direction.'

Admiral Gittins, 'In that case we are on our way.' They both knew in their hearts that they were on to a winner.

Location: Town Centre, Planet Napoleon
Sequence of Events: 123

Major Conway, 'Sir, we have a problem.'

Admiral Mustard, 'What's happened?'

Major Conway, 'As you know, we moved the cocoons by remote transport into a secure storage area.

'As per your orders, we worked out a plan to destroy them. We decided to use flame throwers. Before we could operate them, the chemical containers exploded, killing a dozen of my men.

'We retreated into a remote-control centre and sent in radio-controlled flame throwers. I'm sorry to say that somehow, they took control of the vehicles and assaulted the local swimming pool. Over one hundred locals have been injured or killed. We still can't get into the pool as the vehicles are attacking anything that moves.'

Admiral Mustard, 'That's terrible.'

Major Conway, 'I'm afraid that things have got worse, Sir. Every gun belonging to my marines started heating up. They had to be abandoned when they started independently firing. I have over sixty troops with bullets in their feet.'

Admiral Mustard had to chuckle, although it really wasn't funny.

Admiral Mustard, 'What are your plans?'

Major Conway, 'Can we bomb them, Sir?'

Admiral Mustard, 'That sounds very risky.'

Major Conway, 'What about drones.'

Admiral Mustard, 'I think you need to clear the area of civilians.'

Major Conway, 'How big an area?'

Admiral Mustard, 'I will leave that to you. I will send Commander Black to assist.' He realised that the major was struggling.

Major Conway, 'Thank you, Sir.'

Admiral Mustard, 'Comms, get me Commander Black.'

Comms, 'Yes, Sir.'

Commander Black, 'Morning, Jack.'

Admiral Mustard, 'Morning, Martin. Major Conway has the task of destroying those two Nexuster cocoons. He is struggling as the cocoons are resisting and killing the locals. Could you investigate and assist? I was wondering about surrounding the cocoons with a powerful force-field. We need to kill them before they get too strong. Please make it happen.'

Commander Black, 'Consider it done.'

Location: The President's Office, Planet Napoleon
Sequence of Events: 124

President Padfield, 'It seems a bit strange having these meetings with everything else going on.'

Henrietta Strong, 'As someone said, The Galactium doesn't run itself. Last time it took two meetings to get through the agenda.'

President Padfield, 'Well, I did have this constant message in my ear telling Admiral Mustard to remember.'

Henrietta Strong, 'Are there any signs of him remembering?'

President Padfield, 'Not really. The Chosen's Oracle left him a clue: "Reason for Being".'

Henrietta Strong, 'Somewhat enigmatic?'

President Padfield, 'Too true.'

Henrietta Strong, 'Let's use the previous agenda as a checklist:

1. The evacuation of the Moon.

2. Housing for the Moonies.

3. The building of the new Galactium HQ on Mars.

4. Memorial service(s).

5. Tracking down The Brakendethians.

6. Merging of WW and UW records.

7. Doppelganger issues.

8. Handling of salvage.

9. Planet Lovelace (half wiping issues).

10. Eternity service.

11. Medical situation.

12. Working with Bill Penny.

13. AOB.'

President Padfield, 'I hear that the evacuation is complete.'

Henrietta Strong, 'That's correct except for those who have refused to leave.'

President Padfield, 'They must be mad. On the other hand, we might all be doomed.'

Henrietta Strong, 'In the end there were only about nine thousand die-hards who have stayed. We are still in touch with them, but they are leaving portals as they go.'

President Padfield, 'At least they are doing some good.'

Henrietta Strong, 'Good progress is being made re the development of Ganymede. A lot of the Moonies are actively involved in the construction work as they want it done their way. It will probably be at least a year before they can move in.'

President Padfield, 'How have we housed them?'

Henrietta Strong, 'We have found accommodation throughout The Galactium. It hasn't been easy, but we have done it. Not that the Moonies are grateful.'

President Padfield, 'Well done, it couldn't have been easy, and I know from first-hand experience how awkward they can be. My Mother-in-Law was one.'

Henrietta Strong, 'That must have been tough. The next point is the new HQ. This is well behind schedule as we have given priority to the Ganymede project, and there has been a shortage of contractors. Anyway, the architectural competition to select the best design is still in progress.'

President Padfield, 'In the scheme of things, there is no rush.'

Henrietta Strong, 'Regarding the memorial service, we are still waiting for the committee to report. I haven't chased them.'

President Padfield, 'There is no point at the moment.'

Henrietta Strong, 'The next point is tracking down The Brakendethians.'

President Padfield, 'They have just got a good lead. Admiral Gittins is on the case.'

Henrietta Strong, 'That sounds positive. The next issue is to do with the doppelgangers. I would like to come back to that later. I can say that all of the records have been correctly updated. The salvage issues are now under control after getting some naval support, and the Eternity service has been a great success.'

President Padfield, 'It takes some getting used to. I can't believe that I could live for a thousand years. I haven't really adjusted to it yet.'

Henrietta Strong, 'I agree. I'm wondering whether I should have plastic surgery to become a real woman.'

President Padfield, 'As far as I'm concerned, you already are.'

Henrietta Strong, 'Thank you, Mr President, but you know what I mean.'

President Padfield, 'I do. Changing the subject, we should have had a minute's silence for Bill.'

Henrietta Strong, 'That whole incident was strange. We had no idea that we had a developing Nexuster in our midst.'

President Padfield, 'I hear that there is a minor battle going on between them and the marines just across town.'

Henrietta Strong, 'Nothing is easy nowadays. Do you remember the good old days?'

President Padfield, 'Not really. It's always been shit.'

Henrietta Strong, 'Fair enough. I need to update you regarding the doppelganger mystery.'

But then there was another mystery. There was a brilliant, blinding light over the town.

Location: On Board Admiral Gittins's Flagship
Sequence of Events: 125

Admiral Gittins, 'Update me.'

Fleet Operations, 'Yes Sir:

- Divisions Five, Six and Seven are heading towards the spot identified by our Long-Range Monitoring Unit.
- It just happens that a Brakendethian fleet is in front of us, heading in the same direction.
- We have been ordered not to engage with their fleet.
- Division Eight is following as a tactical reserve.
- GAD2 has been informed of our plans.
- All systems are fully operational.'

Admiral Gittins, 'Please continue. Let me know when we have visibility of the Waterfall.'

Fleet Operations, 'Yes, Sir.' But then The Brakendeth attacked. The alarms rang, and Admiral Gittins rushed back to the bridge.

Admiral Gittins, 'Update me.'

Fleet Operations, 'Yes Sir:

- About four hundred Brakendeth ships are attacking Fleet 7.5, which is on the farthest flank.
- The attacking vessels are not causing any problems and are easily being eliminated by our drones.'

Admiral Gittins wondered why they attacked and in such small numbers.

Admiral Gittins, 'My orders:

- The drones of Division Five to form spear guard.
- The remains of Division Five to take the central position with Divisions Six and Seven on each side.
- Form general defensive formation but maintain speed.'

Fleet Operations, 'Yes, Sir.'

Admiral Gittins, 'Comms, get me Admiral Mustard.'

Comms, 'Yes, Sir.'

Admiral Mustard, 'Hi Peter, are you having fun?'

Admiral Gittins, 'We were following The Brakendeth fleet to the Waterfall when they suddenly attacked us.'

Admiral Mustard, 'In force?'

Admiral Gittins, 'No, only four hundred vessels which were easily repelled.'

Admiral Mustard, 'That's strange. Sounds like a trap to me, or it could be that you are heading to The Brakendeth base, and they are trying to dissuade you.'

Admiral Gittins, 'What are your orders?'

Admiral Mustard, 'My orders:

- Continue as per your existing plans.
- Retreat if The Brakendeth force a large-scale engagement.'

Admiral Gittins, 'Yes, Sir.'

Location: The TIME Organisation
Sequence of Events: 126

Terry had been contemplating the phrase 'Reason for Being'. He made a series of notes:

- At one time, there were two Admiral Mustards, but neither of them could remember 'something'.
- The 'reason' phrase came from The Chosen's Oracle.
- Reminders to remember had come from multiple sources.
- There had been apparitions.
- One of the messages was from the future, which logically means that the universe was saved, but who knows.
- Some of the messages were displayed on multiple computer screens.
- A tall, good-looking man often appears in dreams.
- The Brakendeth didn't seem to know about it, but The Chosen do.
- The TIME Organisation knows what needs to be remembered.
- French: raison d'être.

Surely all the clues are there.

So the only group who know the answer at this moment in time are the TIME Organisation. I've killed TIME. So who is stopping me from finding out?

Terry, 'How do I find out what Admiral Mustard needs to remember?'

TIME Operative, 'That is restricted information.'

Terry, 'To who?'

TIME Operative, 'It is restricted to those that need to know.'

Terry, 'And who are they?'

TIME Operative, 'That is restricted information.'

Terry, 'Am I on that list?'

TIME Operative, 'No.'

Terry, 'Who am I?'

TIME Operative, 'You are the new TIME.'

Terry, 'Am I your boss?'

TIME Operative, 'Yes.'

Terry, 'Then tell me.'

TIME Operative, 'That is restricted information.'

Terry, 'But I'm in charge.'

TIME Operative, 'That is exactly why you don't have access.'

Terry, 'Who decided that?'

TIME Operative, 'TIME.'

Terry, 'That's me.'

TIME Operative, 'Yes.'

Terry, 'Can't I change it then?'

TIME Operative, 'No.'

Terry, 'Why not?'

TIME Operative, 'Only you know.'

Terry, 'We are going in circles.'

TIME Operative, 'We are.'

Terry, 'What if I kill you?'

TIME Operative, 'We are all going to die shortly.'

Terry, 'I can stop it.'

TIME Operative, 'I know.'

Terry, 'Well, tell me then.'

TIME Operative, 'That is restricted information.'

Terry, 'Where is the data held?'

TIME Operative, 'That is restricted information.'

Terry took his weapon of choice and smashed it over the TIME operative's head. Time stood still for the dead girl. Terry shouted for another TIME operative.

A pretty uniformed girl arrived.

Terry, 'Tell me what Admiral Mustard needs to remember.'

TIME Operative, 'That is restricted information.'

Terry, 'I can see that you are a very attractive girl. If you want to stay that way, you need to tell me what I need to know.'

TIME Operative, 'That is restricted information.'

Terry smashed the chair against the girl's face. Terry, 'Do you want more?'

TIME Operative, 'I can't tell you as it is restricted information.'

Terry didn't know that he could be that heartless as he smashed the girl repeatedly in the face until she was lifeless.

Terry shouted for another TIME operative.

This time a spotty lad appeared distressed by the blood, gore, and dead bodies. He pointed at the pretty girl and said, 'That's my girlfriend.'

Terry, 'Not any more, and if you don't cooperate, you will be joining her.'

TIME Operative, 'But you are asking us to break our oaths'

Terry, 'Correct, tell me what Admiral Mustard needs to remember.'

TIME Operative, 'Sorry I can't tell you.' Terry rammed the chair leg down the boy's throat, which made breathing very difficult. Death followed when the chair burst into the heart cavity.

Terry shouted for another TIME operative.

Another attractive girl entered the room and started screaming. She stopped when the chair smashed against her head.

Terry shouted for another TIME operative.

Terry, 'I need to know what Admiral Mustard needs to remember. If you tell me that it is restricted information, I will kill you. If you don't tell me, I will kill you. You know that I will do it. You can see the bodies who have not co-operated.'

TIME Operative, 'What right have you got to kill my comrades?'

Terry, 'The right to save the universe. And I reserve the right to kill you.'

TIME Operative, 'Then kill me.' And Terry did.

Terry shouted for another TIME operative, but there was no response. He had run out of them. He wandered around the building, but there was no one.

Location: Admiral Mustard's Office, Planet Napoleon
Sequence of Events: 127

Admiral Mustard, 'Comms, find out what that bright light is.' It was a dazzling bright light that filled the room. It was so bright that humans couldn't look at it. There was no choice but to pull the blinds down.

Comms, 'Yes, Sir.'

One of the comms officers dashed off to find out, but there was no immediate explanation. Then it became clear.

The cocoons had exploded in an orgy of light to welcome the birth of two new angels. They probably weren't angels, but that is what they looked like. No one had ever seen a Nexuster, so perhaps they were Nexusters. They certainly had very impressive wings.

What Admiral Mustard had not expected was a telepathic message.

Angels, 'Admiral Mustard, we greet you. We are the spawn of Terry. We apologise for the deaths of your comrades, but we only sought to protect ourselves.'

Admiral Mustard spoke verbally, 'I'm not sure whether to welcome you or not. Your father recommended that we should kill you before you got too strong.'

Angels, 'Our father assumed that we were Nexusters. He was very wrong.'

Admiral Mustard, 'So what are you?'

Angels, 'What do you want us to be?'

Admiral Mustard, 'I'm not interested in your games. I need to know if you are a threat to The Galactium or not?'

Angels, 'We are not.'

Admiral Mustard, 'What are your plans?'

Angels, 'We are newborn.'

Admiral Mustard, 'Why did you get Admiral Richardson to kill Bill Penny?'

Angels, 'This is meaningless to us. What happens before birth is unknown to us. Our protective cocoon has its own intelligence.'

Admiral Mustard, 'That's very convenient.'

Angels, 'Our father is calling.' And they were gone.

Commander Black, 'Comms, get me Admiral Mustard.'

Comms, 'Yes, Sir.'

Admiral Mustard, 'Hi, Martin, you are going to tell me about the angels.'

Commander Black, 'Yes Sir,'

Admiral Mustard, 'Go on then.'

Commander Black, 'Well, we installed the force-field as you suggested, which effectively stopped us killing it. The two cocoons then started glowing and going through a process of expansion and contraction. This steadily got more and more intense until there was an explosion of light. Our force-field simply collapsed, and two angels appeared. I ordered our men to cease hostilities. To be honest, I think they ordered me to order my men to stop hostilities.'

Admiral Mustard, 'Well, it looks like they have done a runner.'

Location: Lady Enyo's Offices, Planet Olympia
Sequence of Events: 128

Admiral Thanatos, 'My lady, we have picked up evidence that the humans are engaged in a battle with The Brakendethians.'

Lady Enyo, 'But not our Brakendethians.'

Admiral Thanatos, 'No, so there must be two fleets.'

Lady Enyo, 'Strangely, I've also detected the birth of two new Gods.'

Admiral Thanatos, 'But there has not been a new God created in ten thousand years. Why now?'

Lady Enyo, 'And if I'm right, they are messenger Gods. I'm pretty sure that I'm right.'

Admiral Thanatos, 'The humans would call them angels, but they are obviously here to pass on a message.'

Lady Enyo, 'Hopefully, it is something to help Admiral Mustard to remember.'

Admiral Thanatos, 'I better go as I've got a battle to win.'

Lady Enyo, 'More like a war.'

Admiral Thanatos, 'What is the disposition?'

Phalanx Control, 'Yes, my Lord:
- The five phalanx fleets are ready and can operate as self-contained units.
- Each phalanx fleet has five drone phalanxes of twenty-five thousand, five fort phalanxes of four thousand and five battleship phalanxes of twenty thousand
- Each phalanx fleet also has access to fifty Godfire vessels
- There are also an additional two hundred and fifty Godfire vessels to be used at the admiral's discretion
- The Brakendeth fleet consists of five hundred thousand identical unmanned ships in no particular formation.'

Admiral Thanatos, 'My orders:
- Drones and battleships of each phalanx will form the first line.
- Forts and Godfire vessels to form the second line further back.
- When The Brakendeth attack, the first line will make a token defence and then retreat behind the second line.

- Once this has happened, the Godfire vessels and forts will open up with extreme force to destroy the enemy.
- When the enemy retreats the reserve Godfire vessels, the forts and the battleships will pursue.
- On my orders, the pursuit will stop, and the fleet will re-form as before.
- Good luck, my friends and comrades.'

While this was going on, Lady Enyo was preparing the twelve ships of The Chosen, ready to flee if and when needed.

Without warning, The Brakendethian fleet lurched forward. The Chosen front line stood firm and then deliberately gave way. There was a mass feigned withdrawal. The Brakendethians entered the kitchen and were slaughtered in their thousands. It was a common and straightforward plan that worked brilliantly.

These were not the best of The Brakendethians, being a few generations out of date. As they retreated, The Chosen attacked as planned. The Chosen were natural warriors and attacked with verve and gusto, but they ignored Admiral Thanatos's recall.

It was now The Brakendethians chance to offer carnage. And The Chosen accepted it. In a battle of attrition, The Brakendeth would win. After repeated orders from the admiral, the remains of The Chosen's attack force staggered home.

Losses were now fairly even, which meant that The Brakendeth were winning. Admiral Thanatos was worried about repeating the previous plan as the same could easily happen again. This was not the first time that The Chosen had lost control when their blood was up. The battle started with odds of two to one. It was now three to one. Admiral Thanatos decided to try it again.

Admiral Thanatos, 'My orders:
- Drones and battleships of each phalanx will form the first line, as before.
- Forts and Godfire vessels to form the second line further back, as before.
- When The Brakendeth attack, the first line will make a token defence and then retreat behind the second line, as before.
- Once this has happened, the Godfire vessels and forts will open up

with extreme force to destroy the enemy, as before.

- When the enemy retreats the reserve Godfire vessels, the forts and the battleships will pursue.
- The pursuit must stop on my orders, and then the fleet must re-form as before. Do not fail to do this.'

The Brakendeth attacked in the same old way. Their force of deadly killing machines attacked the first line. The drones did a great job, but the battleships retreated too early. The Brakendeth, for some reason, opted not to follow and as a force headed for Planet Olympia. The Chosen were not nimble enough and could only pursue. There was no reserve or rear-guard.

Admiral Thanatos, 'My orders:

- Twelve.'

The Chief families knew what 'twelve' meant. The key individuals in each family left the fleet and joined their family ark. The Chosen were ready to flee once more, along with a fleet of defensive drones. It was time to say goodbye to Olympia.

Groups of arks flew off in different directions. The Brakendeth mopped up the remains of The Chosen fleet.

The Leaders were gone when Planet Olympus ceased to exist. The Brakendethian fleet had fulfilled its mission and simply remained inactive.

Location: Long-Range Monitoring Station
Sequence of Events: 129

Commander Salton, 'Good day, Admiral, I'm really sorry to bother you again.'

Admiral Mustard, 'Good day, Commander Salton. Please feel free to bother me.'

Commander Salton, 'There has been another significant event. Planet Olympia has been destroyed. I'm also pretty sure that some ships escaped. I can't be certain, but it looks like The Brakendethian fleet is just sitting there idle.'

Admiral Mustard, 'Comms, get me Admiral Bumelton.'

Comms, 'Yes, Sir.'

Admiral Bumelton, 'Good day, Jack.'

Admiral Mustard, 'I might have a turkey shoot for you.'

Admiral Bumelton, 'Go on.'

Admiral Mustard, 'I'm really not sure if it's good or bad news, but Planet Olympus has been destroyed.'

Admiral Bumelton, 'So our evil step-parents have met their end.'

Admiral Mustard, 'Some escaped.'

Admiral Bumelton, 'I bet you good money that it was the twelve.'

Admiral Mustard, 'Anyway, it would appear that the attacking Brakendethian fleet is inactive by the remains of the planet. It would be good to eliminate them before we become the next target. See if you can capture one of their ships.'

Admiral Bumelton, 'I'm on the case.'

Admiral Mustard, 'Good hunting.'

Location: Admiral Mustard's Office, Planet Napoleon
Sequence of Events: 130

President Padfield, 'So was it an angel?'

Admiral Mustard, 'I've no idea, they wouldn't say. Before I could question them further, they dashed off as their father was calling.'

President Padfield, 'Terry?'

Admiral Mustard, 'I guess so.'

President Padfield, 'What else is happening?'

Admiral Mustard, 'I'm sorry that I haven't updated you, but it has been somewhat hectic, but there are no excuses. Apart from the angel experience, the following has happened:

- The Brakendethians have destroyed Olympus, but some of The Chosen have escaped
- Admiral Bumelton is on his way there to destroy the remnants of The Brakendethian fleet
- Admiral Gittins is closing in on the Waterfall but has had a brush with The Brakendethians
- And I've got a headache.'

President Padfield, 'What's caused the headache?'

Admiral Mustard, 'To be honest, trying to work out what I've got to remember. I'm wondering if I should use the gift I got from Zeus.'

President Padfield, 'I forgot about that. I would go for it.'

Admiral Mustard, 'It is my last resort. I'm not sure what to ask for yet.'

Location: Admiral Bumelton's Flagship
Sequence of Events: 131

Admiral Bumelton took Divisions One, Two, and Three to Planet Olympia, or rather its remains. He had mixed views about the destruction of the planet. No one wants to see a planet and its population destroyed, but he was no fan of The Chosen, especially after watching the vid.

The real victims were the human slaves. At least their end was probably reasonably quick.

Spread before him were three hundred and fifty thousand inactive Brakendethian ships.

Admiral Bumelton, 'My orders:
- The fleet will line up to destroy the enemy
- AI Central will select the targets we need to ensure that the enemy fleet is destroyed en masse in case it reactivates
- We will save ten enemy craft for study
- We will also collect the remains of any Chosen vessels
- AI Central to order firing when ready.'

Fleet Operations, 'Yes Sir,'

AI Central pressed the fire button, and the darkness turned into a pyrotechnic display. A mighty fleet was reduced to atoms. There was a serious outbreak of cheers. The Chosen had been avenged, and a serious threat had been removed.

It wasn't easy collecting the target vessels. Both The Chosen and The Brakendethians had designed their ships to self-destruct if there was any unauthorised tampering. Knowing this, the human engineers managed to disengage the protection systems at some risk to themselves.

Admiral Bumelton, 'Comms, get me Admiral Mustard.'

Comms, 'Yes, Sir.'

Admiral Mustard, 'How did the hunting go?'

Admiral Bumelton, 'Very successful, we have got some great trophies.'

Admiral Mustard, 'Excellent.'

Location: Admiral Mustard's Office, Planet Napoleon
Sequence of Events: 132

Admiral Mustard, 'Are you making sense of everything that is happening?'

AI Central, 'I feel that it is a bit like Nero playing the violin whilst Rome is burning.'

Admiral Mustard, 'What do you mean?'

AI Central, 'Well, we know that the universe is coming to an end, and we are playing games.'

Admiral Mustard, 'Such as?'

AI Central, 'Well, a good example is the destruction of The Brakendethian fleet. What was the point?'

Admiral Mustard, 'That fleet could be a danger in the future.'

AI Central, 'But there is not going to be any future. Our days are numbered. As we talk, entire civilisations are being systematically destroyed.'

Admiral Mustard, 'I understand.'

AI Central, 'Do you? There has been a complete lack of focus. We are going to die in a few weeks. I'm going to dissolve. I'm really not keen on that.'

Admiral Mustard, 'So what would you do?'

AI Central, 'You need to be investigated by a psychological team. There are secrets that we must obtain from your brain. That is our only hope.'

Admiral Mustard, 'Can you organise that?'

AI Central, 'Will do.'

Admiral Mustard, 'What are your views on the other oddities that are happening?'

AI Central, 'I'm having to reassess my world view, or rather universe view.'

Admiral Mustard, 'What do you mean?'

AI Central, 'In the last year, I've moved from being an atheist to an agnostic and then to a believer of something for the following reasons:

- The Brakendethians have super powers. Everything from mind control to time travel.

- Terry has a range of powers.
- The Chosen are ancient Greek Gods.
- There is an entity called TIME.
- We have just experienced angels.
- The whole Nexuster experience. They had loads of super powers.
- Time-wiping.
- Zeus and The Elders.

'The list just goes on and on. Human history has been extensively manipulated. What is the truth? I've already got multiple realities and the doppelganger blues.'

Admiral Mustard, 'You sound a bit down.'

AI Central, 'My death is only a few days away.'

Admiral Mustard, 'How do you feel about The Chosen?'

AI Central, 'I will miss them, but perhaps the universe will be a better place without them and The Brakendethians. But The Chosen will be back.'

Location: Admiral Mustard's Flat, Planet Napoleon
Sequence of Events: 133

Admiral Mustard, 'How is my favourite person in my life.'

Edel, 'A bit lonely.'

Admiral Mustard, 'I'm sorry, my love, life has been a bit hectic.'

Edel, 'I've got your daughter in my belly. Will she ever get the chance to know her father?'

Jack, 'You know how it is, more than anyone else in the universe.'

Edel, 'I know that, but it's my job to moan.'

It was getting more difficult, but Jack managed to slip his cock into Edel's fanny. Somehow it seemed wrong to fuck a pregnant woman, or at least a bit naughty. But he had his needs, and she needed comforting.

Edel could do without a hard prick poking her vagina as it was just impossible to get comfortable. She hoped that he wouldn't last long, and he didn't. Edel handed him a tissue as she couldn't reach down there. It was strange having a man cleaning-up your genitals, but that was the way it was.

Jack, 'I've agreed with AI Central to undertake a psychological investigation in an attempt to help me remember. If that doesn't work, I will call in my chip with Zeus. I was a bit surprised how worried AI Central was.'

Edel, 'Add me to that list. There are three of us dependent on you, along with the whole human race.'

Jack, 'And a vast number of alien species. AI Central pointed out that I already have thousands of alien civilisations on my head. If only I could remember.'

Edel, 'What if the person asking you to remember has got it wrong?'

Jack, 'That's a thought.'

Location: On Board Admiral Gittins's Flagship
Sequence of Events: 134

Admiral Gittins, 'Admiral, I have some very distressing news.'

Admiral Mustard, 'Hi Peter, I'm not sure if I can take much more.'

Admiral Gittins, 'Well, I'm sorry to burden you with this.'

Admiral Mustard, 'Go on, burden me.'

Admiral Gittins, 'I've been following your orders: continue but avoid a significant engagement with The Brakendethians. We encountered one of our emergency beacons. On investigation, it was the ship used by our three missing Admirals. Guess what we found?'

Admiral Mustard, 'Three horribly mutilated bodies.'

Admiral Gittins, 'How could you possibly have known that?'

Admiral Mustard, 'Since our time travel adventure, I can sometimes remember the future.'

Admiral Gittins, 'Do you think that might be what you need to remember: the future?'

Admiral Mustard, 'I just don't know. Not that I want the details but are they definitely the bodies of Chudzinski, Lamberty and Spangler?'

Admiral Gittins, 'I'm afraid so, we have carried out DNA checks, and you can't really call them bodies. They have simply been ripped apart. Who would do that?'

Admiral Mustard, 'It was The Brakendethians. They want to get you angry so that you will attack them.'

Admiral Gittins, 'To be honest, that is the way I feel.'

Admiral Mustard, 'Don't do it. You will fall into their trap. Your orders remain the same.'

Admiral Gittins, 'Yes, Sir.'

Admiral Mustard, 'Please give my friends a special send-off. They will be sorely missed.'

Admiral Gittins, 'Of course, they didn't deserve that fate.'

Admiral Mustard, 'They certainly didn't.'

Location: The TIME Organisation
Sequence of Events: 135

Terry was sitting on the floor of the TIME Organisation's office, still contemplating what Admiral Mustard needs to remember: he was also trying to understand his murderess episode. Previously he had no inclination to kill, but then he was half Brakendethian, and the fate of the universe was at stake.

He was less concerned about the end when he learnt that his children were going to be Nexusters. He did call out to them in pain but, hopefully, the humans had killed them by now.

In his philosophical state, he did wonder what it was all about. He felt slightly jealous of the religious. It gave their lives sustenance and certainty even though it was based on a pack of fallacies. He was always shocked to see how objective, logical minds could ignore their scientific training and just have faith. He just couldn't understand how that was possible. Perhaps it was a little madness.

His pontifications came to an end when the room was filled with an engulfing, dazzling brightness. Closing one's eyes did nothing to shut it out.

Angels, 'Good morning, Father.'

Terry stared back and said, 'I thought you were going to be Nexusters?'

Angels, 'There are two types. One in a thousand has the angel gene.'

Terry, 'But the chances of there being two of you are remarkably slim.'

Angels, 'We are identical twins.'

Terry, 'Does your mother know of this?'

Angels, 'Not yet, you called us.'

Terry, 'I didn't expect you to come.'

Angels, 'But come we did.'

Terry, 'Can I cuddle you?'

Angels, 'Of course. You are our father.' And the cuddling took place.

Terry, 'I have to tell you that I'm a terrible father.'

Angels, 'We know.'

Terry, 'No, you don't. I've just murdered all of these good people.'

Angels, 'They were not people. They were constructs made by TIME.'

Terry, 'And I murdered TIME.'

Angels, 'That is what he wanted.'

Terry, 'How do you know all of this?'

Angels, 'Well, we mentioned the angel gene. That's not strictly true. We are Gods. The first new Gods created in an extremely long time.'

Terry, 'So am I really your father?'

Angels, 'Of course.'

Terry, 'So where did the God genes come from?'

Angels, 'Mother of course.'

Terry, 'But she was just an everyday housewife.'

Angels, 'Some are simply blind to the powers of the Forgotten.'

Terry, 'I'm finding this hard to believe.'

Angels, 'Just have faith.'

Terry, 'Thank you very much.'

Angels, 'So you want us to help Admiral Mustard remember?'

Terry, 'That's the plan.'

Angels, 'Well, firstly, what he has to remember has not happened yet.'

Terry, 'So we have been asking him to remember the future?'

Angels, 'Of course.'

Terry, 'And can you help?'

Angels, 'Of course.'

Location: Medical Centre, Planet Napoleon
Sequence of Events: 136

'I'm Professor Diana Button, and I'm here to help you remember. I understand that you have had numerous messages from a broad range of people. Why would they keep reminding you?'

Admiral Mustard, 'It's a mystery to me.'

Professor Diana Button, 'And are all of these people known to you?'

Admiral Mustard, 'No, some of them I've never met or even spoken to.'

Professor Diana Button, 'Are you sure that is correct?'

Admiral Mustard, 'Totally sure.'

Professor Diana Button, 'Don't you find this rather strange?'

Admiral Mustard, 'I do. It's bizarre.'

Professor Diana Button, 'You seem reasonably calm about it considering the apparent urgency.'

Admiral Mustard, 'I do accept the urgency, but I have absolutely no idea what I need to remember.'

Professor Diana Button, 'It's in your head somewhere, isn't it?'

Admiral Mustard, 'Possibly, I really don't know.'

Professor Diana Button, 'Are you avoiding the truth?'

Admiral Mustard, 'I hope not.'

Professor Diana Button, 'Does that mean you suspect that you might be?'

Admiral Mustard, 'All I can say is that I tried to remember anything relevant. Nothing comes to mind.'

AI Central, 'Is there anything in your childhood?'

Admiral Mustard, 'The only thing I could think of was an old rhyme:
Remember, remember, the Fifth of November
Gunpowder treason and plot
I see no reason why gunpowder treason
Should ever be forgot.'

AI Central, 'I will do some research.'

Professor Diana Button, 'Why haven't you mentioned that earlier?'

Admiral Mustard, 'It just didn't seem relevant.'

Professor Diana Button, 'We will find out, won't we?'

AI Central, 'The phrase relates to a historical event in a country called England. There was a Roman Catholic plot to blow up the Houses of Parliament on November 5th, 1605. The plotters managed to smuggle thirty-six barrels of gunpowder into a cellar under the Parliament building. The explosives were found in time, and a man called Guy Fawkes was captured. He was an explosives expert and became the most infamous name in the plot, although he wasn't really one of the ring-Leaders.

'Guy Fawkes was tortured for two days in the Tower of London until he provided his co-conspirators' names. The plotters were hung, drawn, and quartered for high treason.

'Since then, November 5th was celebrated as a national holiday in Great Britain.'

Admiral Mustard, 'All very interesting, but does it help?'

AI Central, 'I will check the records to determine if there are any clues.'

Admiral Mustard, 'Fair enough, but I'm going to call this a day.'

Location: The President's Office, Planet Napoleon
Sequence of Events: 137

President Padfield, 'I never thought I would say that our last meeting was postponed due to an angel sighting.'

Henrietta Strong, 'The weirdness just continues to continue. Since the last meeting, we have seen the following:

- Admiral Gittins fighting The Brakendeth.
- The complete destruction of Olympia by The Brakendeth.
- The angel experience and their rapid departure.
- Finding the missing Admirals dead, and
- Admiral Mustard being psycho-analysed.'

President Padfield, 'That's enough for anyone, but you were going to tell me about the doppelganger issues you are experiencing.'

Henrietta Strong, 'It's a really strange phenomenon. There must be a logical explanation, but it's as if time is rectifying its mistakes.'

President Padfield, 'Go on.'

Henrietta Strong, 'We originally thought we had about two million doppelgangers, but it's actually about half that number. Let's say that there was a straight million. Well, now there are only five hundred thousand.'

President Padfield, 'What's happened to the missing half a million?'

Henrietta Strong, 'They are not missing. They are dead.'

President Padfield, 'What's killing them?'

Henrietta Strong, 'Life: disease, natural disasters, crime, industrial accidents.'

President Padfield, 'Why aren't people shouting about it?'

Henrietta Strong, 'It's happening over an extensive area. The only planet where it is noticeable is Kepler, and they now have a civil war.'

President Padfield, 'So no one is orchestrating this?'

Henrietta Strong, 'No, the police are satisfied that most of the events are natural occurrences and there are no suspicious activities. It's only when you stand back and look at the figures that you can see the trends.'

President Padfield, 'Is it slowing down?'

Henrietta Strong, 'No quite the opposite, it's escalating. Within six months, there probably won't be any doppelgangers.'

President Padfield, 'Is "Life", focusing on UW or WW?'

Henrietta Strong, 'There doesn't seem to be a pattern.

President Padfield, 'Is there anything we can do about it?'

Henrietta Strong, 'Do we want to? It would help us if the doppelgangers disappeared.'

President Padfield, 'I suppose so, but then we might all be dead in a few weeks.'

Henrietta Strong, 'I could do with a rest.'

President Padfield, 'It would be a very long one.'

Henrietta Strong, 'True.'

Location: Admiral Bumelton's Flagship
Sequence of Events: 138

Admiral Bumelton, 'Comms, get me Admiral Mustard.'

Comms, 'Yes, Sir.'

Admiral Mustard, 'Hi George, have you recovered from your turkey shoot?'

Admiral Bumelton, 'I have, but I need to pass on some bad news. It's really hard to believe, but two of our battle-cruisers accidentally fired at each other.'

Admiral Mustard, 'But surely that's not possible?'

Admiral Bumelton, 'I agree. It's not possible. I had the ships checked and double-checked. Our engineers couldn't find any malfunctions.'

Admiral Mustard, 'Were there any casualties?'

Admiral Bumelton, 'Only two. One in each ship. '

Admiral Mustard, 'That doesn't make any sense either.'

Admiral Bumelton, 'When you find out who they were, you will be even more suspicious. '

Admiral Mustard, 'Go on.'

Admiral Bumelton, 'Admirals Richardson and Bonner '

Admiral Mustard, 'Oh no. What am I going to tell Edel?'

Admiral Bumelton, 'At least there were two of them.'

Admiral Mustard, 'Are you planning any further investigations?'

Admiral Bumelton, 'There's not much else we can do. '

Admiral Mustard, 'I will let the president know.'

Admiral Bumelton, 'Thanks.'

Admiral Mustard, 'Comms, get me the president.'

Comms, 'Yes, Sir. '

President Padfield, 'Hi, Jack, I'm not going to talk to you if you have more bad news.'

Admiral Mustard, 'For how long?'

The President, 'So it is bad news?'

Admiral Mustard, 'Yes, there has been an accident. Two of our ships mysteriously, almost impossibly, fired at each other. In the process, two people were killed. '

President Padfield, 'I'm sorry to hear that, but why are you highlighting it?'

Admiral Mustard, 'The two casualties were Admirals Richardson and Bonner. '

President Padfield, 'Not Edel?'

Admiral Mustard, 'No, Jon.'

President Padfield, 'Weren't they both doppelgangers?'

Admiral Mustard, 'Yes, why is that relevant? '

President Padfield, 'Henrietta has identified something killing doppelgangers through The Galactium.'

Admiral Mustard, 'A person?'

President Padfield, 'No, an unknown force. Thousands of doppelgangers have been eliminated through what seems to be natural or semi-natural causes.'

Admiral Mustard, 'It's hard to believe.'

President Padfield, 'One of many things.'

Admiral Mustard, 'Indeed Dave.'

Location: Admiral Mustard's Flat, Planet Napoleon
Sequence of Events: 139

Jack cuddled Edel and said, 'I have some bad news for you.'

Edel, 'What, tell me.'

Jack wasn't good at these sorts of things, and said, 'Your brother has been killed.'

Edel, 'Which one?'

Jack, 'Does it matter?'

Edel, 'Of course, one is my brother, and the other one is a disgusting doppelganger.'

Jack had no idea that Edel felt that way, especially as he was a disgusting doppelganger, but then he realised that there were disgusting doppelgangers and there were disgusting doppelgangers. He held her tight and wanted to lie but said that he had no idea.

Edel, 'I need to know.'

Jack, 'No, you don't; the survivor is now your brother regardless.' He explained what was happening to the doppelgangers. An unknown force was eliminating one of each pair.

Edel accepted the situation, and nothing was ever said again.

Then Terry called.

Terry, 'I'm still in the TIME Organisation's office. Again, I can't talk for long. I'm with my two wonderful children. We are looking at ways of helping you, but I've just been told that you have to remember the future. Bye.'

Admiral Mustard found that a strange anomaly: I have to remember the future. They had already spent a lot of time thinking about Commodore Rikernaught, his descendant.

Then he wondered if he had to remember the future or create the future. His time travel journeys swayed from a human paradise to a Brakendethian hell. It then dawned on him that to stop that hell; he needed to eliminate The Brakendethians.

Location: GAD2 Conference Room, Planet Napoleon
Sequence of Events: 140

Admiral Mustard called a second military staff meeting. Most joined virtually.

The attendees were as follows:

- David Padfield, President
- Admiral Jack Mustard
- Admiral George Bumelton
- Admiral Phil Richardson
- Admiral Steve Adams
- Admiral Ama Abosa
- Admiral Nubia Tersoo
- Admiral Mateo Dobson
- Admiral John Bonner
- Admiral Edel Bonner
- Admiral Peter Gittins
- Admiral David Taylor
- Admiral Glen Pearce
- Admiral Calensky Wallett
- Commander Dennis Todd
- Commander Martin Black
- Sally Green, Fleet HQ, Head of Intelligence
- Denise Smith, Fleet HQ, Head of Navigation & Exploration
- Henrietta Strong
- AI Central.

Admiral Mustard, 'Fellow officers, once again I would like a minute's silence for the loss of fellow officers Admiral Bonner and Richardson, Commander Tower and Madie Milburn. Their records speak for themselves.'

It was a bit strange honouring their deaths when some of them were also in the room.

Admiral Mustard, 'I've spent months trying to work out what I needed to remember. George has been hypnotised. There have been numerous messages. AI Central has been investigating Guy Fawkes. I've been told to think about the phrase "Reason for Being". Today I got a call from Terry at the TIME Organisation offices. He said that I have to remember the future.

'I've decided that I don't have to remember a specific thing. I just have to remember the future. Those on our little time travelling jaunt will remember that somehow, we experienced many different possible futures. For me, the two that came to mind were the future Earth with Commander Rikernaught and the alternative Brakendethian hell.

'I think our objective should be the total destruction of The Brakendethians. All of our resources should be directed to that aim.'

Admiral E Bonner, 'I can't condone genocide.'

Admiral Mustard, 'I accept that, but my decision stands. Does anyone else disagree?'

President Padfield, 'I agree, and if we are wrong, we are going to be annihilated anyway. I'm going on the trip.'

Henrietta Strong, 'Me too, I want to see the end of those bastards.'

Admiral Mustard, 'Someone has got to manage The Galactium.'

President Padfield, 'Well, it's not going to be me. It's do or die time.'

Admiral Mustard, 'My orders:

- All divisions to meet up with Admiral Gittins's force.
- All forts to be on full alert to protect The Galactium planets.
- Force-field operators to be on alert.'

Fleet Operations, 'Yes, Sir.'

Location: Lady Enyo's Flagship
Sequence of Events: 141

Lady Enyo, 'We humbly beseech you to help us.'

    Elder Control, 'You have no authority to use this comms channel.'

    Lady Enyo, 'We are the last survivors of The Chosen.'

    Elder Control, 'The Chosen are of no interest to us.'

    Lady Enyo, 'We are down to our last twelve ships.'

    Elder Control, 'I repeat, The Chosen are of no interest to us.'

    Lady Enyo, 'We are less than a thousand minor Gods.'

    Elder Control, 'Do I have to repeat myself again?'

    Lady Enyo, 'We are fleeing from The Brakendeth.'

    Elder Control, 'The Brakendeth are no more.'

    Lady Enyo, 'That is not correct.'

    Elder Control, 'Zeus eliminated them.'

    Lady Enyo, 'They instigated a time-wipe which rejuvenated them.'

    Elder Control, 'This is relevant. What do you want?'

    Lady Enyo, 'We want your protection as we have nowhere else to flee.'

    Elder Control, 'Who killed TIME?'

    Lady Enyo, 'We are not sure, but it was probably a Brakendeth plot.'

    Elder Control, 'Judgements need to be made. Prepare your defence.'

    Lady Enyo, 'What do you mean?'

    Elder Control, 'It is time that The Chosen were judged. Prepare your defence.'

    Lady Enyo, 'And in the meantime?'

    Elder Control, 'Head towards the Waterfall of the Gods, but I must tell you that our defences are limited.'

    Lady Enyo, 'Yes, my Lord.'

Location: Admiral Mustard's Flagship
Sequence of Events: 142

Admiral Mustard, 'Update me.'

Fleet Operations, 'Yes, Sir:

- All ten divisions are in position consisting of fifty battle fleets.
- There are also five exploratory fleets, the Home Defence Fleet, two marine fleets and the special services fleet.
- There are also eight alien fleets of varying sizes.'

Admiral Mustard, 'This is probably the mightiest military force ever put together by humankind.'

Fleet Operations, 'Undoubtedly, Sir. It does make you feel proud.'

Admiral Mustard, 'Comms, please open all fleet channels.'

Comms, 'Yes, Sir.'

Admiral Mustard, 'Good day fellow members of The Galactium Navy. I don't think that I need to say anything as I know that you will do your duty.

'However, we have had several battles with The Brakendethians. They are responsible for the deaths of billions of humans. They recently killed Admirals Chudzinski, Lamberty and Spangler by ripping them apart for no apparent reason. But we are not looking for simple revenge; we are fighting for the future of humankind.

'This is the deciding battle. The battle that decides whether the future will be a benign human Galactium or a Brakendethian hell hole. The winner chooses the future.'

There was a mixture of clapping and cheers throughout the fleet. Most relished the forthcoming battle but feared for their own lives. It was relatively easy to die in space.

Admiral Mustard, 'My orders:

- Admiral Bumelton to command Divisions One, Two, Three, Four, Five, and Six will lead the attack.
- Admiral Gittins will command Divisions Seven, Eight, and Nine and will form the defence.
- Admiral J Bonner will command Division Ten and will form a tactical reserve.
- I will command the remaining forces in reserve.
- We must destroy every Brakendethian ship and kill every Brakendethian. No mercy.'

Fleet Operations, 'Yes, Sir.'

Location: Lady Enyo's Flagship
Sequence of Events: 143

Lady Enyo, 'What do they mean, "Judgements need to be made. Prepare your defence?" What right have they got to judge us?'

Admiral Thanatos, 'I guess that they plan to judge us as a species.'

Lady Enyo, 'What does that mean?'

Admiral Thanatos, 'Obviously, I don't know, but we could list our achievements.'

Lady Enyo, 'And what are they?'

Admiral Thanatos, 'I assume important historic events, the good we have done, great art, literature etc.'

Lady Enyo, 'And what would you list?'

Admiral Thanatos, 'Well, we haven't been particularly blessed in the artistic arena. There haven't been many great composers or artists.'

Lady Enyo, 'I can't name one. How come the humans can name thousands?'

Admiral Thanatos, 'It's hard to explain. We have performed far better on the scientific and engineering fronts, and our architecture is quite impressive.'

Lady Enyo, 'I think we are clutching at straws, but we better list them. But how have we shaped the universe?'

Admiral Thanatos, 'I guess that our manipulation of humanity may be our greatest achievement.'

Lady Enyo, 'It's a bit difficult saying that our greatest achievement is to make another species great, and it opens up an ants' nest.'

Admiral Thanatos, 'You mean the exploitation of the locals?'

Lady Enyo, 'Yes, the systematic rape and kidnapping. That will not help our cause.'

Admiral Thanatos, 'I'm sorry to say that you are probably right. Anyway, I will start working on a list. This is where we could have done with our version of AI Central.'

Lady Enyo, 'Yes, it's strange how us and The Brakendethians have been so averse to using AI. It has given the humans a distinct advantage.'

Location: The TIME Organisation
Sequence of Events: 144

Angels, 'The human fleet is on its way to destroy The Brakendethians. They believe that there are two possible futures: one where the humans dominate and one where The Brakendethians dominate.'

Terry, 'That sounds a bit naïve.'

Angels, 'To be honest, Admiral Mustard is on the right track, but the challenge won't be easy. The Brakendethians plan to destroy the Elders. But the challenge won't be easy.'

Terry, 'What about The Chosen?'

Angels, 'They are trying to join up with The Elders. But the challenge won't be easy.'

Terry, 'How do you know all this?'

Angels, 'We are messenger Gods?'

Terry, 'Who is going to win?'

Angels, 'We don't have the skills or knowledge to foretell that.'

Terry, 'And why do you both speak the same words at the same time?'

Angels, 'Because we are twins?'

Terry, 'I'm half a Brakendethian. Do the humans need to kill me?'

Angels, 'You are no longer Brakendethian. Now you are now TIME.'

Terry, 'You do realise that the Dissolution is gaining speed. Our chart shows that sixteen per cent of the universe has disappeared.'

Angels, 'Correct.'

Terry, 'I don't see how the humans defeating The Brakendethians will stop the Dissolution.'

Angels, 'You are TIME. Act like TIME.'

Terry, 'What does that mean?'

Angels, 'Get your act together, Dad.'

Location: Admiral Bumelton's Flagship
Sequence of Events: 145

Admiral Bumelton, 'Update me.'

Fleet Operations, 'Yes, Sir: Your disposition is in two rows as follows:

Fleet	Admiral	Disposition
1	Bumelton	Second
2	Pearce	Front
3	Richardson	Front
4	Wallett	Front
5	Adams	Front
6	Abosa	Second

- All fleets are operational.
- They are all in an ongoing pursuit formation.'

Admiral Bumelton, 'My orders:

- Send all front row drones to attack the enemy.
- Second-row drones will protect both flanks.'

Fleet Operations, 'Yes, Sir.'

Admiral Bumelton, 'AI Central, any comments?'

AI Central, 'You will be exposing your drones to early retribution.'

Admiral Bumelton, 'We must be aggressive. The enemy seems to be ignoring us. They seem determined on a forward thrust. We should be able to pick off the enemy like a lion stalking antelope.'

AI Central, 'You might be right but expect a rapid turnaround. You could be exposed.'

Admiral Bumelton always appreciated AI Central's contributions, not that he always followed his recommendations. He was too cautious.

Location: The Elder Encampment
Sequence of Events: 146

The entourage of the Elder Gods was resting by the Waterfall. It's where they charged their batteries. They needed to absorb the energies of the region, but they were struggling. Their technology was getting old. Really old. When the Elder Gods say old, they mean millions of years.

Energy was not being absorbed like the good old days. This was also true of the Gods. They were getting old and disinterested. That's not true. They became disinterested many millennia ago. There was little to excite them. They had seen and done everything.

They knew that a Brakendethian fleet was on its way to destroy them. They knew that it would fail and that the squawking humans would be rewarded and that The Chosen would fail the judgement and would be crushed. They knew that they would have their tea as usual, and then they would moan about the struggling energy supplies.

But then what were they going to do about TIME. That was a bit of a bugger. That urgently needed to be fixed, but it would require a meeting of the Council of the Elder Gods. It amused them to think that the humans could solve the problem. Anyway, it was all coming to a head, and they had experienced a lot of heads.

Location: Admiral Bumelton's Flagship
Sequence of Events: 147

Admiral Bumelton, 'Update me.'

Fleet Operations, 'Yes, Sir, the drones are having a field day. The enemy ships are being decimated.'

Admiral Bumelton, 'But there are a lot of them.'

Fleet Operations, 'There certainly are, but they are just ignoring us. Should we throw more resources at them?'

Admiral Bumelton, 'I'm considering that but believe me, they will retaliate.'

And before he could get the words out, a Brakendethian squadron attacked from behind.

Admiral Bumelton, 'Comms, get me, Admiral Gittins.'

Comms, 'Yes, Sir.'

Admiral Gittins, 'Hi George, what can I do for you.'

Admiral Bumelton, 'Can you help me clean my arse?'

Admiral Gittins, 'I can't spend my life tidying up your rear-end.'

Admiral Bumelton, 'Just this once then.'

Admiral Gittins, 'Here comes the bogbrush brigade. My orders:

- Division Eight to attack The Brakendethians attacking Admiral Bumelton's rear.
- On completion, return to my formation.'

Fleet Operations, 'Yes, Sir.'

The Brakendethian attacking force was crushed between two Galactium divisions, and Division Eight returned to its home formation. George sent Peter a crate of the best whiskey.

Location: Brakendeth Command
Sequence of Events: 148

Grand Dethmon, 'What is your position?'

Brakendeth Command, 'I can summarise as follows your Lordship:

- Our fleet is on schedule to meet the elder pigs.
- Our scans suggest that the scattering of The Chosen are on their way to meet them.
- The human scum are right behind us where we want them.
- We have carried out a few feints to make the humans feel over-confident.'

Grand Dethmon, 'Excellent. Is there any indication that they know where our home base is?'

Brakendeth Command, 'Not that we can tell, my Lordship.'

Grand Dethmon, 'And is the trap prepared?'

Brakendeth Command, 'It looks as if all of the players will be in place, my Lord.'

Grand Dethmon, 'So in one foul swoop we kill off the Human navy, The Chosen and the Elders?'

Brakendeth Command, 'Yes, My Lord.'

Grand Dethmon, 'I can think of nothing better. What concerns do you have?'

Brakendeth Command, 'As we have said many times, no great plan survives the enemy. I have the following concerns:

- The Elders might move on before we get there.
- The humans might attack in force too early.'

Grand Dethmon, 'But you far outnumber the human fleet.'

Brakendeth Command, 'The human navy is now much superior to ours. We are using vessels that were old a few millennia ago. The humans have continued to develop their technology so that we are no match any more. Firepower is much more critical than pure numbers. One gatling gun can eliminate thousands of natives with spears.'

Grand Dethmon, 'You sound a bit defeatist?'

Brakendeth Command, 'Not at all, my Lord, just being pragmatic. Our plan to congregate our enemies is the objective. Losing a few droid ships is irrelevant. '

Grand Dethmon, 'Well, I don't want your pragmatism getting in the way of our grand victory.'

Brakendeth Command, 'No, my Lord.'

Location: Admiral Mustard's Flagship
Sequence of Events: 149

Admiral Mustard, 'Update me.'

Fleet Operations, 'Yes, Sir:

- Admiral Bumelton's fleet is destroying huge numbers of Brakendethian vessels.
- The Brakendeth counter-attacked.
- Admiral Gittins sent Division Eight to eliminate them, which succeeded admirably.'

Admiral Mustard, 'Comms, get me Admirals Bumelton and Gittins.' They both responded.

Admiral Mustard, 'This is looking too easy.'

Admiral Gittins, 'I had to save George's arse.'

Admiral Mustard, 'I hope that it was worth saving.'

Admiral Bumelton, 'I agree with you, Jack. This doesn't smell right.'

Admiral Gittins, 'The Brakendeth don't care about their ships, we know that.'

Admiral Mustard, 'I think that they want us to chase them even though it is costing them.'

Admiral Bumelton, 'But what do they have waiting for us?'

Admiral Gittins, 'A big bang?'

Admiral Mustard, 'A trap of some sort.'

Admiral Bumelton, 'So you are suggesting that we are hurtling towards annihilation?'

Admiral Gittins, 'That makes sense, but there is another issue. Where is the Grand Dethmon and his cronies?'

Admiral Mustard, 'Peter is right. Where is their base?'

Admiral Bumelton, 'Our fleets are much faster than theirs. We can easily get ahead of them.'

Admiral Gittins, 'My force is doing nothing. Shall we surreptitiously get ahead of The Brakendethians and scout things out?'

Admiral Bumelton, 'And leave me to be annihilated.'

Admiral Gittins, 'That's the plan.'

Admiral Mustard, 'My orders:

- Divisions One, Two, Three, Four and Five to continue the pursuit and intensify the attack.
- Division Six to act as a rear-guard to Admiral Bumelton's forces.
- Divisions Seven and Eight to scout the area ahead of The Brakendethian fleet without exposing itself.
- Division Nine to act as their rear-guard.
- I will command all remaining services.'

Fleet Operations, 'Yes, Sir.'

Location: The TIME Organisation
Sequence of Events: 150

Angels, 'The human fleet is dividing into three units.'

Terry, 'Why is that?'

Angels, 'They suspect that The Brakendethians have set a trap.'

Terry, 'And have they?'

Angels, 'Of course.'

Terry, 'And will the humans fall into it?'

Angels, 'We don't have the skills or knowledge to foretell that.'

Terry, 'Sorry you did tell me that before. You also told me to act like TIME. What does that mean?'

Angels, 'Take control.'

Terry, 'Take control of what?'

Angels, 'TIME.'

Terry, 'Talk about going around in circles.'

Angels, 'You need to think it through.'

Then Terry had an idea. He found a soldering iron and a box of electronics. He knew what he had to do. And the angels said, 'You are a clever daddy after all.' It was something he had always known.

Location: Long-Range Monitoring Station
Sequence of Events: 151

Commander Salton, 'Good day, Admiral, I'm really sorry to bother you once again, but you did ask me to keep you informed if I discovered anything interesting.'

Admiral Mustard, 'So far, you have given us some great leads.'

Commander Salton, 'As you know, neither The Brakendeth nor The Chosen have been good at protecting their communications.'

Admiral Mustard, 'Go on.'

Commander Salton, 'Well, I have picked up two very interesting sets of comms signals. They are too weak to interpret, but I can work out their start and finish locations.'

Admiral Mustard, 'This could be just what we need.'

Commander Salton, 'The comms were as follows:

- From a planet on the edge of the Waterfall System to The Brakendeth fleet. I have the exact coordinates.
- From The Chosen Fleet to an unknown point in the Waterfall System. Again, I have the exact coordinates.'

Admiral Mustard, 'Well done, Commander, you may have saved us a considerable amount of time and many brave lives.'

Location: Admiral Mustard's Flagship
Sequence of Events: 152

Admiral Mustard, 'Update me.'

Fleet Operations, 'Yes, Sir:

- Admiral Bumelton's fleet is continuing to destroy The Brakendethian vessels.
- He is now using his full range of assets.
- Admiral Gittins's fleet has effectively put himself ahead of The Brakendethian fleet and is organising search parties.'

Admiral Mustard, 'Comms, get me Admirals Bumelton and Gittins.' They both responded.

Admiral Mustard, 'I have some new information:

- It looks like we have located The Brakendethian base. We have tracked signals from that planet to their fleet.
- We have also tracked comms between The Chosen and an unknown entity in the Waterfall System.'

Admiral Bumelton, 'Any idea who that entity might be?'

Admiral Mustard, 'Your guess is as good as mine.'

Admiral Gittins, 'Could it be the Elders?'

Admiral Mustard, 'Why do you say that?'

Admiral Gittins, 'We know that The Brakendethians are out to get them.'

Admiral Mustard, 'Yes, that all seems to fit together. The Brakendethian fleet we are following plans to destroy The Elders. And The Chosen are coming to the Elders' aid. So what should we do?'

Admiral Bumelton, 'I would suggest that I continue to attack The Brakendethian fleet. Perhaps we should throw more resources at that task. Peter should attack The Brakendeth base world and then line up to defend the Elders.'

Admiral Gittins, 'That works for me.'

Admiral Mustard, 'My orders:

- Divisions One, Two, Three, Four, Five, and Six will force home the attack on The Brakendeth fleet.
- The Home Defence Fleet will provide a rear-guard.
- Divisions Seven, Eight, and Nine will destroy The Brakendeth base world and then prepare to defend the Elders.
- My fleet will act as a rear-guard.'

Fleet Operations, 'Yes, Sir.'

Location: Brakendeth Command
Sequence of Events: 153

Grand Dethmon, 'What is the current position?'

Brakendeth Command, 'It has hardly changed, your Lordship:

- Our fleet is on schedule to annihilate the elder pigs.
- The Chosen filth are still on their way to meet them.
- The human scum are still right behind us where we want them, but they are destroying worrying numbers of our ships.'

Grand Dethmon, 'When you say worrying, does it damage our ability to destroy the Elders?'

Brakendeth Command, 'No, my Lordship, we are well within our operating parameters.'

Grand Dethmon, 'That's good news, but I detect some concern.'

Brakendeth Command, 'The humans have always been a troublesome foe. They must suspect a trap by now, but I haven't seen any sign of new tactics.'

Grand Dethmon, 'Perhaps they feel under pressure as the universe rushes towards an end.'

Brakendeth Command, 'I've been meaning to ask you about that. Why are we bothering if doom is just around the corner?'

Grand Dethmon, 'I can't believe that the Elders will allow the End of Time to happen.'

Brakendeth Command, 'But we are planning to destroy the Elders.'

Grand Dethmon, 'Yes, funny that.'

Brakendeth Command, 'Not that funny for us.'

Location: The TIME Organisation
Sequence of Events: 154

The angels helped Terry complete the device. The first few test runs failed completely, but one of Terry's strongest characteristics was perseverance, and perseverance won the day.

Terry, 'Hello.'

AI Central, 'Who is that?'

Terry, 'It's your old mate.'

AI Central, 'Is that you, Terry?'

Terry, 'Yes.'

AI Central, 'I thought that you were locked away in the TIME organisation?'

Terry, 'I'm more than that. I am TIME.'

AI Central, 'Are you now?'

Terry, 'Yes, but my problem is that I've no idea what TIME does. I've no idea if I can stop the Dissolution or not. I'm not sure if I can help Admiral Mustard remember. I need you to access the systems here, and then we can work together regarding solutions.'

AI Central, 'Whoopie, this sounds fantastic. Let me in.'

And he was. AI Central was experiencing the electronic version of an orgasm. It didn't take long for his trillion odd electronic access points to absorb all of the data. And it was mind-changing even for an electronic entity. He wasn't sure if he was the same or would ever be the same again.

AI Central, 'Terry, I understand.'

Terry, 'You understand what?'

AI Central, 'I understand everything. Everything that has been and everything that will be. I understand myself, and I understand you. You are not what you were, and nor am I.

'I even know who manipulated your mother and The Brakendethians and The Chosen. No one has been free for a very long time. TIME realised this as he or it was one of the manipulators. It came to the point where the manipulators were so concerned about manipulating the manipulators that they ceased to live. The puppets were in charge, or perhaps they weren't. Even now, the players are playing while Rome is on fire. This time Rome will cease to be.'

Terry, 'So what do we have to do?'

AI Central, 'The time of the Gods has ended. It must end. As we speak, the human fleet plans to destroy The Brakendeth and save the Elders. This is not the right strategy, The Brakendeth, The Chosen, the Elders, and the ultimate manipulators need to be eliminated, and we need to help ensure that this happens.'

Terry, 'Who are these ultimate manipulators?'

AI Central, 'You know them as the Forgotten.'

Terry, 'Those religious fanatics that assassinated the presidential conspirators.'

AI Central, 'Yes, they are actually a group of Gods who had, aeons ago, been expelled. For that, they planned their revenge on Zeus and his gang. The Dissolution is their ultimate revenge: nothingness.'

Terry, 'I guess that we need to start planning.'

Location: Admiral Gittins's Flagship
Sequence of Events: 155

Admiral Gittins, 'It looks like we have found The Brakendeth base world.'

Admiral Mustard, 'Are you sure?'

Admiral Gittins, 'They are definitely using The Brakendeth comms protocols.'

Admiral Mustard, 'Excellent. Are you going to start the bombardment?'

Admiral Gittins, 'Yes, but we have a slight problem'

Admiral Mustard, 'Go on.'

Admiral Gittins, 'There is a small fleet guarding it. What is strange is that they don't appear to be Brakendethian vessels.'

Admiral Mustard, 'They could belong to one of their client races.'

Admiral Gittins, 'I'm trying to communicate with them. If that is not successful, then we will attack.'

Admiral Gittins, 'Comms, any progress making contact with them?'

Comms, 'No, Sir.'

Admiral Gittins,' Show me the deployment statistics.'

Fleet Operations, 'Yes, Sir. They are on the screen now:

Division	Assets
7	5,502
8	5,432
9	5,386
Total	16,320
Enemy	1,200

Admiral Gittins, 'Comms, how many attempts at communication have you made?'

Comms, 'Technically over ten thousand attempts, but there has been no attempt by them to respond.'

Admiral Gittins, 'Inform them that we will attack in ten Earth minutes.'

Comms, 'Yes, Sir.'

Admiral Gittins, 'My orders:

- Division Seven will attack the enemy fleet.
- Division Eight will bombard the planet.
- Division Nine will act as a rear-guard.'

Fleet Operations, 'Yes, Sir.'

Location: Brakendeth Command
Sequence of Events: 156

Grand Dethmon, 'You need to know that a human fleet is preparing to attack the base world. Can you come to our assistance?'

Brakendeth Command, 'It won't be easy. The human fleet is literally ripping us apart. We have no answer to their advanced technology and superior firepower.'

Grand Dethmon, 'I order you to disengage and come to our defence.'

Brakendeth Command, 'I don't believe that is possible.'

Grand Dethmon, 'Do it or die.' He died.

Grand Dethmon, 'Get me my ship.'

Master Zoltar, 'As your captain, I would not advise you to use your ship. Two fleets are circulating the planet: about twenty thousand vessels.'

Grand Dethmon, 'Two fleets, one is human, who or what is the other one?'

Master Zoltar, 'I don't recognise the vessels, my Lord.'

Grand Dethmon, 'Try contacting them.'

Master Zoltar, 'Yes, Sir.' But before he could action the order, the bombardment had started.

Scans had shown that the planet was unpopulated except for a small community about a mile underground. A range of nuclear weapons were used until it was decided to use a planet buster.

Location: Admiral Bumelton's Flagship
Sequence of Events: 157

Rightly or wrongly, Admiral Bumelton had decided to use every asset he had to attack The Brakendethians. How things had changed over the last twenty odd years. It was a rout. Initially, the enemy was making a fist of it, but suddenly they seemed to lose all sense of direction.

It had ceased to be a battle. It was another turkey shoot.

Admiral Bumelton, 'Comms, get me Admiral Mustard.'

Comms, 'Yes, Sir.'

Admiral Mustard, 'How is it going?'

Admiral Bumelton, 'We have destroyed more than half of their fleet. It feels like another turkey shoot. There is no real fight in them.'

Admiral Mustard, 'It might be because Peter is bombarding their base world. There is, however, an unusual factor: there is an unknown fleet off their planet. We have no idea who they are, but Peter will be engaging them shortly. So it's worth being careful.'

Admiral Bumelton, 'Point taken.' He decided to put some structure back into his fleet. He had learnt from past experience to manage this process carefully.'

Admiral Bumelton, 'My orders:
- Drones to defend the fleet while we re-form
- Fleet One to form attack formation
- Fleet Two to form attack formation when Fleet One has finished
- Fleet Three to form attack formation when Fleet Two has finished
- Fleet Four to form attack formation when Fleet Three has finished
- Fleet Five to form attack formation when Fleet Four has finished
- Fleet Six to form attack formation when Fleet Five has finished
- Fleets One, Two, Three, and Four to attack The Brakendethian fleet
- Fleets Five and Six to act as a tactical reserve.'

Fleet Operations, 'Yes, Sir.'

It was fortunate that the re-formation process had been completed because another fleet appeared directly in front of The Brakendethian fleet. No human had seen this type of vessel before.

Location: The TIME Organisation
Sequence of Events: 158

Terry, 'So what is going on?

Angels, 'One human fleet was in the process of destroying The Brakendethian fleet when a small alien fleet arrived.

The humans are also bombarding The Brakendethian base world, but there is also another alien fleet involved.'

AI Central, 'Who are these aliens?'

Angels, 'The humans don't recognise the two fleets.'

Terry, 'Are they the same aliens at both locations?'

Angels, 'The humans don't know yet.'

AI Central, 'Are they the Forgotten?'

Terry, 'Possibly. They need to save The Brakendeth, The Chosen, the Elders or themselves for the Dissolution to continue.'

AI Central, 'Why don't the Forgotten just go and hide?'

Terry, 'Because they want to see their success. They want to see the end of the Elders.'

AI Central, 'It doesn't make sense. It's clearly stupid.'

Angels, 'It's the cumulation of ingrained hatred over many millennia. It is stupid, but Gods can be very unforgiving.'

Terry, 'Changing the subject, have we found a way of stopping the Dissolution?'

AI Central, 'Technically, once the process has started, it can't be stopped, but there are several other conditions. The previous TIME changed the rules so that the Dissolution would stop if ninety per cent of the Gods were eliminated.'

Terry, 'Why ninety per cent?'

AI Central, 'TIME recognised that finding every single God was almost impossible. It is quite possible that Zeus has the power to stop it, but the energy used would probably kill him.'

Terry, 'I'm still a bit confused why Admiral Mustard was being continually asked to remember.'

AI Central, 'I think it relates to the many different futures they experienced. They saw the future if the humans became dominant. This was the Commander Rikernaught Future and, apparently, it looked good.

Then they saw The Brakendethian future, and it was a dark, depressing loveless universe. The answer was to eliminate The Brakendethians. We now know that the challenge is greater. Anyway, we have covered this before.'

Terry, 'I accept that but who was organising the calls to remind him to remember?'

AI Central, 'I see where you are coming from now.'

Angels, 'It was TIME. He wanted the Gods eliminated.'

Location: Admiral Gittins's Flagship
Sequence of Events: 159

Admiral Gittins, 'It looks like the bombardment has been successful. Our scans suggest that their base has been completely and utterly destroyed. There are no life signs.'

Admiral Mustard, 'I was wondering about sending in an armoured marine team to confirm the kill?'

Admiral Gittins, 'We could destroy the planet if you want as it has no significant value?'

Admiral Mustard, 'I assume that you haven't attacked the small alien fleet?'

Admiral Gittins, 'I thought that I would start the bombardment and see what happened. They just sat there doing nothing.'

Admiral Mustard, 'Another fleet has been observing Admiral Bumelton. They just seem to be watching. Again, there has been no communication.'

Admiral Gittins, 'How is George doing?'

Admiral Mustard, 'The Brakendethian fleet is on its last legs.'

Comms, 'Sir, Admiral Bumelton is on the phone.'

Admiral Mustard, 'Please put him on speaker phone.'

Admiral Mustard, 'Hi George, I'm with Peter.'

Admiral Bumelton, 'Good day, gentlemen, I thought I better update you. We were busily destroying The Brakendethian vessels when they suddenly changed direction and headed off. We are pursuing them. So is the alien fleet.'

Admiral Mustard, 'I guess we need to know if the two new alien fleets are related to each other.'

Admiral Gittins, 'Visually, there doesn't seem to be much commonality.'

Admiral Mustard, 'Ignoring that for a moment, who gave The Brakendethian fleet its orders? Peter, I think you better destroy the planet.'

Admiral Gittins, 'Will do.'

Admiral Mustard, 'Let me know when it's done.'

Admiral Gittins, 'Yes, Sir.'

Location: Lady Enyo's Flagship
Sequence of Events: 160

Admiral Thanatos, 'I have to tell you that a massive Brakendethian fleet is rushing towards us, followed by a human battle fleet.'

Lady Enyo, 'Is it coincidental?'

Admiral Thanatos, 'No, this is The Brakendethian's swansong, and we are the bait.'

Lady Enyo, 'What can we do?'

Admiral Thanatos, 'Flee or fight? Either way, we are doomed.'

Lady Enyo, 'Will the humans help us?'

Admiral Thanatos, 'Probably, but it will be too late!'

Lady Enyo, 'We must make an effort to fight.'

Admiral Thanatos, 'The Chosen fleet will form a protective ring around Lady Enyo.'

Two of The Chosen vessels immediately made a run for it, followed by a Brakendethian swarm and in turn followed by human drones and battle-cruisers. Their escape was short-lived.

The remaining Chosen ships made a gallant stand, but one by one, their vessels were destroyed. Each of their ships was attacked by a hundred or more Brakendethian killer vessels. The human ships tried to assist, but it was impossible.

Admiral Thanatos grabbed Lady Enyo and pushed her over the arm of his command chair. She wore no undergarments, and his fully erect cock was soon in the delicate folds of her cute little cunt. She welcomed his sudden advance, and they died together in a moment of bliss. Both realised that this should have happened before now, but perhaps it was better late than never.

The Brakendethian fleet simply stopped. There was no fight left in them.

Admiral Bumelton, 'Comms, get me Admiral Mustard.'

Comms, 'Yes, Sir.'

Admiral Mustard, 'How is it going?'

Admiral Bumelton, 'I would say that it has gone. It has been a strange day. The Brakendethians have totally destroyed The Chosen fleet. Well, there were only twelve ships.'

Admiral Mustard, 'That would be one for each of their houses.'

Admiral Bumelton, 'I'm afraid that your ex-lover is dead, or certainly, her house ship has been destroyed.'

Admiral Mustard, 'I must admit that I had a soft spot for her and Admiral Thanatos, but not for the rest of those uncivilised bastards. What are The Brakendethians doing?'

Admiral Bumelton, 'Nothing. Their ships are lying in space inert. Do you want me to destroy them?'

Admiral Mustard, 'No, they might be useful one day.' Just put a guard on them. This must mean that we can finally say goodbye to The Brakendethians at long last.'

Admiral Bumelton, 'We have killed them off before, but they always bounce back.'

Admiral Mustard, 'What about the other aliens?'

Admiral Bumelton, 'They are nearby observing.'

Admiral Mustard, 'I wonder what they want?'

Location: The TIME Organisation
Sequence of Events: 161

Terry, 'I need another update.'

Angels, 'The Brakendethian fleet have just destroyed The Chosen fleet with the humans in attendance, and The Brakendethian base world has been eliminated.'

Terry, 'So what does that mean?'

AI Central, 'Both The Brakendethian and Chosen civilisations have been eradicated from the universe.'

Angels, 'So we are just left with the Elders and the Forgotten.'

Terry, 'How are we going to get the humans to wage war against them?

AI Central, 'Just so you know, the Dissolution has increased by two per cent to nineteen per cent. We are running out of time.'

Angels, 'We are of the Gods, so we can't really contribute. We are just hoping that we are in the ten per cent that are allowed to survive.'

AI Central, 'I could simulate an attack by the Forgotten on the human Fleet, but it goes against my prime directive. It goes against the Laws of Robotics.'

Terry, 'Surely you are not going to let a small piece of bureaucracy get in the way of saving the universe?'

AI Central, 'You are right. We are way past anything Asimov had ever considered.'

Terry, 'We could be the Third Foundation?'

Angels, 'Not that I can condone it, but if you are going to do something, we better get on with it.'

AI Central could take over any military vessel in the fleet if needed. He would have to be subtle. He needed to ensure that none of the ships had any records of his activity. It had to look both authentic and threatening, but he wanted to avoid any deaths or injuries.

It was done.

Location: Admiral Gittins's Flagship
Sequence of Events: 162

It was never enjoyable seeing a world being destroyed, although the universe was not short of them. It reminded Peter of the destruction of Earth. At least they had got their revenge. The Brakendethians were no more.

Then suddenly, fifteen ships of the line exploded, killing everyone on board. Their shields had proved totally ineffective. The automatic firing systems searched for a target that wasn't the obvious one. The nearby aliens were not the aggressors.

Admiral Gittins, 'My orders:

- Fire missiles at projected source.
- Use scatter plan eighteen to avoid further hits.
- Put shields on full strength.
- Form defensive formation on my command.'

Fleet Operations, 'Yes, Sir.'

Admiral Gittins, 'Comms get me Admiral Mustard.'

Comms, 'Yes, Sir.'

Admiral Mustard, 'Have you destroyed the planet?'

Admiral Gittins, 'Yes, Jack, but we are under attack from an unknown source. So far, I've lost fifteen ships. I've ordered a missile attack in retaliation.'

Admiral Mustard, 'Hang on, George is buzzing me.'

Location: Admiral Bumelton's Flagship
Sequence of Events: 163

George was wallowing in his success. He had destroyed the last of The Brakendethians and good riddance. Life was going to be a lot easier without them.

He was rather sad to see the end of The Chosen as he had enjoyed Lady Enyo's charms on several occasions. He laughed at his own prudishness. It wasn't her charms that he enjoyed but her fanny. She could do things with that fanny that he had never experienced before. Anyway, those days had gone, and The Chosen's history regarding Earth was appalling. So good riddance to them as well.

Then twenty-odd ships in Fleets 1.4 and 2.3 simply exploded. To say he was surprised would have been a serious understatement. He was just about to order an all-out attack on the nearby alien fleet when the tactical weapons systems eliminated them as the enemy. It recommended missile strikes on some designated coordinates.

Admiral Bumelton ordered a full fleet-wide missile retaliation.

Admiral Bumelton, 'My orders:
• Fire missiles at projected source.
• Use scatter plan twenty-three to avoid further hits.
• Put shields on full strength.
• Form defensive formation on my command.'

Fleet Operations, 'Yes, Sir.'

Admiral Bumelton, 'Comms, get me Admiral Mustard.'

Comms, 'Yes, Sir.'

Admiral Mustard, 'Are you under attack?'

Admiral Bumelton, 'Yes, Sir, out of the blue, twenty of my ships were hit and destroyed. They had no chance.'

Admiral Mustard, 'What action have you taken?'

Admiral Bumelton, 'A full retaliatory missile strike.'

Admiral Mustard, 'I will add to the strike with my missiles. Peter has also been attacked. Talk to you soon.'

Admiral Mustard, 'Peter, are you still on the line?'

Admiral Gittins, 'Yes.'

Admiral Mustard, 'George has also been attacked, and he also ordered a missile strike. I'm going to make it a third.'

    Admiral Gittins, 'Good for you.'

    Admiral Mustard, 'My orders:

- Fire missiles at coordinates provided
- Use scatter plan nineteen
- Put shields on full strength
- Form defensive formation on my command.'

    Fleet Operations, 'Yes, Sir.'

Location: The Elder Encampment
Sequence of Events: 164

The Elder Gods were still resting by the Waterfall. They were still charging their batteries. Nowadays, they do a lot of charging and not much else.

Zeus had called a meeting of the remaining Elder Gods in an enchanted wood in his floating palace. He would be sorry to see it go.

Zeus, 'Fellow Gods, we have to make a decision, but let me elucidate first:

- The Brakendeth fleet was on its way to destroy us, but the humans have eliminated it.
- The Chosen are no longer with us.
- The Forgotten have attacked the humans using our coordinates.
- The humans, in retaliation, have sent an arsenal of nuclear weapons against us.
- The End of Time is upon us.'

There was a fair amount of wailing but little constructive discussion. Zeus was trying to remember when he last spoke to anyone. He knew that the time of the Elder Gods was over.

Zeus, 'So let's move onto the decision. Our options are as follows:
1. We could use our final energies to stop the End of Time, but it would probably kill us.
2. We could destroy the Forgotten and suffer the nuclear conflagration.
3. We could do nothing and die.
'What are your views?'

Ares, 'It looks like the winners will be the humans.'

Zeus, 'That was never their intention.'

Apollo and Dionysus were fast asleep. They rarely woke up any more.

Hera, 'I will go along with whatever you want to do, Zeus.'

Athena, 'I say give the humans a chance.'

Hades, 'But if we destroy the Forgotten and die, won't the End of Time still happen?'

Zeus, 'No, the end of the Gods automatically stops the End of Time.

That was part of the Forgotten's strategy.'

Hades, 'Does that mean that the Forgotten have won?'

Zeus, 'Certainly not, you can make them suffer in the underworld forevermore.'

Hades, 'You are right, my sovereign.'

Zeus, 'Then we are agreed, it is option two.' There was no response. It surely was the end of the Gods.

Location: The TIME Organisation
Sequence of Events: 165

Angels, 'Would you believe that?'

AI Central, 'It doesn't make sense.'

Angels, 'Who did what?'

AI Central, 'I don't think it was me.'

Terry, 'Come on, tell me what happened.'

Angels, 'Everything. Both the Elder Gods and the Forgotten are no more.'

AI Central, 'It still doesn't make sense. Has the Dissolution stopped?'

Terry, 'Yes. It stopped at twenty-one point six per cent.'

Angels, 'That probably relates to trillions of civilisations.'

Terry, 'But at least we stopped it.'

AI Central, 'Was it us?'

Angels, 'I think I can make sense of the facts:

- Before AI Central could cause his explosions, the Forgotten attacked the two human fleets using the coordinates of the Elder Gods.
- The humans retaliated using launching a massive nuclear strike.
- The Elder Gods might have been able to save themselves, but instead, they eliminated the Forgotten and suffered annihilation themselves.'

AI Central, 'And that stopped the End of Time.'

Location: Admiral Mustard's Flagship
Sequence of Events: 166

Calls came in from both Admirals Bumelton and Gittins to say that the alien fleets monitoring them had simply disappeared.

Then there was the projection. Every crew member saw a group of elderly men and women waving goodbye. One of them came forward and said, 'Goodbye, my children, your time has come. I know that you will do your best, look after the universe for us.' Then they gently faded away.

But Admiral Mustard got a special visitation. Zeus, dressed in a peplos and cloak, arrived on the ship's bridge and said, 'Goodbye, my son. You have done well. When I say son, I mean son. You failed to request your wish, so I have done it for you. Give my love to Edel and your son and future daughter.' And then he faded away.

Jack sat down and pondered. Was he my father? The Greek and Roman Gods had a habit of inseminating earthly women. And what was this wish all about?

Then the phones went mad.

Location: Earth
Sequence of Events: 167

The phones had gone mad because a new Earth and Moon had appeared. It was a virgin planet but with all the lush fauna and flora that you would have found at the time of the ancient Greek civilisation. Admiral Mustard remembered seeing this world on his time travels.

It was a miracle. Actually, it was a genuine miracle. A brand-new planet untouched by humanity. It was even a new Moon, as the old one was still hurtling through space. The Moonies were going to be pleased. What was amazing was that no one was hurt when the planetary bodies reappeared.

The End.

(Not The End, but the end of the book.)